The Coney Island Book of the Dead

An Illustrated Novel

Sheila Martin

First Edition 2016

Narrioch

Books

Narrioch was the Canarsee tribe's word for Coney Island.
It means the place without shadows.

ISBNs
978-0-9972822-0-7 (trade paperback)
978-0-9972822-1-4 (hardcover)
978-0-9972822-2-1 (e-book)

Cover art and illustrations by Sheila Martin

For my husband Jim Blythe, who keeps me from ever being lonely,
and my cousin Marilyn Schorr,
my best friend for as long as I can remember.

And in memory of:

My bubbie: Rose Mangel, who made my childhood a joy, my father:
Abe Mangel—if ever there was a sweeter, more optimistic person, I've
never met them. I found an early draft of this novel open on his coffee
table when he died in 2001 in a car accident at the age of ninety—my
mother: Frances, my favorite aunt: Auntie Ada, my mother-in-law: Ann
Blythe, my old friend: Ryder Syversten, who died in 2015—he always
made me laugh—and saddest of all, Marilyn and Steve's child, my young
cousin Emma Nervosa/David Feldheim—a talented writer who died the
same year when he was only twenty-three.

List of Illustrations

All illustrations are gouache and watercolor except the map. The map is an 1873 depiction of Coney Island and environs and comes to us from Wikimedia Commons.

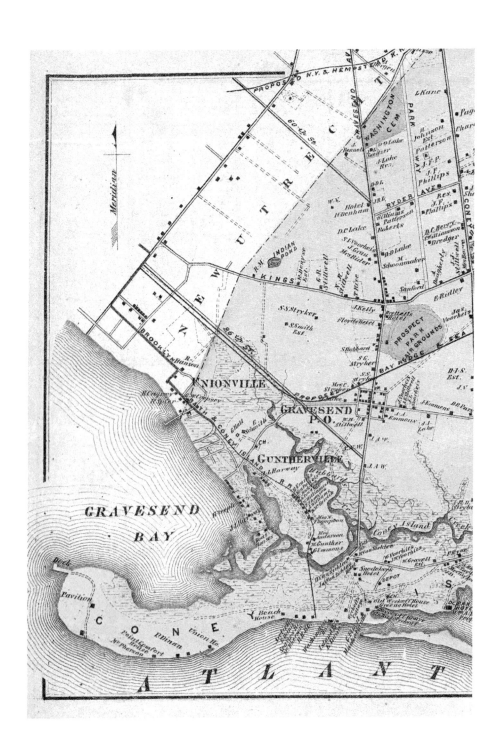

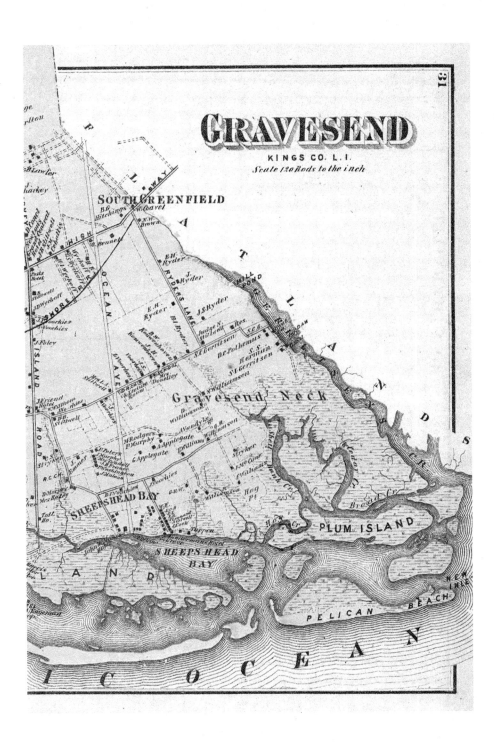

GRAVESEND

KINGS CO. L.I.
Scale 120 Rods to the inch

SOUTH GREENFIELD

Gravesend Neck

SHEEPSHEAD BAY

SHEEPS HEAD BAY

PLUM ISLAND

PELICAN BEACH

NEW INLET

ATLANTIC OCEAN

One

CONEY ISLAND ≈ Memorial Day, 1957

The kind of night when neon signs dust the boardwalk with light like powdered jewels, when foghorns and roller-coaster screams drown out the brush-beat of the surf, when the ocean's salt breeze smells of vast windy skies, great clouds of mist roll in on the waves, and the lighthouse at Norton's Point shines a beacon for ships lost at sea.

It was that kind of night—a night like every night in the City of Fire.

An old man lurched out of the shadows.

"Give me two dollars for this gold doubloon!" he shouted. His face was smeared with dirt, his white beard matted, his eyes smoldering. "No, three dollars! No, one dollar! You, sir." He poked his finger at a heavy-set man. "You buy it. I built the Half Moon Hotel, now look at me."

The heavy-set man kept walking.

The beggar made a grab for a woman's arm, but she dodged out of reach.

"You, lady, buy it or I'll suck your brains out with a straw!" She walked faster.

"Hey, don't run away like I'm a leper or something." He turned and looked at me like he would suck *my* brains out with a straw. "How about you, girlie?" It's a real pirates' doubloon. Fifty cents."

I grabbed Mom's arm, so skinny it felt like it might break. She jerked it back. "Don't cling," she said.

She'd been like this for a while now, ever since Dad's mama, my bubbie... Just skirting the memory crushed my chest.

Mom was wearing a lace-trimmed blouse too dressy for the boardwalk, even I knew that. It kept slipping off her shoulder, exposing her bra strap. She didn't notice.

She was still taller than me, but I was growing fast, would probably overtake her. I was skinny too, but normal skinny, kid skinny. I had her green eyes and rich dark hair, but mine was a little more red and I had a smattering of freckles like my dad.

"Mom?" I tugged at her arm again, got a whiff of her Arpège perfume, rose and jasmine. "Mom!" I shouted.

"What now!"

"When are the fireworks going to start?"

"Stop it, Sarah!" She pried my fingers off. "How should I know?"

She started scanning the boardwalk for Dad, trying to spot his red hair in the crowd, his sweet-natured face. He was out there somewhere, making the gears turn, but not for us.

"Sinners!" shrieked a preacher. He waved his hand at the crowd. "Filthy degenerates!" He pointed a tremulous finger at the saloon, brazenly open to the boardwalk, its crimson neon sign glowing: Max's Place. Dark and smoky, wallpapered in a flocked pattern of blood-red fleurs-de-lis, it had a horseshoe-shaped bar at its center, wrapped around a raised stage now in shadow. Max's reeked of whiskey, beer, and cheap perfume, the whole place pulsing with drunken laughter. I could just make out my gangster uncle Max, tapping his cigar into an ashtray at a table near the back. Of course he owned the joint.

Mom sighed. The saloon used to be her hangout, was where she met Dad, the beginning of everything as far as my existence goes.

"Blasphemers!" the preacher ranted. "Drunkards! Fornicators!" His eyes scanned the boozers inside the saloon. "You!" He pointed at a platinum blonde on a barstool. She was leaning forward, reaching for her drink, her low-cut dress barely able to contain her heaving white breasts. "Filthy whore!" he shouted. "Jesus died for your sins, yet you entice men to defile you!"

The lady took a sip of her highball with one hand, patted her stiff tower of bleached hair with the other.

A ceiling spotlight sliced a cone out of the curling smoke to reveal the singer on stage, seated at a baby grand. Lenny was a dreamboat in his black tuxedo and bow tie, his shiny dark hair casually tossed back.

"I used to date him, you know," Mom whispered, as though everyone didn't know that. He was in love with her before Dad stole her away.

Lenny glanced my way for the briefest of moments, his teeth flashing white against his tanned skin, eyelids half-closed. He tapped the microphone. Boom! Boom! Boom! The drunken laughter dropped away.

"Evening, ladies and gents." He took a slurp of martini. "I can't tell you how ring-a-ding-ding it is to be back here in crazy old Funville, U.S.A. Got my start here, you know, right here in Max's Place, where the broads are stacked and the gasoline's high octane. Hey, you." He pointed at a bald man slouched against the bar. "Don't stop guzzling on my account. You know what I always say, don't you?"

"What, Lenny?" the platinum blonde called out.

"You're not drunk…" He winked at her. "If you can lie on the floor without holding on." He raised his martini glass with a flourish. "This song's for you, baby. With a pair of charlies like you have? Va va va voom! You'll never be lonely.

"And now…" Lenny's fingers tickled the keys. He crooned "One For my Baby."

His voice mesmerized me, pulled me into the broke-down world of grownup love. I wished it was me up there, emptying my heart out, but I was just a kid, I wasn't even *allowed* in there.

As he sang he inserted new lyrics:

> It's not time to go
> I got a story, Sarah, that comes from below…

WHAT! *That's my name!* He was singing to *me!*

> We'll drink little girl
> To the end of someone you know…

Two

"B utwhat'dLennymean?" Marilyn said, so fast her words blurred together.

"I've been trying to figure it out."

Marilyn was my best friend and cousin, maybe the cutest kid in the world with her dimples and big brown eyes. We were born just five weeks apart (me first!) and lived next door to each other. Her house was a rundown boarding house—actually it was just a regular house, but Marilyn's mom, Evil Aunt Suzie, had turned it into a boarding house even though they could have lived off Uncle Nat's income as an accountant.

I was in its living room with Marilyn and Duchess—her adorable, but fiercely loyal little mutt. Duchess was so loyal she wouldn't even let anyone else pet her. Try it and she'd snap at you. We were hunkered down in a tent we made of three cots balanced against each other like a house of cards roofed with a white damask tablecloth Evil Aunt Suzie inherited from Grandma Lena, but never used, not even once.

"All I can come up with is, he was warning me that someone might die. I don't understand why my mom claims she didn't hear it. I have to go to Uncle Max's and ask Lenny what he meant."

"Don't! I hate that place, it's like a house of horrors!"

Marilyn hated it, but I was drawn to it. It felt magical and its magic was music.

"Why don't you come with me?" I said.

"No!" She rubbed her eyes and sniffled.

"Then I'll have to go myself."

"Don't you dare. If you go in you might never come out. Ever since Bubbie died, all we have is each other."

"Don't say that," I said. "We still have our dads."

"Lot of good it does, mine can't get upstairs and yours is so busy."

Oh yes, the busy season, when Dad disappeared to keep the rides running. Of course it was like this every year, but this summer it felt worse because of Bubbie.

Just then we heard the front door bang open, shoes clomping on the linoleum and then on the carpet, closer and closer, until the tablecloth ripped off our tent to reveal Evil Aunt Suzie's face glaring down at us.

We jumped up. Marilyn grabbed my arm.

Suzie, in her ratty old housedress with nylons rolled up under her fat knees, stared at the tablecloth she was holding. Then flung it to the floor, clamped her hands over her ears, and screamed.

"Get out of my head!"

Aunt Suzie wasn't just evil, she was kind of crazy, but I'd never seen her this bad before.

"You made it dirty!" She pointed at the tablecloth, now among the dust bunnies and pizza boxes. "You little shits!"

She lurched, but I jumped over one of the cots and got away. She grabbed Marilyn's arm in a death grip.

I ran into the hall. Suzie, still gripping Marilyn's arm, picked up a heavy glass ashtray with her other hand and hefted it up and down. That thing could bash Marilyn's skull in.

Duchess went berserk, barking, growling, making a lot of noise for such a small dog.

"Run!" Marilyn yelled.

Suzie lifted the ashtray over her head. She looked back and forth from one of us to the other. Then she swung her arm back and hurled her weapon at me.

I ran, heard a clunky splintering noise, then a yowl of anguish.

I saw Marilyn fly out the door after me. She caught up at my side door. She had flecks of blood on her face.

"How'd you get away?" I asked.

She held up a finger, made me wait until she caught her breath.

"I bit her."

Three

The next afternoon I stopped at Marilyn's house, rang the bell, then stood there studying the white paint peeling off the front door. I'd tried to call her last night and this morning, but no answer.

It seemed like forever, but finally the door banged partway open on a chain lock. Evil Aunt Suzie frowned out at me.

"Can Marilyn come out?" I said.

"No."

"Why not?"

"She bit me!"

"Yeah, but you tried to *kill* me."

"Drop dead!" She slammed the door in my face.

I'd been hoping I could talk Marilyn into coming with me to Uncle Max's. Instead I walked down the stoop, along the street, and turned right when I got to Brighton Beach Avenue in the shadow of the el, and kept walking until I crossed Ocean Parkway. There was a shantytown there—a single line of shotgun shacks one block long running between Ocean Parkway and West Fifth. They had chickens in some of the yards and one of them had a real live goat.

Everything started shaking and rattling, banging and clanking. But it was just the train pulling into Ocean Parkway. I crossed under the el, passed an art deco apartment building with salt water baths, then followed Ocean Parkway until it turned into Surf Avenue, which led me around Seaside Park with its ancient sycamore trees.

The names in Coney Island had a ghostly presence to me— Dreamland, Luna Park, the Half Moon Hotel, Gravesend Cemetery— as if the past never really went away.

I was soon in the amusement area, fourteen blocks wide and a long avenue deep, running along the boardwalk. I passed the Cyclone roller-coaster, Feltman's Beer Garden, Blue Bird Casino, Harry's Poker, and Fascination Arcade, until I reached Stillwell. Across Surf Avenue lay the yawning subway terminal, gateway for the millions.

The aroma of grilling hot dogs wafted toward me from Nathan's Famous. I turned toward the beach.

I walked to the end of Stillwell Avenue, up the ramp to the board-walk, around the corner, and there I was, in front of Uncle Max's. The entrance was closed with tall, red, narrow panels that opened like an accordion. I heard music seeping out, but it wasn't Lenny. It was a deep twangy guitar and a man's gravelly voice like nothing I'd ever heard before.

> Well, I'm a pooooor boy, a long way from home
> I'm such a pooooor boy, a long way from home
> I'm headed someplace, where I'll never be alone.

The song seemed to come from a different world, somewhere hotter and harder and slower than New York. It pounded in my blood. I never thought I'd hear a better singer than Lenny, but I was listening to one now.

I cracked the accordion doors open and peeked in. I could just make out the singer in the crimson light of the EXIT sign. He was sitting at one of the tables in the back, picking a guitar. And at his feet was a huge... well, it looked like a wolf.

He started up again:

> Watch out little gal, there's danger to come
> I say watch out little gal, there's danger to come...

It felt like *he* was singing a message to me too.

> Oooooh, no, no, no, I don't know why
> But by the last day of summer
> Someone's gonna die.

I stood there between the partially open doors, my heart pounding like the Brighton Express pulling in.

I pulled the doors open a little more. As my eyes got accustomed to the darkness I saw stools upturned on the horseshoe-shaped bar, baby grand on the stage, microphone on its stand, everything washed in crimson light.

I looked around carefully to make sure Uncle Max wasn't in sight. If you knew him, you'd be careful too. Uncle Max used to be a hit man for Murder Incorporated until he got caught. Then he had to pay off some judge, which cost him a mint, so he decided it would be more profitable to open a bar on the boardwalk. This according to Mom.

The man finished his song and looked up.

He was old—a thin black man wearing a tattered white shirt and suspenders. He had a gray felt hat on the table.

The wolf ran right over to me. He had the thickest fur I'd ever seen, silver on the surface, with a cream-colored undercoat. I wanted to bury my face in his neck. He looked at me with amber eyes so bright they seemed to glow, then he started dancing around, panting, poking me with his muzzle, licking my hands.

"Hi, boy," I said, roughing up the top of his head. "You're a good boy, aren't you."

Follow me, he seemed to be saying, making invitational runs to the back, wagging his tail.

I walked over to the table and planted myself on the edge of one of the red crushed-velvet chairs. The wolf settled on the floor in front of us, still panting and smiling.

"Hi," I said. "What a great dog. Is he a wolf? He looks like a wolf."

"Not likely," the man said, half laughing. "He sure enough likes you. Most folks he don't take much notice of."

I loved the man's face. He had skin like a crumpled brown paper bag, white hair, and sad eyes sunk deep. And he had an inner light like Bubbie.

"Can I ask you something?" I said.

"Sure enough."

"What did you mean when you sang: 'Watch out little gal, there's danger to come?'"

"Pardon me?"

"When you sang those words, did you mean me?"

He frowned, then shook his head.

"I don't rightly see how I could have, since I ain't never laid eyes on you 'till this minute."

"Then why'd you sing them?"

"Sometimes words just come out my mouth. May of heard them somewhere."

"So you don't know who's going to die?"

He shook his head. "Ain't nobody going to die. It's just a song."

"It scared me."

He sighed. "Sorry 'bout that."

"Did you write that song about the poor boy a long way from home?"

He shook his head again. "That there's a blues song old as the hills. But everybody who sings it does it their own way."

"Can I sing it?"

"Hold on." A worried look fell over his face. He squinted at me. "You allowed in here little girl?"

"My Uncle Max owns this place."

"You don't say. He was just here, said he'd be back in a spell. Hired me to play this evening. Trying me out."

"So you're new around here?"

"Just blew into town. Rented me a little house."

"What's your name?"

"Mississippi." He patted the dog on the side. "And this here's Cerbie. Best friend I ever had." The dog was smiling at me which made me feel safe.

"My name's Sarah. You been on the road long, Mississippi?"

"Just about all my life. I'm like Cain in the Bible, cast out of my home and forced to wander all my days."

"You sound a little like Elvis Presley."

"Funny you should say that. I met him once."

"Really?" I could hardly believe it.

"One night I was picking out a tune in a dive on some empty back street not a block from the Mississippi River. Memphis, it was. I'm strumming along when I hear a vroooooom from a motorcycle, a bang like a shotgun, then this here boy comes flying in through the front door. White boy, leather jacket, tight dungarees, greasy blond hair in a pompadour."

"Wait a second," I said. "Elvis isn't blond."

He held up a finger.

"Don't know how he ever found the place," he said. "There weren't no sign outside.

"He's strutting right up to me, grinning this lopsided grin, introduces himself and says, 'I came to sing with the master, sir.' Somehow he heard of me.

"'Sure enough,' I say, so I tell him the words to a song Big Mama Thornton taught me. Then I start strumming and he sings 'Hound Dog.'"

"You taught him that song!"

He held up a finger and went on:

"'I ain't never heard that song before,' the boy says. 'That's a great song. Thank you very much for teaching it to me, sir,' talking real polite like his mama taught him. 'We'll meet again someday, the good Lord willing, and when that day comes I'll be rich and famous, sir.'

"'I got three things to tell you, boy,' I say. 'Three pieces of advice on singing the blues. So listen up.

"'The first is—blond boys don't sing the blues."

"Do girls from Brooklyn sing the blues?" I said.

"Beg your pardon?"

"Girls from Brooklyn, do we sing the blues?"

"I don't see why not." He smiled. "So long as you got a voice and a soul, you can sing the blues."

"What other pieces of advice did you give him?"

"The second piece of advice was: if you want to be rich and famous you got to change that trashy name. Elvis? Oh, Lord. What kind of a name is that for a blues singer? Call yourself Memphis.'

"'But I ain't from Memphis, sir,' he says, real earnest-sounding.

"'You're from someplace, ain't you?' I say. 'Call yourself after whatever town you're from.'

"'What's the third thing, sir?' he says.

"'The third's the most important. It goes against everything your mama ever taught you and your daddy, too. But whatever else you do in life, if we ever meet again or not, don't you never, ever, call me 'sir' again. No one else, neither.'

"'Yes sir, I mean, thank you sir, I mean thank you Mr. Mississippi. I'll take that advice to heart, sir, I mean mister. Should I call you mister, sir?'

"He just couldn't help it. I had to feel sorry for him.

"We never did meet again, but he did take my advice—about the hair color, that is. I often wonder how much more famous he'd be today if he'd called himself Tupelo."

"I'm changing my name to Brooklyn," I said, "so I can sing the blues too."

Suddenly a loud voice shouted, "What the *hell's* going on here?"

It was Uncle Max, standing in the doorway in his black suit, waving his cigar. With his pale skin and straight black hair he looked like an undertaker.

He walked over, pointing at the door.

"Get out of here."

I started to leave, but he grabbed my arm.

"Not you." He swung his head. "Him. And take that mongrel with you."

Cerbie stood up, rigid, ears erect, and stared coldly at Uncle Max. Mississippi put on his hat and picked up his guitar.

"What time should I be back for the first set?" he asked.

"Sorry," Uncle Max said. "Turns out I can't use you."

"That's so unfair," I managed to squeak. For a minute I was afraid I would burst into tears.

"I don't need no boss man nohow," Mississippi said, then left with Cerbie.

"That wasn't right!" I yelled at Uncle Max.

"What wasn't?"

"Firing him. He didn't know I wasn't supposed to come in here."

"That's not why I changed my mind. It's his music—makes people sad. I just booked a mambo band, something you can dance to." He looked down at his huge mitt gripping my upper arm and let go. "What are you doing here? Why were you talking to that man? Don't you know guys like him are dangerous?"

"Guys like what?"

"Drifters. They could do anything, then disappear. I guarantee he'll be gone by tomorrow. Didn't your parents teach you anything?"

"No he won't, he rented a house," I said. "He told me."

"And don't ever come in here again. Now scram."

"Uncle Max? I just want to tell you I think you're making a big mistake. He's the best—"

"Don't press your luck, kid."

"Uncle Max?"

"What?"

"Can I ask you one question?"

He looked at the ceiling, let out an impatient huff.

"Make it snappy."

"Did you hear Lenny sing 'One for my Baby' last night?"

"What do you think, I'm deaf or something?"

"In the song he sang 'It's not time to go, I got a story, *Sarah*, that comes from below.' He used my name! Then he sang, 'We'll drink little girl to the end of someone you know.'"

Uncle Max looked at me like I was crazy.

"You heard it wrong, he just sang the regular words."

"Do you know when Lenny's coming in?" I said.

"Stay away from him. You got no business bothering him."

"Could you do me an itty bitty favor?" I said.

"Spit it out."

"Could you not mention to my mom that I came in here?"

"Sure," he said. "Anything not to have to deal with her. Now get the hell out of here before I change my mind."

I headed for the door, but when I got there I called out to him.

"Uncle Max? I think Mississippi is the greatest singer you'll ever—"

"I'm gonna strangle you!"

I took off running.

four

"But why can't we get a dog?"

This was the next afternoon, and I was sitting at the round kitchen table with its map-of-Florida tablecloth, the victim of Mom's daily three o'clock milk-drinking torture. I knew I was whining, but I couldn't help myself.

"Marilyn has a dog," I said.

Mom banged her balled-up fists on leaping swordfish, flamingos, and palm trees.

"You know I'm terrified of dogs." She crossed her stick-thin legs, bony knees protruding from her Bermuda shorts.

She had been Miss Coney Island once, won the title on the stage of Uncle Max's where they held the contest. That was before I was born and ruined her figure.

Her bra strap slipped off her shoulder from under her sleeveless blouse. She put it back, then ran her fingers through her short permed hair. How could I have turned out so different from her? It seemed everything I loved—animals, music, long hair—she hated.

I looked down at the kitchen floor. In one of their lunatic attempts at home renovation, my parents had tiled the kitchen, hall, and bathroom floors in a random mix of colors, the result of a very good sale on tile remnants at Pintchik's. While they were at it, Dad cemented a glittery piece of white linoleum to the bathroom ceiling, which kept falling down. The whole house was crooked and rambling. That's because Mom's parents built it without a blueprint, without a ruler even.

Mom was staring at the round white kitchen clock, floating like an unblinking eye on the pink and gray plaid Sanitex wallpaper—4:30.

"If it was our dog," I said, "you'd like it. Why can't we just try?"

She sighed and her gaze fell on the tall, sweating glass of calcium-packed, vitamin-enriched, homogenized, pasteurized—yuck, yuck, yuck, yuck—milk, towering like a monument to strong bones on the kitchen table.

We had a seemingly endless supply of Mallomar cookies, but could I have one with the milk? No, that would be too enjoyable.

"Because you're skin and bones," she said.

"You're the one who's skin and bones. You used to be the prettiest mom on the block!"

"You need strong bones and you don't have any color. Why can't you be a normal kid?"

"I didn't ask why I had to drink the milk," I said. "I asked why we can't get a dog."

"And that personality of yours—no cheerful chit-chat out of *you*."

"But Mom, you're always telling me I talk too much."

"Ever since your bubbie passed away—"

I put my hands over my ears.

"You used to always be over there, pestering her night and day. Now you're always here, singing those depressing songs."

I loved to sing, but the only one who ever liked my singing was Bubbie.

"If you want to get rid of me," I said, "it's easy, just stop forcing me to drink the milk and I'll go out—"

"Listen, Sarah—"

"Brooklyn," I said. "I told you to call me Brooklyn from now on."

"Fine. Brook-lyn." She put her hands on her forehead. "Just drink the goddamned milk, Brook-lyn. Before I have a nervous breakdown, Brook-lyn. Where'd you get this crazy name from anyway?"

"Won't you just tell me why we can't at least try a dog? You can pick it out."

"Do you really want to know how a dog destroyed our family?"

"Yes!" I pounded my grimy little fists on the table.

"Drink your milk and I'll tell you."

I made gagging noises, then gulped it down.

"Okay, okay," she said, a nervous edge to her voice. "If you must know, it all started with my little sister Suzie. She had the cutest dimpled cheeks and twinkling eyes you ever saw, just like Marilyn. Heart of gold. We all loved her."

"Aunt Suzie?"

Mom raised a finger. "She was the shining light of our family.

"We had a dog back then, a cute little beagle. Prince, his name was. It's hard to believe we had a dog considering how crowded it was on the Lower East Side. Let's see, there was Mama, Tata, us seven kids, plus a boarder. Oh, and there was my hundred-year-old great-grandmother, but she just sat kvetching in her ratty old armchair in a dark corner of the kitchen."

"What was her name?" I asked.

"Her name? That's what you want to know! We didn't know her name. We didn't even know how many greats she was. She was so old that all the people who knew her name had passed away or forgotten it, and she refused to tell us. She said Molech ha-Movess, the Angel of Death, couldn't get her if he didn't know who she was."

"There's an Angel of Death?"

"Noooo." She waved her hand. "She was mushuga, completely

nuts. She thought Prince was possessed by a dybbuk and there were cats screeching in the walls."

"What's a dybbuk?"

"Stop interrupting. It's a demon or something. Anyway, she was always flicking her hand at the door saying, 'Shoo, shoo, go away. The lady for whom you are looking is not here.' But she was just talking to the air. Mama told us, 'She's never going to die, but some day she'll shrink away to nothingness.'

"Anyway there were ten of us, eleven if you count *her*. All of us in a five-room railroad flat with a bathtub in the kitchen, but at least it was facing the street."

"So you're much better off now," I said, "in this big house with just us."

"But I loved it there," she said. "Mama was so steady and strong. And could she cook! And Tata? Always jolly with his rosy cheeks and big belly laugh. We knew everyone in the neighborhood, Italians, Germans, Irish, it was like the whole Lower East Side was my family. Then Mama and Tata sent me away to be a slave to my older sister, Anna—"

"Mo-omm," I said. "The evil dog?"

"You never give up, do you? You want evil dogs? I'll give you evil dogs." She jumped up, dashed into the bathroom, and came back shaking a few Happiness Pills into her hand. Then she mixed a whiskey sour, gulped the pills down, and lit a cigarette.

"All right," she said. "Here goes.

"We were little kids, sitting around the kitchen table on a cold rainy afternoon. Mama always had a big cauldron of stew bubbling on the back burner. She just kept throwing things in—table scraps, gristle from the butcher shop, whatever was left over.

"That afternoon the kitchen was nice and warm. Little Suzie, Max, and I have our heads cradled on our arms, and Prince-the-beagle is curled up in front of the oven. Mama's rolling dough into plump rugelech cookies when out of the blue, we hear a loud voice.

"'Phooey!'"

"Mama drops the rolling pin and shouts, 'Oy!'"

"There in the shadows is a wrinkled-up face the color of waxed paper.

"'You should excuse my saying,' it says, "but better you shouldn't put in so many raisins.'

"'Too many raisins!' Mama yells. 'You don't say a word to me for months then the first thing out of your mouth is too many raisins?'"

"'Also, it wouldn't hurt a few more walnuts.'

"'More walnuts!" Mama shouts. "More walnuts too you want? Maybe instead of kvetching you could lift a finger.'

"'But I'm a hundred years old!'

"'Again with the hundred years old.' Then Mama's jaw drops. 'Wait a minute. The grandmother I knew in Russia hated walnuts. And you say you want more?'

"'So who said anything about liking? Feh, feh, feh, take it out of my sight. Walnuts? Nothing but tsuris for old ladies. But for the children, they need more walnuts for strong bones.'

"Suddenly Prince springs up, gives a strangled little bark, and flies into a frenzy—knocking over chairs, growling like he never did in his life. It could have been any of us, but he lunges at little Suzie and bites her ankle. She lets out a horrific scream. Mama grabs a cast iron frying pan and bam! slams Prince against the oven. He falls to the floor. For good."

"Wait!" I cried. "So the evil dog was the cute little family beagle?"

"He wasn't so cute anymore."

"And that's how Aunt Suzie got mean?"

"Oh, no. My little sister Suzie could never have been mean. Even though she was just a kid, she took care of all of us. When Shirley had rheumatic fever, Suzie stayed by her bed day and night."

"Aunt Suzie?" I couldn't believe it.

"Day and night."

"Was Shirley all right?"

"She lived, but she died young."

"What about Suzie?"

"The bite was nothing, just a scratch. Great-grandmother kept saying we should take little Suzie to the doctor, but Mama put her homemade salve on it, and it healed up. Soon everything went back to normal.

"Two or three months later little Suzie told Mama, 'My ankle feels funny—look.' She pointed at the spot where Prince had bitten her, but there was nothing there. A few days later we're at the kitchen table eating lunch when all of a sudden Suzie screams, 'Mama! Help! I can't swallow.' So Mama puts a glass of water to her mouth and tries to pour it in, but Suzie spits it out, grabbing her throat, gagging.

"'Get the doctor!' Mama shouts at me.

"She grabs little Suzie in a bear hug and lifts her up kicking and crying. I run out the door. Soon I'm back, dragging old out-of-breath Dr. Hauser.

"By then poor little Suzie is flat on her back in bed, her big brown eyes terrified, arms stiff at her sides. Funny thing is, she looks especially healthy because her cheeks are so rosy.

"Mama tells the doctor the whole story and he sits there at the table shaking his head.

"'I'm so sorry,' he says. 'I'm very, very sorry. I wish there was something I could do.'

"'Gotenyu!' Mama screams. 'What's wrong with her?'

"'Rabies,' he says.

"'That's impossible. She was fine half an hour ago. She was fine for over two months. It was just a little bite. Besides, Prince was *our* dog.'

"'If only you'd come to me sooner," the doctor says. "There are two ways rabies can progress. One is excitation, the other is paralysis. If it's excitation she'll pass away sooner. There's no point in taking her to the hospital, there's nothing they can do.'"

"There must have been *something*," I said.

"There wasn't. After that the little sick room was always crowded. Shirley stayed by Suzie's side, holding her hand, just like Suzie did for her. Mama kept trying to spoon chicken soup into her mouth, but if she swallowed even a few drops it made her choke.

"The rabbi of our storefront schul asked everyone to pray for a miracle, and everyone did. But on the fifth day little Suzie starts thrashing, jerking her arms and legs, banging into the wall."

"But—"

"We lost her," Mom said. "She passed away right in front of our eyes."

Just then the front door banged open, which made us jump up. Evil Aunt Suzie stomped through the hall and into the kitchen. Today she looked worse than usual, as if she hadn't changed her housedress in a week. There was a dirty bandage around her forearm.

Mom and I both glared at her.

"Fran!" Suzie shouted. "You have to do something about—"

"When are you going to let Marilyn out?" I shouted louder.

"What happened to your arm?" Mom shouted even louder.

"She'll get out when I say so!" Suzie shouted so loud it hurt my ears.

"Put your hearing aid in!" Mom shouted directly in her ear. "Anyway, what do you want?"

"I want Marilyn to apologize."

"I mean what do you want from us?" Mom said. "Why are you here?"

"I can't visit my own sister?"

"You said I had to do something about something."

"Oh, you have to discipline— "

"Oy!" an old lady voice called out. We turned and looked down at the Boarder, hands on hips, standing in the doorway. The tiny old lady didn't seem to have a name, not even on the mailbox. She scurried in like a troll, her white hair sticking up in clumps. Mom didn't like her in our kitchen, but there was no stopping her. I wasn't even supposed to talk to her. Sometimes I tried to peek in her room when she opened her door, but all I ever saw was a pile of junk.

The Boarder started jumping up and down.

"The meshuga sisters! It's like a side show."

Suzie grabbed hold of the Boarder's shoulders like a giant grabbing a gremlin.

"Why don't you get rid of her?" She shoved her at Mom.

"You think I want her?" Mom shoved her back.

"Gevalt!" the Boarder yelled.

"Stop it!" I cried. "She's an old lady, you'll hurt her!"

The Boarder broke loose and fled upstairs.

"Get rid of her!" Evil Aunt Suzie yelled at Mom.

"You know what we promised Mama."

"You should drop dead!" Suzie shrieked. "All of you. My useless husband and my rotten kid included." She ran out, slamming the front door behind her.

"You hear that?" Mom cried out with glee. "She wants us to *die*! Her own *family*!"

We sat back down.

"Mom, I don't get it. You told me your sister Suzie died."

"So?" She looked puzzled, then, "Ohhhhhhh." She bounced her hand off her head. "That was the so-called miracle.

"When little Suzie died Mama took her hand and passed it over our heads, so Suzie's good qualities would be given to us. Then we walked around the block three times and threw black cloth over the mirrors. The next day we took seven horse-drawn carriages to the old cemetery in Brooklyn. Little Suzie was the first one buried in our family plot, the first to die in the New World.

"Back home we sat shiva on hard benches, low to the ground to be closer to the world of the dead, though I doubt it made much difference on the fifth floor."

"Then what happened?"

"Great-grandmother stayed in her corner muttering. 'Enough already with the sitting shiva,' she said. 'Suzileh? She's not dead even. Just wait. She'll be back. Molech ha-Movess made for himself a mistake. Two mistakes. With this one it makes three. Like it's my fault?'"

"So she came back from the dead?"

"If you stop interrupting I'll get to it!

"One year later, we went back to the cemetery for the unveiling of her gravestone. When we got home Tata gathered us all in the living room and passed out glasses of Manischewitz wine. He held up his glass and said, 'Let's have a toast to my beautiful wife Lena. She's making for us a miracle, just like Sarah in the bible. She's going to have another baby. Can you believe it? Another baby at age fifty.'

"So Mama had a baby girl and they named her Suzie after the one we lost, so she'd live on. The second little Suzie was as rosy-cheeked and cute as the first, but the resemblance ended there. We got the meanest, nastiest, most selfish little Suzie there ever was. You never heard a baby scream so much! Well, that's it. End of story."

"Thanks, Mom," I said. "But can I have a dog if it isn't a beagle?"

She glanced at the clock, got up, and headed for the front door.

"Where're you going?" I said.

"I can't stand being trapped in this house another minute."

"Wait," I said. "What happened to your great-grandmother? Did she really shrink away into nothingness?"

"I should have such luck."

"Then where is she?" But Mom was already closing the door behind her.

Five

Mom started shutting herself in her room every day and Marilyn was still in lockdown, so I didn't have anybody to talk to. I tried to find Lenny so he could explain his secret message to me, but Uncle Max's always seemed to be empty during the day. I kept an eye out for Mississippi and Cerbie, but Uncle Max was probably right, and they were long gone.

My big discovery was a blues station I found on the kitchen radio. The trouble was it didn't always come in and when it did it sounded faint, far away, and staticky, which almost made it better, more mysterious, hard to hold onto. I'd lost it and was trying to find it again, turning the dial back and forth, when I heard a gravelly voice singing:

> Got them boxcar blues
> Got them in the soles of my travelin' shoes
> And when the train horn blows, I'm gonna go
> Oh! Lord! Bzzzz… Never going to lose
> Those mean old… Bzzzzzzzzz, bzzz, bzz, bzzzzz.

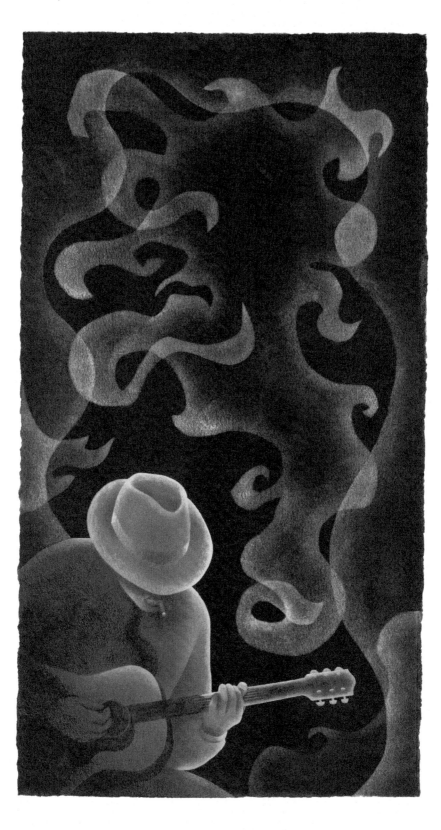

Lost in static. But no one in the world sounded like that except Mississippi.

I could just see him and Cerbie rambling down lonely dirt roads, singing in honkytonks, riding the rails. I wanted to be with them so bad it hurt.

I started rambling myself, in deserted places just outside the crowds: the dank dunes and pillars under the boardwalk, little alleyways off the walks, service corridors behind the rides, and the overgrown Coney Island Creek under the Belt Parkway. From there I roamed the tracks in the train graveyard. I could almost hear that lonely whistle blow.

And while I did, I wailed my song:

> I'm just a poor girl, a long way from home
> Such a poor girl, a long way from home
> I'll ramble all my days
> Without a tooth in my comb.

Scuffling and yelling in the hallway woke me up after a long day of lonesome rambling.

It was really late. Really, really late.

I hugged Bubbie's patchwork quilt, pressed it against my face—the dark red velvet patch the softest thing in the world.

There was the yelling again.

"Let go!" Mom cried. "Yuck, it's filthy, it died in there. It's crawling with germs."

"It wouldn't kill you to let go first," the Boarder yelled.

I cracked open my bedroom door and peeked out. There in the crooked, shadowy hall were Mom, looking like a stick insect in her pink satin pajamas, and the Boarder, half Mom's height with her white hair in snarled clumps. They were having a tug-of-war over poor Goldie's birdcage.

"What are you trying to do?" Mom cried. "Kill us?"

"Again with the killing? Kill-schmill."

"We'll get cock-a-roaches!" Mom wailed.

"Gey in drerd!" The Boarder's wrinkled brow was knotted into a tight vee.

"Why can't I throw anything away?" Mom shouted. She seemed to be gaining the upper hand. "Don't you ever sleep?"

"Gey kocken oyf der yam!" The Boarder's face flushed scarlet and the knuckles on her knotty old hands were white.

"Will you just. Let. GO!" Mom shrieked.

Suddenly the Boarder *did*—which sent Mom flying backwards, slamming against the wall.

The Boarder clutched her chest.

"Gevalt!" she shrieked as she keeled over sideways, landing on the floor with a thump.

Mom stood there, her free hand on her neck, gasping, then glanced over at me, standing in my doorway. She sighed, put down the bird-cage, and leaned over the Boarder.

"Fine." She rolled her eyes. "You win." And stomped off into the bedroom.

I inched into the hall.

"Excuse me," I said.

The Boarder's eyes were rolled up so only the whites were showing, and her tongue was hanging out the side of her open mouth.

"You all right?" I asked. "Should I wake my dad?"

She popped up like toast. I staggered backwards as she grabbed the birdcage, scooted through her door, and slammed it shut—BANG!—behind her.

Mom stuck her head out.

"You happy now?" she said. "Go back to bed this minute or you're going to catch it in the morning."

Six

I rambled day after day until I was so weary I could die. Mom—who knows why?—started emerging from her room again. She went back to making me breakfast like she used to before she stopped eating—bacon and eggs and fresh squeezed orange juice. She wasn't eating herself, but it seemed like progress.

Marilyn was still under lockdown. You'd think Uncle Nat would stand up to Evil Aunt Suzie and help his daughter, but he literally couldn't—he was in a wheelchair from multiple sclerosis and Marilyn's room was on the second floor.

I walked across the hall to Mom's room and stood in the doorway. She was wearing her pink satin pajamas and hadn't combed her hair or put on makeup, which made her look kind of unfinished. She was staring into the mirror on her fancy burled wood vanity. I noticed a bottle of Happiness Pills there. She leaned forward and frowned at herself.

"Where'd you go?" she asked her reflection.

"Mom?" I said.

She jumped with a start, then let out a sigh.

"Don't sneak up on me like that."

"The door was open."

She frowned at me and put her hands on her hips, which were practically nonexistent.

"Did you want something?"

"Why can't you talk Aunt Suzie into letting Marilyn out?" My voice rose to a squeak. "It's been forever. She might not even be alive any more."

"Not now." A huge sigh. "I have problems of my own."

It was just like her. She didn't care about Marilyn, didn't care about me.

"Fine," I said. "Stare at yourself in the mirror all day. I'm going to the boardwalk."

"Don't forget to eat lunch." She took a dollar out of her pocketbook, handed it to me. "And be back for your three o'clock milk."

"Gee, thanks." I left the house by the side door.

We had a large cement backyard, more of a side-yard really, bordered on its front by rickety cabanas my grandparents used to rent out. Along its back was a broken-down chain-link fence separating it from a huge overgrown vacant lot.

I walked down the path between the house and the garage to the street, past Marilyn's house, fronted by Evil Aunt Suzie's lush rose garden. As was my habit, I kicked her chain link fence.

Why would someone like Evil Aunt Suzie plant a rose garden? you might ask. Then it might occur to you that maybe she just needed some beauty in her angry, bitter world. But Mom considered Suzie's garden to be an act of war. That's because Mom is cursed with hay fever, so roses make her sneeze.

There were lots of kids out that day, trading baseball cards, playing stoop ball, hit the penny, redlight/greenlight. I remembered that strange pastime: playing.

Joanie waved and said, "Hi, Brooklyn." (Word of my new name had spread.) "Want to play cowboys and Indians?"

As long as I'd known Joanie, which was practically all my life, the only thing I'd ever seen her wear was cowboy outfits. She was wearing one now, a skirt and blouse with suede fringes.

"Not today," I said.

I took the usual route to Surf Avenue, turned on Stillwell, up the ramp to the boardwalk, and there I was—but Uncle Max's was closed and bolted, no one in sight.

I turned toward the ocean and walked over to the railing. Once there was nobody here but the Canarsee Indians. They saw the same ocean I was seeing, heard the same surf. It was whispering to me. *Swim out, swim out, swim out, little girl—*

I heard singing on the boardwalk—and took off running.

Been riding down that long railroad track, Lord, Lord
Been riding down that long railroad track...

Then Cerbie was bounding toward me. He jumped right up on my shoulders to lick my face, almost knocking me over, and we danced around together. He was smiling, wagging his tail, spinning in circles, barely able to contain his joy. I roughed up the top of his head.

"Good boy!" I hugged him around his neck, burrowing into that thick soft fur. "You're such a good boy, Cerbie. I missed you, you big bad wolf."

Then we ran over to where Mississippi was sitting on a folding stool, winding up his song:

Don't go, oh no, no, don't you go, old friend

Don't go, don't you never leave my side
If you go, if you go, if you go, my life'll end
And I'll die on this long and lonesome ride.

Mississippi had set himself up three blocks down the boardwalk from Uncle Max's. It seemed like the perfect place for him, the salt breeze, crashing surf, his voice blending with the distant clank-clank-clank-eeeeeeeeeeek! of the Cyclone roller coaster. He was wearing his tattered white shirt and suspenders, the gray felt hat at his feet. I plopped down on the edge of the bench next to him.

"Hey, Mississippi, I'm so happy you're still here." I gave him a big smile. "I thought you left town."

"Brooklyn." He gave me a wonderful smile back. His eyes crinkled, his face glowed. "Ain't you a sight."

We were both smiling and smiling like our faces would break.

"Did that song mean something?" I asked.

"Pardon me?"

"The song you were just singing. You know, about an old friend never leaving your side? Did you mean Cerbie?"

He shook his head. "I just made up that verse, don't expect it means a thing. Don't you worry none, Cerbie wouldn't never leave me."

"Okay," I said, but the song was still in my head and made me uneasy. "So where've you been?"

"After your uncle fired me I started going into Manhattan trying to find me some work, didn't have no luck. Bar owners these days seem to want cheerful songs, but my heart ain't in it."

"I hate fake cheerful," I said.

"So I come back here." He shrugged.

I glanced down at his hat and saw coins in it, mostly dimes and nickels.

"Cerbie picked out this spot." He gave his dog a smile. "Didn't you, boy?"

The dog grinned back.

"Could I be Cerbie's godmother?" I said. Cerbie came over and planted his head on my lap. "You know, in case you can't take care of him some day?"

"Well, that's the nicest thing anybody ever offered us. But the sad truth is, I'm on the run. If I had a choice, I'd stay right here. But sooner or later a certain sheriff will be along and I'll have to take off running."

"Coney Island doesn't even have a sheriff," I said. "It's not that kind of place."

We were facing Jones Walk, a walkway connecting the boardwalk to the midway. Jones was my favorite walk, with its red THRILLS arrow pointing at the Wonder Wheel soaring 150 feet in the air. As it turned, its cars rolled down internal tracks, swinging back and forth. Behind the Wonder Wheel was a maze of back alleys, and the gearboxes, motors, and lift chains that made the rides run.

"No sheriff?" Mississippi said. "That's hard to believe."

"I'm a Coney Island insider." I puffed up. "My dad makes the rides run, and my bubbie used to…"

Mississippi leaned toward me and squinted.

"You all right, Little Sugar?"

"Did you know Coney Island was always burning down?" I said.

"You don't say."

"There used to be a hotel in the shape of an elephant! Then one day, poof, it went up in smoke. And you know Steeplechase?"

"That big thing over yonder?" He pointed toward the parachute jump, which was in front of the amusement park.

"Steeplechase was named for its mechanical horse race that goes around that big glass building," I said. "I've gone on it lots of times.

It's so much fun. They have huge spinning barrels you try to run through, and really high slides that dump you onto a spinning floor, and a maze that lets you out on a stage where a clown tries to hit you in the tush with a paddle, but the clown never gets me because I'm so skinny I can run back and squeeze through the turnstile the wrong way."

Mississippi laughed and laughed.

"Ain't you something."

"Anyway," I said, "it burned down too, lots of times. But they kept rebuilding it. It was the first amusement park built and the only one that's still here."

"You sure do know a lot about Coney Island."

"Yeah, my dad tells me stories when it's not the busy season."

"You a lucky girl."

Just then I noticed a cop looking at us. He glanced over at the No-everything sign, then back to us, then back at the sign. He frowned, as if he was running through the list of things not allowed. I knew these included soliciting and dogs.

I pocketed Mississippi's change, put his hat on, and ran over.

"Hi, Officer O'Levy. Like my new hat?"

"Very becoming." He smiled and walked on. I ran back to Mississippi, sat down, and returned the hat and change.

"Don't worry, I know him. If any of the policemen say you have to take Cerbie off the boardwalk, just tell them he's your Seeing Eye dog."

"You something, all right." Mississippi grinned. "You a little charlatan, ain't you?"

"Thanks." I grinned back. Now I noticed Lenny standing on the other side of the boardwalk, smoking a cigarette. He kept glancing at his watch like he was waiting for someone.

"Look, Mississippi." I pointed. "That's Uncle Max's singer, Lenny."

"Heard him sing the other night. That man was blessed with a fine voice."

This was my chance. I could go over right now and ask him what he meant by his song. But just as I started getting up, Cerbie put his paws on my legs and pressed down. I roughed up the top of his head.

"Okay, boy, I'll stay right here." I turned to Mississippi. "On Memorial Day Lenny sent me a secret message in a song he was singing in Uncle Max's. I think I was the only one who heard it."

"Why you so sure he was singing to you?"

"He used my name! He sang 'I got a story *Sarah*,' and then he sang it was the end of someone I know! And the next day you sang almost the same message but you didn't say my name."

"Two secret messages? You ain't pulling my leg, are you?"

"Mississippi, look at me." I stared him straight in the eyes. "If I was kidding you'd know it."

He looked. He saw.

"Well, that's the damnedest thing I ever heard."

"Did that ever happen to you before? Sending secret messages through songs?"

"I ain't even sure it happened this time," he said. "Might not mean a thing." But he frowned.

Just then Cerbie jumped up and looked at Lenny, tail low, ears pointing forward, fur bristling. He let out a few short barks.

Lenny chuckled and walked away.

Cerbie watched him go, his eyes slanted back, tail still. He emitted a low growl.

"Cerbie!" Mississippi said.

He turned and licked Mississippi's hands, then mine.

"I love you too," I said and kissed him on the head. He sat back down.

"I don't know about no secret messages," Mississippi said, "but I do reckon fate brought me and Cerbie here to Coney Island for some special reason."

"How come you left home?"

He shook his head. "I had to run away."

"Oh, no. What happened?"

"It started with a murder committed a hundred and fifty years ago," he said, "when my great-great-granddaddy shot a sheriff in the heart and ran off to be a sailor before they could lynch him.

"Where I come from we had to pick cotton till our fingers was all blistered and bleeding. Be hotter than a fever in hell, and we'd be dragging them cotton sacks like they's a ball and chain, never stopping 'less we passed out. Didn't hardly get no pay, neither."

I leaned in closer, dangling my flip-flops back and forth on my toes.

"The worst was one long hot summer when it never did rain but once. The earth got scorched up so hard and so dry them cotton plants looked like they's made out of hay, but we harvested as best we could. I was just a boy back then, not much older than you, but my daddy was dead, which I guess made me the man of the house. When Mama sent me over to the bossman's place to get our share for the year's work, he told me, 'Wait here,' and goes back into the big white house, slamming the door in my face. I waited and waited. After a long spell he come back, but instead of the money he owes us he gives me this sack of his wife's old dresses, and there weren't a thing I could do about it."

I sucked in a breath, couldn't believe anyone would be so mean.

"Is that why you hit the road?" I said.

"Good Lord, no. I was just a kid, never once left that little town before. Catfish Eddy, it was called. My family goes way back, hundreds of years. Dragged there in chains by the first white folks. Then around 1800 the master freed my great-great-granddaddy, educated him, and left him the farm when he died, slaves and all. That's because he was the master's only surviving child. Looked just like him, too, only darker.

"But this don't set well with the sheriff, the master's cousin. So he destroyed the real will and forged a fake one leaving the farm to his own self."

My throat and chest filled with a wet kind of anger. I was glad his great-great-granddaddy shot the sheriff.

"But that was long before I came along," he said. 'I sure loved it there."

"What was it like?" I said.

"It was on the Mississippi, zippered right down the middle by freight-car tracks—white folks on the north side in their nice houses and us coloreds on the other. There was a little cemetery behind our church with mossy gravestones, all falling over, carved with names like Yates, Kurtz, Campbell, the same exact names as in the white folks' graveyard. Them white folks would of denied it but we had the same great-great-granddaddies as they did.

"What did you do there?"

"On Sundays Mama'd stick a big creamy magnolia flower in her hair and put on her pale blue dress with the lace trim, and she was the most pretty mama in town. And when she give you a hug, you felt so safe and treasured. She had this strong, sweet singing voice, used to sing us to sleep when we were babies." He started singing: "'Hush-you-bye, don't you cry, go to sleepy, little baby. When you wake, you shall have, all the pretty little horses.'

"I learnt that song from her and do believe I was the first one ever to sing it north of the Mason Dixon line."

The look on his face made me hurt for him—and for me, because I wanted my bubbie so bad.

"I bet you miss her," I said.

"Always will. Miss my three sisters, too. In my head they still young, all sitting around the kitchen table after church, looking so pretty in their Sunday dresses, laughing and deviling my older sister, Pearlene, because she's sweet on some boy. Then Mama would bring the food— crispy fried chicken, turnip greens, mashed potatoes with gravy, and home-baked cornbread so good you could slap your grandma."

He sighed, then shook his head. I was dying to hear the rest of the story but suddenly I was starving.

"Want to break for some lunch?" I said. "My treat, I have a whole dollar."

This was a fair amount of money, considering a hot dog was a dime and corn on the cob a nickel.

"I sure would appreciate it," he said.

So off I ran, leaving him singing, "Oh, oh, oh, oh, I miss my mama so…"

There were so many choices: oysters on the half-shell, fried frog's legs, chow-mein sandwiches, cotton candy, Hirsch's hand-rolled knishes, Nathan's hot dogs—the best in the world. Nearby was a place called Sodamat, with the motto "Good drinks served right," which meant in paper cups by machines in the walls. You could get exotic flavors like champagne and loganberry. You could also get an egg cream, a drink made with no eggs and no cream but a secret syrup found only in Brooklyn. There were a lot of urban legends about finding the perfect egg cream. Personally, I would vote for Karpkowsky's corner candy store, but that was too far away at the moment.

I ran over to the closest snack bar, loaded up with hot dogs , fries, corn, and sodas, and ran back. Mississippi was still on, "Oh, no, no, no. Left my mama, didn't never say goodbye…" and his voice sounded sadder than I'd ever heard it. But just when I thought it was as deep and as painful as anyone could bear, he glanced up, caught my eye, and slid to, "You got to jump down, turn around, pick a bale of cotton. Got to jump down, turn around, pick a bale a day," his voice as joyous as the tune.

Cerbie jumped up and wagged his tail, grinning and panting, bouncing to the music. So I put the food on the bench and did a little jig with him until the song ended.

"I thought you never sang happy songs," I said.

"I ain't felt like singing that song in maybe ten years."

"I got the two candied apples for free." I was so proud. "The guy said he'd throw in a candied apple if I gave him a smile."

"How'd you get the second one?"

"I asked him if he'd throw in two for a really big smile."

"You *are* a little charlatan." The three of us were grinning to beat the band. I gave my hot dog to Cerbie and just ate the bun and fixings, my favorite part anyway. That and the candied apple filled me right up.

"I just had a horrible thought," I said. "Do you think they put real dogs in hot dogs?"

Mississippi laughed. "Don't you worry yourself none. Hot dogs are made from hog fat and gristle." He held up the soda bottle. "What kind of Coke's this?"

"That's not Coke, that's a Doctor Brown's Cel-Ray Soda. Don't tell me you don't have celery soda where you come from!"

"We sure enough don't."

"So tell me what happened in Catfish Eddy?"

"I come home from the cotton fields one day, weary to the bone, and there on the front porch was our poor old hound dog, head chopped off, big sad eyes staring right at me." His jaw tightened. "The grass-gut who killed her throwed her head on the rocking chair. Poor old dog never hurt nobody."

"That's terrible!"

"We all knew who done it—Bobby Wayne Kurtz, the deputy, a buzzing mosquito of a good old boy, stupid as a sack of hair. He was making a spit cup out of me, sucking up to Sheriff Virgil. Now, Sheriff Virgil was a Yates, same as me. Huge fella with a square jaw like a block of granite. White folks liked him, said he was friendly and aimed to please. But he weren't nothing but a meat-faced grinning pig to me. Weren't nobody meaner. He hated me because it was his great-great-granddaddy who my great-great-granddaddy shot dead. But what made him hate me even more was he thought I low-rated him. I was only fifteen years old, and he was always big-bellying me around, wanting me to call him sir. Yes, sir. No, sir. Whatever you say, sir. But every time I did, he had the suspicion I didn't mean it. After I left, I never call no one sir no more. Not ma'am neither."

"But if you knew he killed the dog—"

"Weren't a thing I could do about it. If I did something they'd come after Mama and my sisters. It's a terrible thing not to be able to protect your family.

"That night, dead tired as I was, I just couldn't sleep. Couldn't even close my eyes, just kept twisting round and round, thinking about Deputy Kurtz. I know it ain't right, but I kept praying something terrible would happen to him.

"Then about midnight I hear something howling in the distance, then closer and closer. I'm shaking, scared to death, reckoning it's a hellhound come to get me for my evil thoughts. Soon it's right at the back door barking and howling, scraping the door with its nails. I just keep digging my fingers into the mattress, too scared to look. Suddenly it stops, just like that, and there's dead quiet for the rest of the night.

"That morning at first light I peeked out, and sure enough there's scratches on the back door."

I shivered and looked around for Cerbie.

"Where'd Cerbie go?" I asked.

"I don't rightly know." Mississippi looked all around, frowning. "He ain't never run off before."

"The song! When you sang, 'Don't you ever leave my side," you must have meant Cerbie!"

"Good Lord." He was worried but trying to hide it, I could tell. "Most likely he'll be right back."

We waited and Mississippi called him and called him, but Cerbie didn't come back. I asked all the people around if they'd seen him, but none of them had.

"That song *was* a warning," I said.

He put his hands over his face and sighed.

"I reckon you might be right, but I don't rightly know what it all means."

A terrible thought occurred to me.

"What if someone kidnapped him?"

He gave a sad laugh. "I can't think why anybody would kidnap a dog. Besides, they'd have to do it right in front of us and Cerbie would put up a fight. He's the strongest dog there ever was."

We decided to search the neighborhood, split up to cover more ground, then meet back at the boardwalk after supper.

I went to some of the places I'd gone to during my rambling days, which led me to my secret hideout—the place where the Coney Island Creek abruptly ended. It was filled with dark stagnant water, a few tires, pipes, and the skeletal remains of a shopping cart sticking out along the left bank. I stood at the railing on the part of Shell Road that had never been paved, under the Belt Parkway, breathing in car exhaust and listening to the whoosh of traffic overhead. In the distance I could see a small pier sticking out into the water.

Strange, but as many times as I'd been here, I'd never seen a person or even a car.

The other side of the creek was covered in a wild tangle of trees and underbrush as far as you could see. Just then I heard something muffled and under the surface, far, far away. Then louder and closer. Barking.

"Cerbie!" I cried out.

It stopped. I heard a bird cawing: wa, wa, wa, like a sarcastic baby crying.

Then there it was again, definitely barking.

"Cerbie!" I yelled as loud as I could. "Is that you, boy? Come here!"

The barking got louder. I saw movement in the thicket, but nothing came out— was he afraid to show himself?

"Cerbie? It's me, Brooklyn."

The movement again. I held my breath, felt a ping of joy when I saw silver fur between the thick leaves and branches. Then a dog broke out of the underbrush and stood there, staring at me.

It was just an ugly gray mongrel, nothing like Cerbie. Sometimes we see things because we want to so badly.

The dog started snarling. I jumped back, heart pounding. There must be hundreds of strays in Brooklyn—which gave me an idea.

Mom hadn't even noticed I missed my three o'clock milk-drinking torture—she was still in her room staring at the mirror. I wasn't sure I was all that happy about this. There was nothing in the Frigidaire, so I headed back to the boardwalk.

When I got there Mississippi looked as worn out as an old shoe. He was sitting on his folding stool, cradling his guitar. I plopped down on the edge of the bench.

He told me he'd covered the midway and the boardwalk and a lot of the streets, calling out Cerbie's name over and over. I told him about the secret places I'd looked and about my idea, which was that the dogcatcher might have scooped Cerbie up in his net and taken him to the pound.

"Well," he said, "I'll check the pound in the morning when they open up, before I come back here." He got up and slammed his folding chair shut. "I got to be going, got to keep searching. I ain't never going to have a minute of peace until I find that dog of mine."

I wasn't either, but I didn't tell him that. It would just make him feel worse.

Seven

Another week went by, and not only had Cerbie not come back to the boardwalk, neither had Mississippi. Even worse, Marilyn was still under lockdown. This meant she'd been literally imprisoned in her room for over two weeks. Between that and everything else, I figured I had the right to sing the blues.

I was stomping back and forth in front of the boarding house. When the mood struck me, I'd wail, "Oh, oh, oh, ooooh, I got the lockdown blues." Then I'd lean over the chain-link fence and glare at Evil Aunt Suzie, who was pulling Japanese beetles off her rose bushes and dropping them in a jar of turpentine. She was wearing her usual ratty housedress, hair uncombed, no hearing aid. The bandage, now filthy and ragged, was still wrapped around her arm.

"See, isn't this nice?" she said to herself. "We can get along when we try."

She didn't take any notice of me. I wasn't surprised. When she wasn't trying to kill me, she usually just looked right through me. We'd seen each other practically every day of my life, but I sometimes wondered if she even remembered who I was.

Anyway, she was doing her favorite thing—killing something—so she had a serene smile on her face. In fact, I'd never seen her look happier. Surrounded by her beloved roses—a lush profusion of reds, pinks, and yellows—she looked, well, almost pretty.

Just then something hard struck my arm.

"Ouch!"

I turned and saw Joanie, wearing chaps and a cowboy hat. She had a thick piece of hemp rope dangling from her hand.

"You trying to break my arm?" I said.

"Sorry. I was trying to lasso you. Want to play rodeo? You be the bucking bronco."

"No, thanks." Then I had an idea. "You think we could use that rope to get up to Marilyn's window on the second floor?"

"Of course not. It's only a few feet long."

"Where'd you get it?"

"Our basement."

Then I had a great idea. In fact, I was an idiot not to have thought of it before.

"Got to go," I said.

I ran down the alley that bordered the left side of our house then turned the corner into a huge vacant lot and after a few feet came to the steps to our basement's back door. I used the spare key we kept under a brick to get inside. Most of the basement was made up of useless hallways and dead ends, home to a recurrent infestation of rats. But there was also a small apartment down there—moldering wallpaper, tarp-draped furniture, piles of books, even a TV—that my parents figured was too awful to rent out.

I was in luck—I found a rickety folding ladder not far from in the entrance. I dusted a big tent of cobwebs off it, carried it to the back of the boarding house, unfolded it, and propped it up under

Marilyn's window. It felt unstable on the bumpy dirt and was a couple of feet short of the window. I looked around, took a deep breath, and up I went.

Through the window I could see Marilyn in her pedal pushers, her shiny straight hair tucked behind her ears. She was sitting on the floor reading a book, her back against the side of her canopy bed. Her room was the opposite of the rest of the house, a wonder of neatness and order. She had an antiqued white bedroom set, a gift from her paternal grandparents, long dead and gone. The canopy bed with its white eyelet-trimmed top was the only possession of hers I envied. It looked so safe and cozy.

I rapped on the glass, which made the ladder shake and Marilyn jump up. I grinned and waved. I was so excited—a real jailbreak! Her eyebrows shot up and her round face broke into the happiest of smiles. How could anyone lock up someone so lovable? She ran right over to the window and opened it.

"I've come to break you out," I said, and climbed into the room.

"Thank you, thank you, thank you!" Her sweet little voice, so different from mine, was squeaky with excitement. She hugged me and we danced around together.

"I've been going crazy in here. How many months has it been? Has school started yet?"

"It's been about two weeks. Let's get out of here before someone sees the ladder."

"Wait. I want to show you my secret weapon." She took a jar out of her dresser and handed it to me.

"What is this? It looks like a dead bug and a piece of bread."

Her words ran together. "It's a bee, it flew in the window, I'm saving it for when my mom brings me dinner then I'll make it sting her."

"Um… Marilyn, it looks dead."

She squinted at it. "It was all right yesterday."

"Come on," I said. "Let's go, before it's too late."

We climbed down the shaky ladder—I went down first and held it steady for Marilyn—folded it up and carried it back to the basement. Then we just stood there in the dimly lit entrance hall.

"Now what?" she said.

"What made your mom so mad? She never locked you up this long before."

"When I bit her? It was so bad she had to go to the emergency room."

"I have a lot to tell you," I said, "but let's get out of here before your mom realizes you escaped."

"Look what she did to me." Marilyn held out her arm. "See? I still have the bruises. She screamed she was going to lock me up for the rest of my life."

"That's not good," I said.

"It doesn't matter now."

"Why not?"

"I'm never going back!" She slammed the wall with her fist. "Whatever you do, don't let them get me."

"Where are you going to go?"

"I don't know. Hide in your room?"

"But they'd find you right away, it's the first place they'll look."

"I'll sleep under the boardwalk if I have to. I'm never going home. Let's get out of here, I'm dying to have some fun, let's go to the midway."

"You mind walking by Uncle Max's? I want to see if Lenny's rehearsing. I still don't know what his secret message meant."

She thought for a minute, then shrugged.

"Okay, I guess." She tiptoed up the basement stairs, looked in both directions, then waved me to follow.

As we walked under the giant sycamore trees in Seaside Park Marilyn was hopping, skipping, twirling around, waving, saying hi to complete strangers, just grinning and grinning.

When she calmed down I filled her in on how the first Little Suzie died of rabies and Mississippi's secret messages and Cerbie disappearing. And how I'd changed my name to Brooklyn so I could sing the blues. It seemed like everything had changed while she was locked up and I was so happy she was here now to help me.

We passed the handball courts and walked up the steps to the boardwalk. It was a perfect seventy-degree day, kids running, skating, eating cotton candy, sunbathers tanning, the smell of Coppertone wafting off the beach. There were even a few swimmers braving the chilly ocean.

We were passing the penny arcades now. I could hear the clank-clank-clank, eeeeeeeeeeeek! of the Cyclone and smell the hot dogs and sauerkraut.

Then there we were, on the boardwalk in front of Uncle Max's.

The accordion doors were open a crack. Through them came Lenny's deep sleepy voice. He was singing "Smoke Gets in Your Eyes."

The words snaked out, encircling me, drawing me in. I pulled the doors open a little more. Lenny was sitting at the piano on the raised stage. When he saw us looking in he winked at us, which made Marilyn wince. I figured he was rehearsing today because it was Tuesday—fireworks night—the most crowded night on the boardwalk.

"Let's get out of here," Marilyn said.

"Wait. I have to ask him what his secret message meant."

Then, he sang some wrong words:

It cannot be denied
Brooklyn you can't hide.

I gaped at Marilyn, but her expression hadn't changed.

"Did you hear that?" I cried. "You *must* have heard it."

"What?"

"He sang that I can't hide. He called me Brooklyn."

"No he didn't."

Oh God. Maybe I *was* hearing voices, just like Evil Aunt Suzie. I took a couple of steps backward, over the threshold. I just had to find out what was going on.

A big hand clamped on my arm. Oh, no—it was Uncle Max, glaring down at me with his icy blues.

"What the hell's going on here?" he asked.

"Run!" I shouted to Marilyn.

"But I…" I could see she didn't want to abandon me.

"Run!" I yelled again, "or he'll call your *mom*!"

Marilyn took off. Uncle Max pulled me outside.

At the end of the building Marilyn stopped.

"I'm never coming back!" she yelled, then she disappeared around the corner.

"Where'd Marilyn go?" Uncle Max asked.

"I don't know."

"And why did you come in? You know you're not allowed in here."

"Did you hear what Lenny sang to me?" It just wasn't fair—nobody believed me. "He said I can't hide." I turned to Lenny. "*Tell* him!"

Lenny looked confused. "You heard me sing *what*?"

"I want you to stop these lies this minute!" Uncle Max shouted at me.

"But—"

"Get lost and don't come back."

Eight

Now all my friends were missing.

It was three whole days now, and Marilyn seemed to have vanished from the world. At first I didn't realize how serious it was, then the police showed up and searched our house top to bottom, paying special attention to the basement with its maze of dead ends. The first thing they searched was my room, but Mom had already done that three times and there was no place to hide there anyway. To make things worse, I was under house arrest—not as bad as lockdown—I could wander from room to room, but I couldn't go out, not even to look for Marilyn. Lucky for me, Mom didn't believe in lockdown. Too much work, she said.

We were in the kitchen, Mom's elbows planted on the map-of-Florida tablecloth.

"Where is she?" she asked for the hundredth time. There were dark circles under her eyes making her look even more like a skeleton.

"I wish I knew." I squirmed around on the red vinyl seat and started chewing a lock of my hair. I kept thinking about each passing moment, the way it just disappears.

"Where is she!" she screamed. I put my hands over my ears. "It's like banging my head against the wall!" she screamed louder.

"It's your fault for not making Aunt Suzie let Marilyn out."

"Are you crazy? You know what she's like."

"You didn't even try!"

"Why won't you tell me?" She tapped her cigarette into the ashtray, then took a drag.

"Because I don't know."

"You'd tell Bubbie, if she were alive."

There she went again, saying it, making it real.

"No, I wouldn't. Because I don't *know*."

"I don't believe you."

"I have an idea," I said, "let's combine the third degree with my three o'clock milk-drinking-torture. That way we won't have to spend all day doing this again."

"You look terrible," she said. "Are you eating? Want some cookies?"

"I'm not hungry and you're the one who looks terrible."

"Don't you care that Marilyn could be in danger?"

The front door banged open and Evil Aunt Suzie stomped through the hall and into the kitchen. I noticed she didn't have the bandage on her arm anymore, but in its place were two ragged red semicircles.

"Where's my baby!" she wailed. "I can't live without her!"

"It's your fault Marilyn ran away," Mom said. "If you didn't lock her up like a criminal—"

I pulled on Mom's sleeve. "For over two weeks," I whispered.

"It's child cruelty!" Mom yelled.

Suzie glared at her. "You're the one who should lock up your daughter. If you disciplined her none of this would have happened. She wouldn't have been breaking into my house, stealing my baby. Now she's lying. She's lying right to our faces. Look at her." She turned to me and yelled, "Liar! Why won't you tell me where my baby is?"

"Child torturer!" I yelled back.

"If Marilyn dies it's on your head!" she cried, and with that she stomped out.

"Why hasn't Marilyn even called?" Mom asked.

"Maybe she's trapped somewhere," I said. "Or lost. Or she doesn't have a dime."

"So where is she?"

"I told you, I don't *know.*" I felt like I might cry any minute. I rubbed my eyes with the back of my hands, sniffled.

"If you knew, you wouldn't tell me, would you?"

"I'd never rat out Marilyn."

"So how do I know you're telling the truth?"

"Because I *am.*"

"Did you eat the whole fruitcake I had in the Frigidaire?"

"Are you kidding? I hate fruitcake."

"That's what I thought." She aimed an angry look up toward the Boarder's room. "Is she ever going to stop making my life miserable?"

"Why do you hate her so much?"

"What am I supposed to do now? Just stay in here and stare at you all day?"

"You're asking *me?*"

"And the cheese. Did you eat the Laughing Cow cheese?"

"I ate a piece yesterday, why?"

"The whole box is gone." She scowled at the Boarder's room again. "That lunatic, always taking. Take, take, take." She stubbed out her cigarette, heaved a sigh, got up and went over to the counter, where she picked up *Peyton Place.* I was reading it too when she wasn't looking, trying to make sense of adult love. But no sooner had she picked the book up than she slammed it back down. She yanked open the kitchen drawer and started thrashing around in it until she latched onto something—Bubbie's sewing shears. Mom snapped them open and closed—snick-snick—then turned towards me.

I jumped up so fast it made me dizzy and backed away.

"I just want to give you a little trim."

I grabbed hold of my hair, held it down with my hands.

"Have you lost your mind? I'll never, ever, ever let you cut it short! You *know* that. Never-ever!"

She slammed the shears on the table.

"Fine," she said, "look like a mangy rat if you want." She picked up her book. "I'll be in the backyard—and don't try to sneak out, I'll be watching."

"Okay," I said, though I didn't see how she could see me from there.

She headed toward the side door, then turned back.

"If I let you out, do you think you can find her?"

"I can go out?"

"Just get back for your three o'clock milk, and this doesn't mean you aren't still being punished."

I ran out the front door before she could change her mind.

There I was again, standing on the boardwalk outside Uncle Max's, the last place I saw Marilyn. The accordion doors were closed and locked. I know, because I tried them. I let out a frustrated huff.

I was about to turn away when the lock clicked and the doors folded open. I found myself facing Lenny, casually dressed today in wrinkled black slacks and a beige sports shirt. He squinted his dark sleepy eyes at me, then smiled.

"Excuse me," I said. "I was wondering, did you see where Cerbie went?"

He frowned. "Who?"

"Mississippi's dog. I saw you across the boardwalk right before he disappeared a couple of weeks ago."

"Oh, the big wolf." He laughed. "Sorry, didn't see where he went but I'll keep my eyes open."

"And how about Mississippi? He disappeared too."

He shook his head. "Got me there."

"Lenny? I have to ask you something important."

"Shoot."

I hesitated, was afraid he'd get mad or say I was crazy.

"Why are you singing secret messages to me?"

"You imagined it."

"Mississippi did it too!"

"What?"

"He sang a message to me."

Lenny looked at me intently.

"He sang that someone's going to *die* the day after you sang the same thing."

"Really?" He sounded interested.

"Yeah. But I don't know who."

"Want to come in?" He waved an arm, taking in the saloon. "Come on, I'll buy you a drink."

"But…" I bit my lip.

"And I'll sing you a song."

He pulled the doors open a little further.

I looked around. The coast was clear so I stepped into the crimson light, felt the shivery thrill of the place.

Lenny stepped in after me and closed the doors, making it even darker. He turned the lock.

"Hey," I said. "Do you have to lock it?"

"Just a precaution. I could get fired for this."

He walked behind the bar while I jumped on a stool and planted my red Keds on one of the rungs. It felt so cozy, just the two of us.

"So what'll it be, kid?"

"Ummm… I don't know."

"How about a Coke."

"Can't I have a real drink?"

"Your uncle would kill me."

"How would he find out?" I said.

"You know, you really are growing up fast." He poured Coke into a glass, then said, "Oh what the hell, life is short." He added a few drops of rum and handed it to me. "Drink up," he said, "for tomorrow… Who knows?"

I took a sip so tiny I wasn't sure any of it really went down my throat.

"Aren't you going to have one?"

"Sure, kid. Why not?" He made his signature drink, a martini with a green olive in it, held it high. "Bottoms up."

I heard a rumbling noise, could feel the place vibrate.

"Does the subway go under here?"

He gave me an odd look and shook his head.

"Of course not. We're right on the beach."

"I thought I heard a train."

"There's no underground in this part of Brooklyn, just the elevated trains."

"That's what I thought, but… how come there's stairs going down, you know, tucked away behind the stairs going up?" I'd only seen the stairs from outside the turnstiles, but I'd explored the cavernous station with its concession stands like I'd explored everywhere else in the neighborhood.

"You saw that?" He templed his hands and brought them up to his chin. "They closed that line years ago."

The rumbling had stopped.

"Can you sing now?" I said.

"Hold on." He thought for a moment. "What's your favorite ride?"

"I guess… My cousin Marilyn and I like the Magic Carpet."

This was just a walk-through, featuring a Laughing Sal, dark mazes, and a couch that dumped riders onto a moving carpet, which in turn dumped them onto the midway. That's the part we liked, being dumped on the midway.

"No, I mean a dark ride," he said. "How about Spook-a-Rama?"

"Yeah!" I said. "I love the way it's in three parts, dark, then sunny, then dark again, like they're three different worlds."

"Excellent." He smiled. "Now for your song." He winked at me, then mounted the stage carrying his martini. He sat down at the piano, flashed those bright white teeth in a big grin, and started playing and singing "Thank Heaven for Little Girls."

This, I decided, would be our song. I wondered if there was a secret message in this song too, but if there was, I didn't hear it.

BRRRRRING!

"Damn it," Lenny said.

He stepped off the stage and answered the phone.

"Yeah," he said. "Yeah, yeah, I'll be here." He hung up. "That was your uncle," he said. "He's coming in. You better skedaddle."

And with that he unlocked the doors and shooed me onto the boardwalk.

Nine

I walked over to the railing, looked out at the crisp blue sky, the waves rolling in, the breakers. The ocean sang to me, calling me to dive in, swim out. On the beach kids were playing tag, tossing beach balls, running and tackling each other, having so much fun that for a moment I almost wished I could be like them. I started singing to myself:

> Oh-oh I woke up this morning, and all my friends were gone.
> I said I woke up this morning. . . .

I remembered Marilyn saying she wanted to hide in my room the day she ran away. I thought of the food disappearing. Maybe she *was* hiding at our house. But the police had searched everywhere, in every closet, even the basement, in every room except…

Oh my God—the Boarder's room!

I ran home, through the front door, the hall, the kitchen, to the side door, where I pulled back the curtain and looked out the window. Good, Mom was still in the yard, sitting on her webbed lounge chair reading her book. I raced upstairs to the second floor and knocked on the Boarder's door.

No response.

"Hel-loooo. Anybody ho-ome?"

Through the open hall window came the xylophony, doodly-doo-de-do music of the Good Humor ice cream truck. I pitched my voice louder (I was good at that).

"It's me, the kid that lives here."

Finally I heard a creak, clunk, crash, tinkling-shattering, ay-yay-yay yay-yay-ing, thumpa, thumpa, swoosh, slide, thwunk!, all getting louder and louder. Until, right behind the door, clank, rattle, boing, squeak, bang...

"Oy!"

The door opened a crack, then the Boarder's bony fingers curled around it, *then* she flung it open. She looked up at me, her ancient head bobbing like a jack-in-the-box.

"Sarileh," she said, "already you're growing up nice and tall, kayne horeh. Maybe a little bit skin and bones. Your mama, she doesn't feed you?"

"My name's not Sarah any more. I changed it to Brooklyn."

"Okay, okay already, Brookileh. I wouldn't say my real name neither. It's too dangerous. What is it you want?"

"Is Marilyn hiding in your room?"

"Marileh? Nooo. Even if she wanted to, I keep the door locked. The police I wouldn't let in even."

"Are you sure?"

"Of course I'm sure." She latched onto my arm, her bony nails digging in like claws. She tried to pull me inside.

"Hey!" I yanked my arm back. "What are you doing?"

"Have a look. You don't believe me, look."

"No," I said. "I believe you."

I'd never seen her this close before. The skin on her face was finely cracked all over, like mud that had been in the sun for a thousand years. She looked a little like a much older Grandma Lena—they both had green eyes, but hers looked shrewd and kind of mischievous.

"You won't come in?" she said. "Fine. Go away, and never darken my doorway again." She started to pull the door closed—then, wham! I had a brainstorm.

I grabbed the door. "Wait."

"What? What is it you want now?"

"Oh my God," I said. It came out as a whisper, so awesome was my realization. "You're not a boarder at all, are you? You're my great-great-grandmother!"

"Oy!" she shouted. "Oy-yoy-yoy!" She grabbed her stomach, tears running down her cheeks, coughing, convulsing. I was about to run downstairs for Mom when she caught her breath, tapped her chest, and said, "I haven't had such a good laugh since that howling beagle dropped dead." She tapped my arm. "So maybe I helped a little. Do me something."

"So are you?" I said. "Are you my long lost great-great-grandmother?"

This sent her into another seizure of oys, stomach-grabbing, coughing, then catching her breath again.

"Ay-yay-yay," she said, "how many greats did you say? Never mind, it makes to me no difference. And even if it did, then still you wouldn't know."

"So you *are* my great-great-grandmother."

She opened the door further.

"You better come in." She looked around. "Quick."

She stepped around a pile of brown-edged newspapers, and in I sailed. The room reeked of mildew and damp paper. She stuck the police-lock bar against the door.

"You can't be too careful these days. There's a certain Molech who wants to kill me, but he doesn't know where I am. Persistent, he is. Smart, he's not."

We were crammed eyeball (hers) to shoulder (mine) into a small vestibule walled by clutter of biblical proportions: leather-bound books piled to the ceiling interspersed with things like a crushed saltwater taffy box, a straw fan embroidered with a flamingo, an unmatched set of crutches, a stuffed baby alligator, pink plastic hair rollers... Hanging on a doll's hand was a beat-up oil painting of a lady with a single thick eyebrow. Everything was coated in dust and dripping cobwebs like Spanish moss.

I was surprised to see many items I thought we'd thrown out over the years, like the busted floor fan and the spark-shooting toaster. Rusty power tools including a drill and jigsaw missing from the garage were on the floor near the door. Next to it was Grandma Lena's Miami Beach lamp, shaped out of scallop shells into a glowing castle (Mom use to call it the Monstrosity before it disappeared). Perched on a white plastic Corinthian column was poor Goldie's birdcage, a scattering of yellow feathers still stuck to its newspaper carpet. Some of my former possessions were in sight, like that square wooden beach pail Mom had thrown away years ago because I brought a dead kitten home in it, and clawing at the side of a dirty juice glass was my pet turtle, who'd disappeared under the dresser just the other day.

Three narrow paths cut through the Junkland Jungle.

"Walk this way." She waved me on, then plunged into the widest trail. No wonder it took her so long to answer the door. The slightest bump could bury you alive.

We turned a corner and I nearly jumped out of my skin. There, propped up on a broom, was a familiar looking electrocuted rubber man. This I knew had gone missing from Spook-a-Rama. The Boarder didn't so much as slow down, so I continued to troop after her.

We turned left off the main trail onto a tributary and soon reached a small clearing. This radiated other trails, but we stopped there. It was furnished with an ancient maroon armchair and ottoman, and a rickety table covered with one of Dad's sport shirts. On it was a small glowing lamp with a milk-glass base plugged into a jumble of patched-up extension cords. A three-foot-square cabinet with a ten-inch television fit neatly into the wall of junk facing the armchair. I noticed Cracker Jack boxes, an old-fashioned standing radio, and some hard canvas valises. Jutting out of one wall was an ornately carved sideboard with three clocks on it: a cuckoo shaped like a thatched cottage, a pendulum in a glass dome, and a ticking alarm clock with a big bell on top. They all read different times.

The Boarder hoisted herself onto the overstuffed armchair and I plopped down on the ottoman, bringing us more or less eye to eye.

"Well, here we are. Home at last." She smiled and tapped my arm. "Can I get for you a nosh? A Saltine, maybe? A Mallomar cookie? Don't be a stranger."

I noticed a squashed box of air-raid crackers among the packaged foods tucked under the dusty table.

"No thanks," I said. "So who's trying to kill you?"

She looked around, then whispered, "This I can't tell you, until it's the right part of the story. How's about a nice glass of schnapps?"

"Schnapps!" *Really* out of bounds. "Okay."

She went over to the carved sideboard, took out a fancy bottle, poured a tiny bit into two shot glasses, gave me one, and hoisted herself back onto her chair.

"L'chaim." We toasted, and I took a sip. It tasted like raspberry syrup spiked with rubbing alcohol.

"So if you're my great-great grandmother, how can you still be alive?"

"Marileh!" she shouted suddenly.

I jumped up and gawked at her.

She added in a singsong voice, "Come out, come out, wherever you are."

"Marilyn?" I called. "Are you here?"

"See?" She shrugged. "What did I tell you. She's not here."

"Why did you just call her like that, then?"

"I just wanted you should be sure. So you wouldn't be suspicious."

"Oh." I sat back down.

"Well, then, on to business." She grinned and rubbed her hands together. Then, "What business was it?"

"You were going to tell me if you're my great-great-grandmother or not."

"Oy, with so many greats already." She chuckled. "*This* is not so easy to tell you."

"Don't you know?"

"Of course I know. But your mama? She would plotz if she knew the truth."

"I won't tell. Really. Cross my heart and hope to die."

"Don't hope to die. It's enough you shouldn't tell."

Then she plunged into her story.

"When I was a young lady, back in Russia, Russia with the czars, I was such a beauty. *Such* a beauty. The most beautiful girl from my shtetl. Long brown hair like silk to the back of my knees. And tall? Tall and skinny like a willow tree."

"*You* were tall?"

"You wouldn't know it now because I've been shrinking, shrinking like wool since I came to this country.

"Most young ladies, they would have been vain, Brookileh. They would want all day to look in the looking glass, to brush the hair, to change the dresses. But not me. I wanted I should study philosophy at university."

"Philosophy?" I found this hard to picture.

"I wanted I should find out the meaning of life. Go sue me. But would they send me to university? Mama says, 'Why do you need university? You've got the sight. You can see Molechs. It runs in the family. I can see them, your grandmother can see them. And her mama, may she rest in peace, also with the Molechs. It goes with the green eyes.'"

"What's a Molech?" I asked.

"A Molech is a big shot in the afterlife. Then Mama she tells me, 'Beware of Molech ha-Movess, the Angel of Death.' But with the meaning of life, my mama was no help."

"So you can see the Angel of Death? Is that who's trying to kill you?"

"Don't rush me. When I went to Tata, he says, 'A girlchik should have babies, that's the meaning of life,' and he goes to a matchmaker and finds for me some schmegegge to marry. They pay a dowry in goats and geese to get rid of me, and that's that. My schmegegge husband has on him big ears like Mr. Potatohead, and I was such a beauty. *Such* a beauty.

"I made with the babies, with the scrubbing floors, with the washing diapers, and my schmegegge husband, he worked at some cockamamie job."

"How many children did you have?"

"You want to know how many children I had? This you want to know? What kind of question is this? Okay, okay already, this I can tell you." She looked up and counted on her fingers, "ayns, tsvay, drei, ummmm, ummmm, ummm, umm—Twenty?"

"Twenty! You had twenty kids?"

"Give or take." She shrugged. "Twenty, it was not so many in those days, what with Cossacks, pogroms, wars, and who knows what else, epidemics, starvation, you name it. Did from this list I leave out anything?"

"Murder?" I said.

"Murder is correct. Pestilence. Accidents maybe? You were lucky if you ended up with half. But that's another story."

"So which one of your children was my great-grandparent?" I asked.

"Oy! You never give up. I'm still telling you how I wanted to look for the meaning of life. For this I had for myself a plan. But first I'm having to stuff the kishkas, stuff the fish, stuff the homentaschen, and take all this stuff and stuff Mr. Potatohead and the twenty or so little schmegegges until they become big schmegegges, get married, and the whole mishagas starts all over again."

"Can I call you Grandma?" I asked.

"Don't jump to the conclusions, Brookileh. You want I should tell you my plan? Or maybe you want a little nosh now? Some khazeray?"

"Okay, tell me your plan. I'm dying to hear it."

"Again with the dying? Don't die, just listen.

"I would wait until the children grew up and left home, and then I would read for myself the books from the greatisha philosophers. I'm figuring that somewhere in there would be the meaning of life.

"So my children, kayne horeh, finally they grew up, got jobs, got married, and all of them moved out except for one boychik. He became a communist and moved to Mexico with Trotsky, but that's another story.

"That's when I start to see the fiddler. Hau boy, what a fiddler! Tall, dark, sexy, with a beard and a vest. Like a movie star he looks.

"First he turns up when the nextdoornic is dying. I'm right there in the room. He walks in, takes from his breast pocket a pince-nez pair of eyeglasses, clips them on his nose, then squints at poor whatever-his-name-was, may he rest in peace.

"The family, everyone there, they don't even look up, it's like he's invisible to them.

"In the room are the wife, four or five grownup children, the rabbi, the doctor, and my husband. All whispering like the poor fellow's sleeping, which he's not.

"The fiddler puts the fiddle to his shoulder and starts playing and singing:

Tumbala, tumbala, tumbalaika
Tumbala, tumbala, tumbalaika
Thumbalalaika, shpiel balalaika…

The family keeps on talking right over it, like they're deaf they act."

"So the fiddler's a singer too?" I asked.

"Of course, what did you think? Just fiddling? It's nothing without the singing.

"So." She held up a finger. "The fiddler looks like he's having for himself a good time, but finally he puts down the fiddle, takes a little black book out of his pocket. In this he runs his finger down a list of names and stops halfway down. Then he takes this same finger and touches it to the forehead of the dying man, and there it leaves a red mark. Then, like he has all the time in the world, which he does, he saunters out."

"Was it the Angel of Death?"

"Wait for the right place to ask that question. 'What's that red mark on the head?' I say to the neighbors, but everybody says, 'What mark? You see maybe some mark? I don't see any mark.'

"The poor schlemiel dies that night. Then a few months later in the marketplace there he is again—the fiddler—singing his song. When he sees me walks right up, squints in my face, and takes from his breast pocket his pince-nez."

"Oh, no!" I cried.

"Oy gevalt!" she said. "That's when I realized who it was." She paused so long I had to jump in.

"Who was it?" I squealed. "Is this right place to ask? Was it him?"

"You want to know who it was? This you want to know? Okay, okay already, I'll tell you. It was Molech ha-Movess, the Angel of Death."

"So you actually saw the Angel of Death?" Boy, was I impressed.

"As clear as seltzer. *And* I could hear him singing, remember, which nobody else could."

This sent a chill through me. "I'm getting secret messages in songs," I said.

"What?"

I told her about the messages I got through Lenny and Mississippi about someone going to die, and how no one believed me.

"Oy gavalt! Must be me. Must be the Molech zeroing in."

"So you believe me?"

"Of course. What's not to believe?"

"What should we do?"

"I'll have to take for myself special evasive actions. Throw him off. This I can't tell you about. It's too risky."

"Are there other big shots in the afterlife?"

"There's a guide there too, also a singer, but that one I never saw. Maybe other ones. I wouldn't know."

"So what happened when you spotted him?"

"So here we are, face to face in the marketplace packed with yentas, fiddlers, peddlers. We're standing in front of the one that sells dill pickles in big wooden barrels, and he's squinting and blinking in my face, taking out from his breast pocket the eyeglasses. I know from what happened to the nextdoornic that if he puts the red mark on my head, I'm a goner. So what could I do?"

"What?" I cried.

"I take my hand and I swipe the eyeglasses with it. Hau boy, is he surprised."

"Did that work?"

"Noooo." She waved her hand. "He's a Molech, with eyeglasses from a different plane of existence. My hand went right through. So I ran away."

"Does that work?"

"Of course. If you can see him."

"So the Molech can take anyone he wants, any time he wants?"

"Nooooo." She waved her hand. "There has to be a slot for you, right time, right place."

"So how did you get away?"

"It comes to me such a brilliant idea. I have the luck of a schlemiel, but the heart of a bonditt.

"So that night, after my schmegegge goes to sleep, I pack up my schmattes and take also a paring knife, a pot of glue, and all the money hidden in the mattress. Then I catch the night train out of there. Comes the morning I get off at some city with big gold domes like onions, get for myself a passport, and catch the next train. But as the train pulls out of the station, the Molech, he's there on the platform waving to me like he's my landsman. They love trains, molechs. They all do."

"So do blues singers!"

"Stop with the interruptions already. So when I arrive at the port of Gdansk there's a ship leaving for America, but they're already pulling up the gangway. 'Wait!' I give a scream, 'It's a life and death emergency,' so they let me jump on. I'm hoping the Molech won't follow me all the way to America, but if he does, I have in my head a plan, and—"

BRRRRRING!

The Boarder jumped up on her chair and started rummaging

through the wall behind her, sending plastic dragons and pairs of eye-glasses flying. Finally she managed to extract an old black telephone.

"So? How's by you?… Of course not… How much do you think a hundred-year-old lady can eat? Leave me alone already… What would your mama say?… No she wouldn't!"

She banged down the receiver.

"I didn't even know you had a telephone," I said.

"Of course." She beamed. "Only in America, kayne horeh. Here everyone has for themselves a telephone and a television. Without, how would I call the weather? Or maybe the operator for a little kibitzing? I call sometimes the television stations to kvetch that Lucy is too much a meshugana. I even call your mama, and she calls me. That was her just now, calling from the kitchen. Her fruitcake she thinks I stole."

"You and Mom call each other? But you live in the same house, why don't you just talk in person?"

"Because she's always hiding in her room. Nerves, she says she has. And she calls *me* a meshugana. But that's another story." A pause, then a grin. "No, it's the same story, but later."

"*Did* you take the fruitcake?"

"You too with the fruitcake? Fruitcake I wouldn't touch. Feh. It has raisins in it. Anyway, I eat like a bird. One Danish, it's enough for the whole day."

"All right," I said, "you find out the Molech's after you and the next day you're on a ship to America without so much as a tooteloo to your husband and twenty or so kids. Right?"

"Exactly, but don't forget my thirty or forty grandchildren, kayne horeh. I didn't tooteloo to them neither.

"So there I am," she continued. "I don't know if the Molech caught the same ship or not, but I'm not taking any chances.

"I was in a big cabin with a dozen or so Ashkenazim families, kids running around like mice, and there's a lady who looks like me. I go over and give a good look. Green eyes, gray hair, not so gorgeous, a little bit too old, and that black old-lady dress? I wouldn't be caught dead in it, but definitely she looks like me.

"I smile sweet and ask her, 'You have family in America?'

"'Do I have family in America?' she says. 'Could Moses make laws? Does Tiffany have eggs? I have such a family, and they're all in America, kayne horeh.'

"'Nu, so tell to me all about them.' I pat her hand. That's all she needs. What a yenta. She kvetches, she kvells, she kibitzes. Hoo-ha. From her I find out everything I need to know, including that she doesn't have any relatives left in the old country, which is why the American granddaughter is sending for her. Also her darling granddaughter hasn't seen her since she was six years old. But to tell you the truth I felt a little guilty. She was a real mensch, and I was a bonditt from drerd."

Suddenly the Boarder jumped up on her chair and smacked the side of her head.

"Gevalt! Do you know what time it is?"

"How?" I said. "Your clocks all say different times."

"Time for your three o'clock milk." She shook a finger at me. "With calcium for strong bones." She pinched my cheek. "Go, Brookileh."

"But I'm dying to hear what happens next."

"Again with the dying? Go already, go drink your milk so you wouldn't grow up to be a dwarf like me."

"Can I give you a hug goodbye, Grandma?"

"Oy, now a hug you want. What next? Kisses? Birthday presents? I ran away from all that. Go already."

"All right, Grandma."

"And don't call me Grandma, not until you find out who I am. And then? Don't do it then neither."

"I'll be back as soon as I can. Then you can tell me how you ended up being my great-great-grandmother. And don't lock the door."

"Okay, okay already. I won't lock any door. And Brookileh, could you do for me a favor and bring maybe a nice Danish from the ice box?"

"I'll try."

"Oh, could you bring for me also *The Daily Mirror*? And maybe a nice cushion for my back? And…"

I staggered onto the trail before she could give me her laundry and dry cleaning.

"Oh, and Brookileh," she called after me, "could you bring with you also a deck of playing cards? I want you should teach me to play poker."

Ten

A few minutes later while I was at my three-o'clock milk-drinking torture, the Boarder came downstairs. She stopped at the doorway to the kitchen.

"Yoo-hoo." She waved at us. "I'm going out."

Rats! I wanted to sneak back up to hear the rest of her story.

"Who cares?" Mom said.

"I have to…" She put her finger to her lips, shook her head at me.

Cover her tracks so the Molech couldn't find her?

"Don't come back," Mom said.

That was yesterday, and the Boarder *hadn't* come back. Not so I could tell, anyway.

Mom had been in her room all day with the door closed. She hadn't said I couldn't go out, so I figured I was still allowed as long as I was looking for Marilyn.

I crept out of the house, down the path, and through the gate. The street was strangely empty. I started walking, looking for signs of life.

Bernie came running up and smacked my cheek with a big kiss. Boys were mostly dreadful, but not Bernie. He liked to hang out with us girls and was just as sweet as can be. Still…

I pushed him away and said "Yuck."

"I just meant it as a fan." Bernie, despite the heat, was wearing crisp navy pants and a short-sleeved flowered shirt. I had on shorts, flip-flops, and pop beads.

"You're famous," he said.

"Huh?"

"You're famous. You know, in the neighborhood. Could I borrow your pop beads as a souvenir? I'll give them back tomorrow."

"Sure." I slipped the string over my head and handed it to him.

"Why am I famous?"

"Because you helped Marilyn escape. We can't stop talking about it. A kid who actually ran away and never returned."

"Has anyone seen her?" I asked.

"There've been rumors, but I don't believe any of them."

"Are there rumors about where she's hiding?"

"Nope." Bernie shook his head. "The police looked all over. Under the boardwalk, behind the rides, and they talked to everyone."

"Why's the street so empty? Where *is* everybody?"

"The beach, of course." He grinned. "It's the first perfect beach day, no one wanted to miss it."

"Why didn't you go?"

"Mono." I jumped back. "Don't worry, it's almost gone. My mom says it's not contagious anymore."

"Keep the pop beads," I said, and off I ran.

When I got to Brighton Beach Avenue I turned right. On every lamp post I saw a poster with Marilyn's smiling face over the words MISSING CHILD and a number to call the police with any information. I crossed Ocean Parkway and kept going, past the shanty town under the el and through Seaside Park.

As I walked I thought of all the places she could hide. During the day there were lots of spots where she could hang out and not be seen, from the train graveyard to the dunes at Plum Beach. But where could she sleep? And what was she eating? I was really worried about this.

I arrived at Jones Walk, where I stood under the huge red THRILLS arrow pointing at the Wonder Wheel—its cars sliding and swinging, slicing up the bright blue sky. And on the other side, Spook-a-Rama ran almost the entire block. This attraction had gone up just last season and they were still tinkering with it, so I didn't even know what all the stunts were. I did know that the cars no longer spun side to side as they whipped around the pretzel track—too much vomiting, I'd heard.

The Cyclone's clank-clank-clank, eeeeeeeeeeeek! was going full blast, and the Virginia Reel was generating loud screams of its own. Between shooting galleries, barkers, and frenzied sound effects, the whole place was exploding with noise. Yet I felt totally alone.

Then my ears started tingling. Cutting through all the noise was a familiar voice. It seemed to be there just for me. Could it be? Yes! It was Lenny singing to the tune of "Thank Heaven for Little Girls." Our song!

Thank goodness for little Brooklyn
Come on this ride and on this ride please stay…

So I did have a friend in the world, my other secret singer.

I made my way through the crowd as fast as I could, until I spotted him. He was selling tickets at the Spook-a-Rama ticket booth.

He paused, handed a lady tickets, then went back to singing at the top of his lungs without piano or microphone or anything.

I ran right up. He stopped singing and smiled down on me.

"Were you singing that just for me?" I asked. But of course I knew he was.

He laughed. "Kind of figured you'd be here today."

"But what are you doing here?" I said. "Where's the regular guy?"

He shrugged. "Just a little freelance work until my singing career takes off." He handed me a ticket. "Next car that returns," he said.

A car stopped and two little boys staggered off. Spook-a-Rama's cars were the plushest on the midway. High-backed and upholstered, they seated two riders and rode sideways on the track. I got in and the attendant pulled the restraining bar down in front of me.

The car lurched into motion and off I went, through the giant legs of the Cyclops, past a life-sized witch, under the waterfall of blood, and Bang! through swinging doors and into total blackness. But I could see after-images—Lenny's smile, the Cyclops' legs—and then I heard something, very faint but unmistakable: *Come to me little Brooklyn...* Lenny, the ghost of his voice.

My car made a sharp U-turn, wheels squealing, then shot down a long corridor and out into the bright courtyard. I was suddenly assaulted by the noises of Jones Walk and a dizzying zig-zag ride past an array of sinister figures, then Bang! straight through the green swinging doors—painted with giant terrified eyeballs—of the main building. The tracks pitched downward into darkness and a world with noises all its own. A light flashed on a figure: Frankenstein's monster, gray and looming. He lurched at me, arms out, bandages unraveling. "Goooood," his deep voice groaned.

This ride was so new Dad hadn't had to fix it yet, but I knew how it worked. Each car, when it reached a stunt, triggered it to come to life. Even with the partitions, you could see flashes of light from different stunts, and with all thirty-six cars in play, wheels squeaking and clanking, sound effects blasting... well, you can imagine.

In the cacophony of sound effects and screams I heard a girl's voice cry out: "Help!"

"Marilyn?" I called into the darkness, but it could have been anyone, anywhere.

A light flashed on, revealing a nasty-looking lizard-man. He lurched toward me, leaving a lady mannequin in a torn bikini frozen behind him. This stunt was accompanied by a Tarzan-like cry.

My car clanked further into darkness, spinning this way and that, then stopped. An overhead light clicked on and a giant rubbery spider fell from the ceiling, almost hitting me in the head. It bounced up and down to horror-movie shrieks.

Over them I heard something that made my heart skip. I became super alert, straining to hear, filtering out all the other noises.

There it was again. A bark—it sounded like Cerbie. Another one.

"Cerbie!" I screamed as loud as I could. "Is it you? Are you there, boy?"

Without a second's thought I flipped open the restraining bar and plunged into the darkness, running toward where I thought I'd heard him. He barked again.

Ouch! I bumped into something hard, skinned my leg. I circled—around it, but which way was I going? I kept on walking, arms outstretched. My hands hit something—a partition. *Feel along it, follow it.* It seemed to end. A sinister laugh engulfed me: Yaaaaah-ha-ha-ha-ha. Yaaaaah-ha-ha-ha-ha-ha. But somewhere out there I heard the bark again. I knew Cerbie's language—he was warning me.

"Cerbie! Where are you?" I plunged on into the void. The barking had come from…

In a flash of light I saw him, at least I thought I did.

Then I heard a growling noise close by. Then—

Someone shoved me. I landed on the floor, shocked, scared. A car sped by and nearly hit me. And I heard a loud series of barks.

Who would do something like that—shove a kid in the dark? I could almost feel the imprint of a big hand on my back. My knee hurt. I touched it—wet and warm. I pushed myself up to a standing position, but everything was spinning. My whole side ached. Which way was which?

Clank! Clank! Clank! Yaaaaah-ha-ha-ha-ha-ha. Yaaaaah-ha-ha-ha-ha. I tried to listen, my ears pounding. A whoosh of air. Yaaaaah ha ha ha ha ha. *Creep along. Just keep creeping along.* It was so dark, completely black. A light flashed on. Around me was a jungle scene. Loud bird noises. A gorilla lunged forward, bumping into me, grunting and snorting, jerking its arms up and down. I backed away.

I started walking straight ahead—as long as I kept going in the same direction, I'd reach a wall. I could feel the tracks under my feet as I shuffled forward, my hands reaching out, waving in the air. But there were tracks everywhere, every inch of floor it seemed.

Through the random din I heard the barking again. Cerbie was still warning me.

"Cerbie!" I yelled. "Where are you?" My hands hit a pillar, felt around it. There was a thick panel with knobs and switches on it. I flipped some of them hoping one would turn the lights on, but instead the stunts and sound effects seemed to speed up. Yaaaaah-ha-ha-ha-ha. Ahhhhhhhh! Yaaaaah-ha-ha-ha-ha-ha. I staggered on. Flashes of bright colors in the darkness. I tripped, yelled "OW!" Landed on my scraped knee. I forced myself up.

I kept walking, bumped into something. No, someone.

A stunt light flashed on. A bug-eyed man gaped at me, his tongue sticking out of the side of his mouth, his head twisted to one side. It was just the hanged man.

A lady and little boy were staring at me from a car.

"Oh my," the lady said. "What are you doing out there?" The room went black again. "You'll get hurt. It's…" The light went off but I heard their car start moving, "very dangerous," she called to me, "you should…" Her voice was drowned out by Aaaaaaahhhhhhhh! Yaaaaah-ha-ha-ha-ha-ha. Yaaaaah-ha-ha-ha-ha-ha.

I felt so lost, lost in every way. Mom told me that when you're lost the best thing to do is to stay where you are. I was shaking, tears running down my face.

Then I heard Cerbie barking again. He was trying to tell me something.

"CERBIE!" I yelled, then started running toward him when— bam! I slammed into something else, something dangling. Clink, clank, it fell to the floor. Now everything started squeaking and squealing, slowing down, the sound effects spreading out, getting deeper. Yaaaaaaaaaaaaa…haaaaaaaaaaaaaaaa…aaaaaaaaaaaaaaaaaaaaa…fading into silence. I heard voices, a lady and kids calling out into the darkness. "What's going on?" "What happened?" A man's voice shouted, "Would someone turn the damn lights on!"

There was a growling noise like a motor revving, a whoosh of air, a whoomph like something heavy slamming into someone, a scream of agony, then a thump on the floor.

"Damn you!" Lenny yelled.

The overhead fluorescent bulbs started hissing and flickering, then all at once lit up the hall with a greenish sheen. I was standing there with a broken skeleton heaped at my feet. The room wasn't as big as I'd imagined, and the stunts looked cheap, phony. Cars were scattered all over the place, their passengers obviously bewildered.

And Lenny was on the ground, holding his upper arm like he was in pain. He stood up, gave me a look of such pure anger I froze with fear.

"You!" he yelled.

I sucked in a breath.

"I'm gonna kill you!" he yelled even louder.

I turned and fled. My knee was throbbing, but that didn't stop me. I skirted the stunts, the cars, the equipment.

"Come back here!" he screamed.

I ran out the back door into the alley, then on to Jones Walk toward the beach. When I got to the boardwalk I just kept going, half running, half limping toward home.

By the time I hobbled through our side door, word of my adventure had reached Mom. I'm sure the whole neighborhood knew.

"You could have been killed!" she kept shouting over and over, then, "They'd blame me, that's who they'd blame!"

Even Dad when he got home from work that night was so mad he woke me up.

"How could you do something so dangerous?" he yelled at me, which wasn't like him at all. He couldn't believe that after all the talks on ride safety I would pull a stunt like this. Mom tried to make him hit me, but he wouldn't. It was her job to get me under control, he told her. Which brought her back to the only punishment I hated, we both hated.

House arrest.

Eleven

Mom was so mad she was barely talking to me. I don't know which made her angrier, the fact that I almost got killed or the fact that she was stuck in the house with me all day. She'd taken a turn for the better, gained a little weight, and bought a new bathing suit. It was a beautiful beach day and that's where she wanted to be, lounging on the sand with her friends, showing off her figure. Instead she was downstairs in the living room drinking a whiskey sour and watching "Queen for a Day" on TV.

"Kvetch for Pay," she called it.

I wanted to get back to the Boarder's story, but as far as I could tell she still hadn't returned.

The doorbell rang. I ran downstairs, but Mom was there ahead of me opening the door.

I sucked in a breath when I saw who it was.

"Well, hello there," Lenny said. He was dressed today in a crisp white shirt, stinking up the hall with his cologne, smiling at Mom. He ran his fingers through his brilliantined hair, patted it down.

"Hey there!" she sang out like he was her best friend. "Long time no see."

Then she did something I couldn't believe—she gave him a kiss on the cheek!

"Don't, Mom." I tried to pull her away, but she swung around and pushed *me* away. Her eyes flared.

"What is *wrong* with you?" she said.

"But Mom—"

"Kids." Lenny chuckled. "Don't worry about it."

"She's been nothing but trouble."

"You look great," he said.

"And you haven't aged a day since I met you," Mom said. "It's amazing."

For some reason he didn't look pleased at this, but then he brightened.

"You're the one who hasn't aged. You're more gorgeous than ever."

"You think so?" She struck a fashion-model pose. "I've been trying to take off some of the weight I gained when I had her." She frowned at me, then pulled at her blouse to straighten it. "If I'd known you were coming, I'd have put on something nicer."

He stood back, looked her up and down.

"Complete perfection." He kissed his fingertips.

"How can you say that?" I said. "She's starving to death. She can't even wear grownup clothes anymore. Those are *my* pedal pushers she's got on."

"Brought you a little present." He handed Mom something in a purple pouch.

"How nice." She gave him the biggest smile I'd seen in a long time. "You shouldn't have."

"Just a little token of my… friendship."

Mom opened the pouch and pulled out a wide flat bottle in the

shape of a crown filled with golden liquid. Royal Crown Whiskey, the label read.

"My favorite! I can't believe you remembered."

"A royal drink for a beauty queen."

Mom tilted her head down, smiled up at him.

"Those were the best days of my life," he added.

"Mine too. Our Rat Pack days."

"You had Rat Pack days?" I said.

"I wish you'd come to the bar like you used to," Lenny said. "Have a drink with your old friends."

"You know I can't. I have her." She tossed her head my way. "So what are we waiting for?" She stepped aside and motioned him in. "I'll pour us a couple of drinks."

"No!" I cried. "He's trying to steal you away from Dad." I tried to block the door.

"Go to your room!" she said. "You always ruin everything." Then to Lenny, smiling, "Why don't you have a nice comfy seat in the living room. I'll be right there."

She headed for the kitchen. I followed.

"Mom, he's been singing me secret messages— "

"Stop it! Don't say crazy things." She took two shot glasses out of the cupboard, carried them to the living room, filled them with whiskey and sat down next to him on the plastic-covered couch in the orange glow of the tangerine-colored lampshades.

I sat down in an armchair and glared at them.

"So how's tricks, Lenny?" Mom took a sip of whiskey.

"Ring-a-ding-ding. Hate to desert your brother, but I finally got some big gigs in the city."

"If anyone deserves it, it's you." She took another sip, then offered him the pack of cigarettes on the coffee table.

He pulled a gold lighter from his pocket, put a cigarette in his mouth, lit it, then handed it to Mom before lighting one for himself.

"Remember that time…" Mom exhaled, a dreamy look on her face. "You know, on the beach, after the bar closed, when we went swimming?"

Yuck.

Lenny grinned. "You mean skinny dipping?"

Skinny dipping! Double yuck.

"I loved the way you used to swim way out," he said. "Just disappear out there."

"It's so peaceful," Mom said. "Just leave everything behind, nothing matters."

I couldn't take it anymore.

I jumped up, said, "What are you doing here!" It came out loud.

He looked at Mom.

"Actually, I came to see how the little lady's feeling." He cast his sleepy eyes at me. "You know, after the accident."

"See?" Mom said. "He just came to see how you are. Aren't you ashamed of yourself?"

"No, he didn't. It's *you* he wants. He gave me rum at Uncle Max's."

She shook her head and tsked.

"I don't know what I'm going to do with you."

"Any headaches?" Lenny asked me.

"Why should I have headaches?" I'd never had a headache in my life.

"Sometimes head injuries can act up later, be very serious."

"I don't know what he's talking about, Mom. I didn't hit my head."

Lenny laughed, then turned to Mom.

"Next she'll be telling you I pushed her on the ride."

"What! I never said that." Then it hit me. "How did you know about that?"

What if Lenny's first message— *we'll drink little girl to the end of someone you know*—wasn't a warning? What if it was a *threat*? The Molech might be after me, too, using Lenny, but Cerbie bit him and—

"Oh my God—it was you!" I was shouting. "You tried to *kill* me!"

"That's enough of that," Mom said.

"Mom, he tried to push me in front of a car in Spook-a-Rama, but a dog attacked him—I heard the whole thing. The dog barked to warn me!"

Lenny laughed. "That was a new stunt, Fran. We just put it in. It's a werewolf barking at the moon."

"Then how did you know someone pushed me!"

"Stop it!" Mom shouted.

"I'm going to call Dad!" I yelled at Lenny, "and tell him you're trying to get Mom drunk!"

"I better go," Lenny said to Mom. "The poor little thing's getting hysterical."

"No!" Mom grabbed his arm. "You just got here. I'm going crazy here all by myself."

"No, really." He pried her hand loose. "I just wanted to see how she was."

He walked out.

Twelve

The *Daily Mirror* ran a story about Marilyn's disappearance, complete with a photo of her adorable little kisser grinning out at us. There was also a picture of me—an old school photo Mom hated because my hair was a mess. How did they even get it? And to make the coverage complete, they included Evil Aunt Suzie and Uncle Nat's wedding photograph.

The story made much of my mischief and Marilyn's parents' plea for any information that might lead to the return of their darling little girl. As an enticement to Marilyn, should she be reading it, they promised to limit her punishment to time served.

Mom cut the story out and pasted it in her scrapbook. Then she scowled at it, ripped it off the page, crumpled it up, and threw it in the trash.

The next afternoon Mom said she had to go to Key Food. Danishes and leftovers were still disappearing from the Frigidaire and the milk situation was critical. I was under house arrest, so Mom enlisted Evil Aunt Suzie to watch over me.

There we were, the Evil One and I, sitting at the kitchen table, loathing each other. I was trying to write a blues song on a scratch pad. *I shot the sheriff,* I wrote.

Just then the front door banged open and the Boarder walked in. She stopped in the kitchen doorway. She seemed to have something hidden under her coat. It was making muffled squawking noises.

"Yoo-hoo." She waved at us. "I'm home!"

"Drop dead," Aunt Suzie said.

The Boarder scurried upstairs.

"You have rats in the basement," the Evil Aunt said. "I hear them squeaking. Go down and look."

"I don't hear anything," I said. "And if there were rats down there, how would you be able to hear them when you can't even hear people talking?"

"I have my hearing aid on."

"You still have trouble hearing us."

"It doesn't amplify talking real good. But the other noises, the little faraway noises, especially high pitched ones… ugh. Every little spoon clink sounds like a gong. And look at all the batteries I have to lug around." She pointed at a tiny bundle on her lap. "So go downstairs this minute and look for the rats."

"I hate rats. Anyway, what do you want me to do? Catch them with my bare hands?"

"Fine. Let them bite you when you're sleeping and give you rabies." Without warning she clamped her hands over her ears and screamed: "I can't stand it anymore!"

"What's wrong?" I asked, my heart thumping. "Is it the high pitched noises? Is that what you hear when it looks like you're hearing voices?"

"None of your business." She gave me a hateful look, then picked up the book she was reading, *The Vixen's Dark Desire*. She frowned into it as if it held the answer to all her problems.

"I think I will look for those rats," I said.

She didn't even look up.

I tiptoed upstairs.

I was reluctant to knock on the Boarder's door, in case knocking was one of the faraway noises Evil Aunt Suzie's hearing aid picked up, so I turned the knob and gave the door a push—good, it opened. I carefully closed it behind me and ran through the Junkland Jungle until I got to the clearing, but it was empty. I started down one of the trails. The walls in this section were made up of books with Yiddish titles. Soon I began hearing a squawking noise coming from the depths of Junkland Jungle, getting louder and louder, then something red, green, and blue came flying around the bend, loudly flapping up a cloud of dust. It flew over my head, through the den, and down one of the other trails.

I coughed.

"Wait for me, birdchik!" And here came the Boarder, limping around the bend, out of breath, tapping her chest. "Oy," she said. "Never a dull moment."

"Where'd the parrot come from?"

"It's where it's going I'm worried about."

"Should I chase it?"

"Don't worry. I have by my chair a birdcage and with it a cracker. When it gets hungry, it'll come over."

I followed her into the den. Sure enough, there was a box of Saltine crackers on the table and poor Goldie's birdcage on the floor. We sat down in our usual seats.

"You want maybe a nosh? Some home-baked rugelech?"

"Not right now," I said. "I was just wondering, did you cover your tracks?"

"What?"

"You know, the reason you went out the other day. You were going to take special evasive actions in case you're the one who's supposed to die this summer?"

She nodded vigorously. "This I did. I put out for the Molech a lot of false leads. He comes looking for me? He'll end up maybe at Stauch's Baths."

She started looking around in the junk piled up behind her.

"Have you seen maybe my blue beaded purse?" she said. "I want I should give to you a little something."

"That's nice, but you don't have to give me anything." I smiled. "It's enough that you're my long lost great-great-grandmother."

"It's a gorgeous purse. Where could it be? Your mama must have stolen it."

"Mom?" I repressed a laugh. "When did you see it last?"

"When did I see it last? Must have been in fifty-four? Fifty-five?"

"1955? Not that long ago, should be on top."

"Not nineteen, 1855. Ay-yay-yay." She furrowed her brow and looked up at the ceiling. Then her eyebrows popped up and she slapped the side of her head. "Nu, I remember, it was in the bundle on the ship to America. I gave it to the Ashkenazi lady, may she rest in peace. Which she refuses to do."

"O-kay," I said. "Now you have to finish the story."

She threw herself into her overstuffed armchair and I plopped down on the ottoman.

"You were on a ship to America," I said. "You didn't know if the

Molech had caught the same ship but you weren't taking any chances so you pumped an Ashkenazi lady for the story of her life."

She pinched my cheek.

"Okay, okay already, so maybe I shouldn't have farpotschket with life and death, but that's what I did.

"On the ship I said to my Ashkenazi lady, 'You look a little chilly. Here, take my shawl, I have shawls coming out from my pupik.' I put it around her shoulders. Then I say, 'Let me comb your hair like mine.'" The Boarder patted the snarled mess on her head. "'Braided around the top, and maybe pull out a few eyebrow hairs, and just a little rouge, and how's about a nice beauty mark right here on the chin.'

"When I'm done with her, her face looks like mine in the mirror. Then I say, 'Take my bed, why don't you? It's more comfortable. I don't sleep anyway.' So she does. Then after everyone goes to sleep I pick up her bundle and take it to the ladies' lav. I take out her passport and with my knife I pry off her picture, and also mine, and with the pot of glue I switch the pictures. That night I put my passport with her picture back in her bundle and return it to where she's sleeping. I then hide myself in a janitor's closet in the hallway. I open the door a crack and peek out, waiting and waiting for the Molech.

"Must have been two, three o'clock in the middle of the night when I finally hear footsteps in the hallway, ta-tap, ta-tap, ta-tap, closer and closer, the footsteps of death."

"Oh no!" I cried.

"Slowly he's taking shape out of the shadows. A creaking door opens somewhere and he steps under a light." She pulled herself to the edge of the chair, reached to the floor, and picked up a dusty Mallomar cookie.

"Here," she said. "Have a nosh."

"No!" I pushed it away. "Could you just get on with the story, please?"

"I could have plotzed. It was just the cabin boy, checking the decks. The next day my Ashkenazi lady is nice and rested, but me? I'm a wreck.

"'Nu, Mamaleh,' I say to my lady, 'did you have for yourself a nice sleep? You're entitled.' Again with the entire life story. What a kvetcher. 'I'm not a well woman,' she says over and over, 'my heart, my stomach, my kidneys.'

"Luckily she goes all day and doesn't have a look at her passport. It comes night, she goes to sleep and I hide in the janitor's closet.

"Again with the waiting. I could hardly keep my eyes open. Then finally the ta-tap, ta-tap, ta-tap, the creaking door, the rattling. But this time the footsteps are slower and heavier. I peek out, and there he is, in the shadows at the end of the hallway.

"Oh no!" I cried again.

"He's carrying with him a book and stopping at each door like he's looking for something. Then he stops in front of my cabin and pushes the door open. He looks in, then jumps back. He closes the door and steps into the light.

"Oy-yoy-yoy. This time it was only a Hinklisha gentleman who got on at Liverpool. He keeps walking until he comes to the men's lav and there he goes in.

"The next day I was a wreck again.

"'So tell me mamaleh,' I say to my lady, 'did you have for yourself a good sleep?'

"'Of course,' she says, and again with the kvetching.

"That afternoon after lunch, the Ashkenazi lady and I are taking for ourselves a stroll around the deck. We're just coming around the back of the ship when I see the Molech standing there in broad daylight."

"Oh, no!" I cried a third time.

"Hoo-ha! I was thinking he would show up in the middle of the night, but that was meshuga. After all he's a Molech, not a vampire.

"So quickly I'm ducking behind a door to wait for him to pass.

"He's strolling along, carrying with him his fiddle. He puts it to his shoulder and makes with the Tumbala, tumbala, tumbalaika, and my Ashkenazi lady is standing there like a schlemiel looking around for me. He finishes his song, walks over to her, tips his cap, and bows. But of course she can't see him. Then he's reaching for his eyeglasses in his vest pocket, but they're not there, so he moves in close and squints in her face. Then he grins. 'Thought you could outrun me?' he says, but of course she can't hear him neither. He tucks the fiddle under his arm, takes the book out of his pocket, runs his finger down a page, stops and nods. Then he puts the red mark on her forehead. He gives a laugh and saunters away, and I jump back on the deck.

"'Nu? Where was you?' my lady asks.

"'Oy. Don't ask.'

"Suddenly she grabs her stomach. 'I don't feel so hot,' she says.

"'Oy vey iz mir. Better you should go to the infirmary,' and I schlep her there myself. The doctor hands her a laudanum pill and a glass of water, so she drinks it. Then she starts saying, 'My heart, my liver, maybe it's…' Suddenly she falls off the chair, out cold on the floor. So he tells me he'll keep her there overnight. The next morning when I go back, he says she passed away in her sleep. 'Heart attack,' he says."

"It was all your—"

"Let me finish." She held up a finger. "I tell him I don't know her, but here's her things, and I give to him my bundle, with my passport, with her photograph pasted on it. And that was the last I ever heard from myself." She shrugged. "I know what you're thinking. You're thinking, what chutzpa, what bonditt."

"No!" I said, "I'm thinking you murdered my great-great-grand-mother and stole her family—my family!"

"Death-schmeath." She waved her hand. "All I did was change a little passport picture. And the family? You call this a family? I threw away better families. Nu? Where are those playing cards? I want you should teach to me how to play poker."

"You just told me you killed my great-great-grandmother and now you want me to teach you how to play poker?"

"What difference does it make, everyone dies sooner or later." She looked around. "Except maybe me."

"What happened to your family in Russia and the son that went to Mexico?"

"What do I know?"

"Then what happened when you got to New York?"

"You can't imagine the tumult at Ellis Island. They're poking at us, looking at our papers with magnifying glasses, some people they won't let in, even. We end up in a big room with the American relatives lined up on both sides. The Kissing Post, they called it. I see there a little family standing in the line. There's a short jolly-looking fellow with rosy cheeks, and with him is his pretty wife, holding in her arms a fat rosy baby. Hau boy, I'm thinking, that looks like the family in the lady's pictures, so I wave and call out.

"'Yoo hoo, mamalehs!'

"The granddaughter, she looks over her shoulder, then points at herself with a questioning look.

"'Lena! Abraham!' I go up to them. 'Give to your old grandma a big hug.' I smile sweetly. 'I'm so happy to finally see you after all these years. You look so well, kayne horeh, and the children?'

"'There must be some mistake,' the granddaughter says, 'you're not my grandmother.'

"'Mamaleh, don't say such things. I'm not a well woman. My heart, my stomach, my kidneys. And I haven't seen you in so long. Since you were six years old back in Russia. So maybe I changed a little. Your darling mama, may she rest in peace, she would want you should welcome me.'

"'No,' the granddaughter says. 'You're not my grandmother.'"

"But if they didn't believe you," I said, "how did you end up in their apartment?"

"I took out the pack of family letters and photographs from the Ashkenazi lady's bundle. The granddaughter looked through them and seemed confused.

"Finally the husband laughs and says, 'Enough already. She's your grandmother. What do you want to do? Send her back to Russia? Give her a hug and let's get out of here.'

"So she pats me on the shoulder and we go back to their farschtinkener railroad flat on Norfolk Street. Crowded like steerage it was.

"She has some faded beat-up photograph of her grandmother and she keeps looking at it, then at me, and shaking her head. For months this she's doing. The husband keeps grabbing it out of her hand and saying, 'It's her. It looks just like her. People will think you don't love her.'

"'Love her!' she shouts, 'I don't even know her. Who in drerd is she?'

"After a while they just forgot I was there. I looked for the meaning of life in the great books and that was that. End of story." She paused. "Well, if you must know, there is something else. Ever since I dropped dead on the ship I haven't slept a wink, and besides, I've been shrinking."

"There's one thing I don't understand," I said. "If the Molech took my real great-great-grandmother instead of you, why are you still running away from him?"

"Because," she held up a finger, "he thought I was dead and she was still alive, so when she was supposed to die he came to the apartment on the Lower East Side where she was supposed to be living with her granddaughter. But I was living in her place."

"So why didn't he take you, if he thought you were her?"

"Better you shouldn't know. In case he shows up. So where are those playing cards?"

"Mom is right," I said. "I shouldn't talk to you any more." And with that I walked out.

Thirteen

Marilyn had been missing for a whole week when I got a message from her. Mom found it in the mailbox on the morning of the seventh day. It was carefully lettered around the margins of a yellowed *Daily Mirror* page dated July 18, 1947.

"Dear Brooklyn," it read. "I have started a new life. Whatever you do, don't look for me in the place I told you about. Please make sure Duchess gets her milk bone every day. Love, Marilyn."

Mom and I ran right over and showed it to Evil Aunt Suzie and Uncle Nat. Aunt Suzie was insulted that Marilyn had chosen *our* mailbox to put it in. She even accused me of stealing it from their mailbox. They all kept asking me what place Marilyn told me about, but I didn't know. All I could think of was her saying she wanted to hide in my room and would sleep under the boardwalk if she had to, but I'd already told them that.

Then Mom drove us all to the police station and we showed it to the policeman in charge of the case. The detective wanted to know if it was Marilyn's handwriting. I said it sure looked like it—big, round, and left-handed. Mom wondered if kidnappers could have forced her to write it, but the detective said it was unlikely since it didn't ask for a ransom.

Of course, none of this brought us one bit closer to finding Marilyn. But I was so relieved by the message, so happy to know she was okay, it almost didn't matter that nobody knew where she was.

So there we were again, Mom and I, facing off across the map of Florida.

It was hot out. Normally on a day like this we'd be at the beach, splashing, swimming, having a great time.

"What was the place she told you about?" Mom said in a toneless voice. She lit another cigarette.

A summer breeze wafted in though the open kitchen window. I could almost feel the sand between my toes, the waves breaking against my knees. But it wouldn't be any fun without Marilyn.

"How many times do I have to tell you?" I said. "I don't know." Instead of chewing my hair I was chewing on the wood of a number two pencil, making gratifying teeth marks in it. For variety I started to push my cuticles back with one of my pointy teeth.

"What do you think happened to the cheese in the trap?" Mom asked.

"A rat must have eaten it."

Suddenly Mom sucked in a startled breath.

"The note, maybe it's some kind of code," she said. "There's a secret message in it."

"You think so?"

This wasn't so far-fetched since Marilyn was known to be a genius in math. But if there was a secret message, what could it be?

Suddenly I had an idea.

"Mom?"

"What?"

"Could I have my milk now?"

"What?" She looked at me like I was crazy. "It's only two o'clock."

"But if I drink it now, you won't have to force me to drink it at three. Then as a reward you can let me go out and look for her. So what do you say?"

She frowned for a minute, sighed.

Okay. Tell her to come home. Make sure she knows they won't punish her."

Mom poured me a glass of milk. I grimaced, steeled myself, then slugged it all down.

Mom reached into her pocket and pulled out a dollar, then she pulled out another dollar and handed both of them to me.

"Be sure she gets something to eat."

"Thanks, Mom."

I passed the Cyclone, turned the corner at Jones Walk, then followed the long stretch of Spook-a-Rama until I got to the red THRILLS arrow, where I turned the corner onto the midway. Marilyn and I had been headed for the midway the day she disappeared, when Uncle Max nabbed me.

Despite its being a weekday, it was packed. A cacophony of hurdy-gurdy music, Laughing Sals, and giggly chatter filled the air. Their laughter didn't even sound real—it sounded like a stuck record in an empty house. I felt like a ghost.

It wasn't them. It was me without Marilyn, without Mississippi and Cerbie. As I walked I sang to myself: "Oh-oh, oh-oh. Oh-oh, oh-oh. /I miss my friends, I miss them so…"

I passed Ripley's Oddities, the Whip, Pleasureland, the Tunnel of Love, Spooks, the Minotaur's Maze.

All the way to the World in Wax Musee, where I walked up to the ticket booth.

"Hi, Mrs. Santangelo," I said.

I'd known her forever. She was the founder, wax artist, and owner of the museum. She looked down at me, then furrowed her brow.

"I heard what you did at Spook-a-Rama," she said.

"I know. That was an accident."

She looked at me doubtfully.

I lifted my hand. "I swear."

She smiled.

"So can I go in?" I gave her a sheepish grin. "Please? I just want to look around."

"Go on." She waved me in.

It was dark and cool inside, with high ceilings in a series of alcoves closed off by low fences. I pictured Marilyn dressed as Little Red Riding Hood, freezing in position every time someone passed.

I turned to the first alcove on my left. It contained a cobblestoned London street dimly lit by a gas streetlamp. There was a man wearing a top hat and black cape. He had one hand clutched around the neck of a terrified-looking lady he was stabbing in the heart with his other hand. Jack the Ripper, the sign read.

I wondered, not for the first time, how Mrs. Santangelo made the faces so life-like. They looked like real people, down to crooked noses and laugh lines. Jack the Ripper had a mole on his chin.

The alcove on my left contained a bulky man in a long black coat and fedora hat. Cold glass eyes stared out of his chubby face. He was holding a machine gun, bracing it against his shoulder, aiming it out at spectators. Al Capone.

Both these displays had been here for a long, long time. I looked around the hall. It wasn't crowded today, just a few gray-faced grown-ups dragging themselves from alcove to alcove.

I stepped up to the next display, and what I saw sent chills through me.

There stood a handsome man at a microphone, relaxed, head thrown back, mouth open as if in song. He was wearing a tuxedo, bow tie, and had a red handkerchief in his breast pocket. Dean Martin, the sign read. But it wasn't Dean Martin—it was Lenny.

I ran back out to the ticket booth.

"Mrs. Santangelo?" I called up to her. "Do you know a singer named Lenny?"

"Of course." She laughed. "Everybody knows Lenny. What a character!"

"The wax dummy of Dean Martin—it looks just like him."

She laughed again. "I should hope so, he's who I used."

"You mean as a model?"

"Sort of. I took a plaster cast of his head, then poured flesh-colored wax into it. That's how I make them. Then I paint them and glue real hair on them. Nothing's too good for my babies."

"I didn't know that."

"Old Dino in there…" she nodded at the building, "he's a big seller."

"You mean you make more than one of them?"

"Sure, if I get any orders. I've sold six Dinos already. One of them went all the way to Japan. Lizzie Borden's a big seller too. She was molded on my sister-in-law."

"If you need someone who's real mean-looking you should use my Aunt Suzie."

She chuckled. "Know anyone who looks like Madame Blavatsky? I'm doing her next."

I shrugged. "I don't even know who that is."

"She's a famous spiritualist."

"Thanks for telling me that." I'd had an idea. "See you later!"

I merged back into the crowd outside and continued down the midway until I could smell the hot dogs grilling at Nathan's Famous. I crossed Stillwell Avenue, passed the Bobsled and the Dragon's Cave—the dragon sign shooting big puffs of smoke—then turned the corner on Schweickerts Walk.

I looked up at the side of the Dunes Residential Hotel. There in a third floor window I spotted what I was looking for—a small glowing green and lavender sign. I entered a peeling gray foyer and walked up two dimly lit flights. I knocked on a door.

"Come in if you dare," a husky female voice said in a really strong New York accent.

I pushed the door open. A large middle-aged women dressed in multiple layers of red, yellow, and green chiffon with big loop earrings and teased black hair was sitting on a ratty couch, magazine in hand. She looked surprised to see me.

"Hi," I said.

"Welcome to the realm of the spirits." She blinked her dark, heavily made-up eyes at me. "You look familiar."

Like most places in Coney Island, the hotel's glory days here were long past, but an attempt had been made to cover the cracks in the dirty walls with taped-on pictures from magazines. The Venetian blinds were drawn and the room was lit by a baroque lamp with a tattered red lampshade that cast ragged shadows on the walls. The place was sweltering and smelled like kitty litter. There was a hot plate on the floor with a burnt pot on it.

"That's probably because I live around here." I gave her a smile.

"My dad makes the rides run, and my grandma used to…" I sighed. "You've probably seen me around. My name's Brooklyn."

"I am Madame Clarissa, medium to all the realms of existence. What can the spirits do for you?"

As she spoke I realized she didn't have a Brooklyn accent but something harsher and tougher.

"I need a reading," I said. "I only have two dollars. Can you help me find my cousin Marilyn for two dollars? I'm afraid she's in danger. She's my best friend and she might be sleeping under the boardwalk or something."

"I know who you are." She jabbed a long red fingernail at me. "I saw your picture in the paper. The little kid with the messy hair."

That accent of hers—New Jersey?

"It was an old photo," I said.

"Everyone's looking for your cousin. Her picture's all over the neighborhood."

"I've seen them." I told her about Marilyn's note.

"You've come to the right place. Tarot cards, palm reading, or crystal ball?"

Bronx—that's what it was.

"Crystal ball," I said.

"A wise choice in the case of a missing person." She pronounced it poysun.

She motioned me over to a small table with a lace tablecloth on which rested a large crystal ball with a gold base of bird's claws. We seated ourselves.

She closed her eyes and made circular motions with her hands around it. She stopped and her eyes popped open. The crystal ball clouded up and she stared into it.

"Hello?" she called out in a loud voice. "Are you there?"

"Who are you talking to?"

"Shhhh." She held a finger to her bright red lips. "Harry? Is that you?" She nodded. "Great. I have a question… Okay." She gave me a helpless look. "She's a little girl named Brooklyn." She listened some more. "That's what I called to ask you about. Can you see the cousin?" She cupped her hand to her ear. "Yes, that's the one. Where is she?"

The ensuing pause was punctuated with screams from the plummeting Bobsled outside.

"Where?… Can't you do any better than that?… Wait—I didn't mean to offend you. Harry? Come back." An exasperated sigh. "He's gone."

"Who was it?"

"That," she said, puffing up her large chest, "was no other than the one, the only, the great Harry Houdini."

"No kidding! What'd he say?"

"He says Marilyn appears to be in a crowded room."

"She's in a room full of people?"

"He said crowded with boxes."

"What kind of boxes?"

"That I don't know."

"You think they're more like shoe boxes or Frigidaire boxes?"

"I just told you, I don't know."

"What else did he say?"

The Bobsled plunged. Kids shrieked.

"That's it. He ran out on me. The dead aren't real good at seeing our world, it's fuzzy and confusing to them. And the longer they're dead, the less interested they are in it. The Place-between-Life-and-Death is what they know. He thought I was criticizing him. He's very sensitive."

"Would you try again? I'm really worried about her."

"Okay. What else do I have to do?" She repeated the circular motions with her hands around the crystal ball. I was fascinated by her blood-red fingernails. They were so long they curved in like talons.

"Hello!" she called into the air. "Anyone there?... Harry? Is that you?" She cocked her head. "Oh, good…" Her voice seemed different, warmer. "What?" She blinked her tarred eyelashes. "I'm sorry. He just showed up again." Beads of sweat were forming on her pancake makeup. "Okay, be that way." She turned to me. "He hung up. He's insanely jealous."

"Houdini?"

"Nooooo." She waved her hand. "Harry-my-husband."

"You're in contact with two dead Harrys?"

"Can you believe it? Millions of spirits in the afterlife and I get two Harrys."

"Is the afterlife the same as the Place-between-Life-and-Death?"

"Harry-my-husband says that after a while spirits leave the Place-between-Life-and-Death, go someplace else. He doesn't know where. But something went wrong, and now a lot of people can't seem to move on, and new ones keep crowding in."

"Do they want to move on?"

"Some can't wait, but most of them need help letting go of this world."

"How did you come in contact with the two Harrys in the first place?"

"Harry-my-husband I've been hearing from for about a year. Ever since he dropped dead fighting over a parking space. He's afraid I'll remarry. Fat chance. And when he doesn't call me, I call him. I sure wish the big lug was still alive. But the strange thing is, ever since I moved into this dump, when I call Harry-my-husband sometimes Harry Houdini shows up."

"There's something I don't understand," I said. "If the spirits talk to you, what do you see in the crystal ball?"

"Well…" She scratched her head. "To tell you the truth…" We waited through another chorus of Bobsled screams. "Nothing."

"Then what's it for?"

"I just thought I needed one. I got it from a catalog." She gave me a sheepish grin. "You press this little button and it clouds up."

"You're new at this, aren't you?"

"I'll have you know I'm a professional," she said.

I swallowed a smile.

"I think after your husband died…" I could see it all. "You were stuck living alone in a Bronx apartment with no income. Your savings were running out, so about three weeks ago you tucked your cat under your arm, moved in here, and opened this fortune-telling business. You don't know how to read palms or tarot cards either, do you?"

A look of amazement spread across her face.

"How'd you know all that?" she said.

"Houdini said never to reveal your tricks." I smiled, then stuck my canine teeth onto my dry lower lip so I'd look like a vampire.

"You're good," she said.

She didn't seem to notice the teeth, so I tucked them back in.

"But the Harrys are real, aren't they?" I said.

"Of course. That or I'm crazy. It was either Bellevue or Coney Island. Was my fortune-telling act that bad?"

"It needs a little work."

"To tell you the truth, you're my first customer. When I rented this dump I thought it was a good location. I put the fortune-telling sign in the window and waited. But it hasn't attracted a single person—except you, and you're only a kid." She blinked her eyes and sniffled. "I used all my savings setting this place up. If I don't get some customers soon I'll be out on the street."

"No one can see your sign from the midway," I said. "Get one of those big standing signs and put it on the corner. The gaudier the better."

"You think?"

"Definitely." I thought for a moment. "And don't bill yourself as a fortune-teller. Call yourself a spiritualist. It's higher class."

"Thanks. Is there anything else I can do for you?"

"I don't think so." I felt a wave of despair. "I just keep wondering if I'm cursed. Everyone I love seems to die or disappear."

"Same here." With her smeared mascara, big red painted lips, and crown of teased black hair drooping to one side, she looked as sad as I felt.

The biggest blackest cat I'd ever seen came flying through the air and landed at my feet. It arched its back, fur bristling, claws digging into the floorboards, and locked its angry yellow eyes on mine. Then it hissed like a motorcycle revving up.

"Madame Clarissa? Could you help me out here?"

The cat batted my leg with its huge paw. She scooped him up.

"Bad Fluffy!" She tossed him into another room, closed the door, and sat back down. There was a screech and some crashing noises.

"He was on top of the chifforobe," she said.

"He hates me."

"I don't know what got into him." She gave me an apologetic smile. "He's usually so friendly."

"That's strange, because I like cats."

"Do you have a dog? He gets crazy around dogs."

"No, but I'm godmother to a dog." I told her all about Cerbie and Mississippi.

"Just a minute." She looked up. "I think... maybe..."

The Bobsled whipped around a bend. Screeches. Screams. Shrieks.

"Does Mississippi usually wear a white shirt?" she asked.

"Yeah." My heart started jumping.

She squinted and looked up some more.

"And suspenders?"

"That's him! Is one of the Harrys telling you where he is?"

"Just a minute, I need to concentrate." She put her hand to her head.

"What's he saying?" I burst out. "Is it Houdini?"

"No, I'm just trying to remember. I think... lunchtime. I might have seen him playing on the boardwalk."

"Oh, my God!" I jumped up and bolted for the door, caught the door frame and swung back around. I pulled the two dollars out of my pocket, dashed back, and handed them to her.

"Thanks," I said. "You're the greatest."

Fourteen

There he was, hunched over his guitar, strumming and singing. Even from a distance Mississippi looked haggard and worn out. I ran toward him along the slats of the boardwalk, heard him singing:

I'll follow him to the station, be the guide down there
Yes, I'll follow him to the station, be the guide down there
You might be sad and lonely, but you got to stay up here.

Just before I got there, he saw me and jumped up.

"Brooklyn!" he cried. A big smile transformed his lined face.

"Mississippi!" I stopped short right in front of him. "I've missed you so much." I would have given him a big hug, but he was still holding his guitar.

"What does the song mean?" I said.

"You mean the one I was just singing?"

"About the guide. It sounded like another secret message."

"That there's a Robert Johnson song." He shook his head. "I don't rightly know why I sung it that way."

"The Boarder in our house can see the Angel of Death! And she says there's a guide in the afterlife, and… and… maybe it's you."

He looked doubtful. "If I am, I sure don't know about it."

My thoughts raced ahead.

"I saw Cerbie on Spook-a-Rama and he attacked Lenny so he wouldn't kill me!"

"*What*! You saw Cerbie?"

I remembered how the stray dog at the creek fooled me.

"Well… I'm ninety-nine and forty-four one hundredths percent sure it was him. I got out of the car because I heard him bark. It was pitch black, but then there was a flash of light and that's when I saw him. But then someone pushed me! I almost fell in front of a car."

"Good Lord!"

"I think it was Lenny—he knew about it the next day, but I hadn't told him."

"You think he might still be in Spook-a-Rama?"

"Lenny?"

"No, Cerbie."

I shrugged. "He wasn't there when the lights came on."

"It just don't make no sense, Little Sugar. Why wouldn't he come back to me if he's right here?" He pointed at Jones Walk. Spook-a-Rama was about a block away.

"You think Lenny would do that? Try to kill me?"

"I don't rightly see why," he said, "but I reckon you're in the gravest of danger."

"What should I do?"

"You need to be real careful. Don't go getting out of no rides in the dark, you hear me?"

I stood there for a few minutes feeling scared and helpless, then sank onto a bench. At least Mississippi was back. I latched onto that thought and held it tight.

He sat back down on his folding chair. He seemed even more troubled than when I got there. I was almost sorry I told him about my brush with death.

"What have you been doing all this time?" I said.

"Been searching high and low for that dog of mine." He rubbed his face with his long bony fingers. "Went to all the dog pounds in all the boroughs, asked everybody, but I ain't had a bit of luck. After a spell I thought I may as well come back here. At least that way, he wants to come back he'll know where I am."

A girl walked by with a transistor radio blasting a rock beat and a female voice singing: *You're a mean old dog/You're always after me...* I could just make out something mixed in—a bunch of short excited barks—which dissolved into static. The song came in clear again and faded as the girl walked away.

"What was that?" I said.

"I sure do love that song."

"No, I mean the barking. It sounded like Cerbie."

"Seemed like that radio was picking up another station."

I bit my lip. "I guess it's possible."

"You best just forget it."

"And you know what? Lenny pushing me? That's not my only problem."

I told him how I broke Marilyn out of lockdown and now everyone was looking for her, including me. Then I told him how Madame Clarissa said Houdini told her Marilyn was hiding in a room full of boxes.

"So what do you think?"

He smiled. "I think you sure do have a lot of stories."

"You can ask her yourself," I said. "She told me how to find you." I let out a big sigh. "But both our best friends are still missing."

Mississippi was quiet for a minute, then his eyes widened.

"She that pretty little gal on the posters?"

"That's her. She ran away and may never come back and it's all my fault."

"No, Little Sugar, I reckon you did the right thing. Everybody need a friend good as you. Sometimes you just got to run—believe me." He strummed a few twangy, heart-tugging bars on his guitar. "Difference is I wished I *could* go home."

"Why did *you* run away?" This had been bothering me for weeks. "You never got to finish the story."

"That there was the saddest day in all my years." He heaved a sigh. "That evening when I come back from the cotton fields I was mighty tired, but it felt so good to be home. I sat down on the front porch and started picking out a tune. I still remember it."

Run, run while you can, there ain't no use in stayin'
Yeah, run while you can, ain't no use in stayin'
Ain't nothing you can do now, no point in even prayin'.

"So you sang yourself a secret message!"

He seemed to consider this, then he nodded.

"You might just be right. But at the time I thought I was just singing what I was thinking—that more trouble's on the way."

"Then what happened?"

"While I played I saw someone running down the dirt road way off in the distance, kicking up a cloud of dust. It was this little freckle-faced white boy, name of Andy. Used to sneak across the tracks to listen to me strumming. He stops to catch his breath and I fly out my chair, heart jumping like a hen on a hot brick. He hollers that some-one kilt Deputy Kurtz, then he starts running again until he's right up on the porch.

"Andy grabs my arm and starts talking fast. Someone ripped the deputy's throat right out of his neck and left him to bleed to death in the exact same field where I'd been working. Then he starts crying and shaking my arm and saying how Sheriff Virgil's coming after me.

"So what'd you do?"

"I looked down the road. It was getting dark, but sure enough there he was in the distance, walking my way, swinging his shotgun. So I just started running right then and there, didn't take nothing but my old guitar. Never did say goodbye to nobody. I regret that, I surely do. But I was just fifteen."

"But Mississippi… couldn't your mom have helped you? Or your sisters?"

"Oh, Little Sugar, you don't know nothing about that place. Any help they tried would of gone against them, put them in gravest dan-ger. Running away was the best thing I could do for my family."

"But where'd you go?"

"Grew up riding the rails. Picking my guitar, passing the hat. Back-dooring for odd jobs and table scraps." He rubbed his eyes and sighed. "Always looking over my shoulder for the sheriff. Every now and then I'd catch a glimpse of his meat-face from a dirty bus window or the back of a pickup truck. That man hates me like I murdered his great-great-granddaddy my ownself."

Close to us a guy let out a wolf whistle so loud it hurt my ears, then ran over to a girl who was smiling at him.

"He'll hunt me down until his dying day," Mississippi said.

"Oh, God," I whispered. "But… when's the last time you saw him?"

"It's been a right long while, but I ain't taking no chances."

"Do you think the station is a train station?" I asked.

"What?"

"Like in the song you sang, 'I'll follow him to the station?'"

"It surely is."

"So why do blues singers like trains so much?"

"I been on the road so long, to me they just feel like home."

He looked down at his guitar, honey-colored wood gradually shading to dark brown around the edge. I didn't know a thing about musical instruments, but it looked like a fine guitar to me. And unlike anything else he owned, it was in perfect condition. He strummed it for a minute.

"It's beautiful," I said. "Your guitar, I mean."

"This guitar was handmade by a master," he said.

"Where'd you get it?"

"One night I was in some pool hall's smoky back room staking the most important thing I had in this world. There was green walls, green lamp shades, table covered in green felt... so much green it look like the bottom of the ocean.

"I was playing seven-card stud with five or six railroad porters and everybody but this rawbony boy and me had folded. He has three tens showing and I got a could-be royal flush out there on the table. Only card I'm missing is the jack of hearts. Aside from some dimes and quarters, there's only two things in the kitty: my old guitar that Mama bought me for two dollars from the Sears catalog and his guitar—that would be this one here. That boy wouldn't know a great guitar from a puked-up hairball.

"I look at the two cards I'm holding and for some crazy reason this canary-gobbling grin spreads across my face. He's blinking and sweating, getting as skittish as a cat on the third rail. I slam down what I already won and say, 'Raise you fifty,' cool as anything. The boy folds.

That's how I won this guitar that he didn't know how to play nohow. You never treasure anything like you treasure something you won fair and square playing poker.

"Did you really have the jack of hearts in your hand?" I asked.

"Well, I'm truly sorry, but I never tell if I been bluffing or not, 'less I have to." He smiled.

"Okay." I smiled back. "So that's how you got this great guitar. Can you teach me how to play it?" I asked.

"Well, now, it ain't easy, playing the guitar."

"Just show me where you put your fingers."

"All right." He placed the fingers of his left hand on the neck of the guitar and held the pick with his right. "You do it like this." He strummed a little.

"Can I hold it?"

"This is an awful big guitar, much too big for a little gal like you."

"But I'm real tall for my age. Look how long my arms are." I held out my skinny arms for him to inspect. "And so are my fingers, see?"

A negro lady and two boys came up to us. One boy was about my age and the other was younger.

"Well, looky who's here." Mississippi got up, laid his guitar on the bench, and gave each of the boys a hug.

"These are my neighbors, Mrs. Jones and her sons Edgar and Clarence. And this," he pointed at me, "is a sassy little gal goes by the name of Brooklyn."

"Hi." I gave them a friendly smile. They looked at each other, then broke into smiles themselves.

"We're out celebrating," Mrs. Jones said. "I bought the boys hot dogs."

"These folks went through a bad spell while their daddy was out of work," Mississippi said, "but he just got himself a good job at the Brooklyn Navy Yard loading cargo."

"Play Jambalaya!" the younger boy cried.

"Sure enough." Mississippi sat down and started playing and singing. The boys started dancing around in a wild burst of energy, waving their arms, kicking their feet. It looked like so much fun I jumped in too, right between them, spinning around, jumping in the air. But just as I was getting started, their mom shouted, "Stop it!" and grabbed hold of them.

"What's wrong, Mama?" the younger boy said. "Why can't we dance?"

"Tell you later." She took them each by the hand, said they had to go, and dragged them away down the boardwalk.

"Was it something I did?" I asked Mississippi.

"Oh no, Little Sugar. Mrs. Jones is just… well, she didn't want them to get in no trouble for dancing on the boardwalk."

"So they're your neighbors?" I know it seems strange, but it hadn't occurred to me that he must have neighbors. "Where do you live?"

"I best not be telling you that. Ain't a good place for a little gal like you to be going."

"Why not?"

"There's some places… it's just ain't a good idea for you to go there."

"But how will I find you if you're not on the boardwalk?"

"My Lord! Look who's here." He pointed at the beach.

"The Good Humor man?"

"How's about I buy you an ice cream?"

"But you don't have enough money for things like that."

"I sure enough do." He handed me a dime. "I would take it as the most grave disrespect if you didn't allow me to treat you. It's my turn."

"You want anything?" I asked.

"No, but thank you kindly. I don't have me much of a sweet tooth."

I ran down the beach and came back with a Clarabelle, a chocolate-coated popsicle shaped like a torpedo with blue and banana ice cream inside. Mom would have worried that a snack this late might ruin my appetite for dinner, but this was pizza night, my favorite. I perched myself back on what I'd come to think of as my bench.

"I have a real pirate's doubloon," I said after I finished my ice cream. I took my treasure out of my pocket and handed it to him. "It's my lucky charm, I carry it all the time."

He squinted at it, then at me.

"Where'd you get this?"

"Found it on the beach." This happened to be true. "It's from the Coney Island pirate's buried treasure."

"And you just carry it around?"

"Why not?"

"This could be valuable. Your folks know you have it?"

"Nope. You want it? I think you should have it."

"Lord, no. I couldn't never accept—"

"Flip it over," I said.

"You little charlatan," he said as soon as he did. "Souvenir of Coney Island. My Lord."

"Would you teach me a song?"

"Why, sure." He strummed a few bars. "This song was taught me by a friend of mine name of Woody, lives over on Mermaid Avenue." He started singing:

> You will eat, bye and bye,
> In that glorious land above the sky;
> Work and pray, live on hay,
> You'll get pie in the sky when you die.

He smiled. "Now you try it."

"All right." I was so excited, my first song with a real guitar. "Here goes…"

He started strumming and I started singing.

You will eat, bye and bye,
In that glorious land above —

"Stop! You ain't doing it right." He pointed at a spot between his chest and his stomach. "You got to sing from here."

I always thought I had a great voice, but now I could hear it through Mississippi's ears and I realized Mom was right—I was wailing, my voice cracking.

"From the inside," he went on. "Not from your throat. Breathe in deep from the belly and lift up your chest. Then think about where you want the sound to go."

He told me to try again, and when I did it felt easier, smoother.

"That's real good," he said. "You got natural talent—just keep practicing and singing from the inside. Go ahead, now, try again. And this time sing what you feel."

You will eat, bye and bye…

I sang while he strummed. This time my voice sounded smooth and strong, as if all the experiences of my life were layered in. But when I got to *You'll get pie in the sky*— he said, "Oh, Lord!" then jumped up, grabbed his things, and took off down the boardwalk.

I looked around and saw the new cop on the beat walking toward me. I didn't know why Officer O'Levy wasn't around any more, but this guy was twice as big, blond with a square jaw. He was slapping his baton against his hand as if he were dying to hit somebody with it.

It had been a long day, and I was down for the count. I went to sleep early, but in the middle of the night something woke me up—a horrific scream. I leapt out of bed and ran downstairs, right behind Dad. He screeched to a halt in the big dark kitchen so suddenly I ran into him.

Mom was standing there in her pink satin pajamas, hand on throat, eyes agog—and no wonder. Standing in the blue glow of the open Frigidaire, a piece of limp pizza dangling from her hand, was Marilyn.

Fifteen

Dad had been out of the house since dawn, even though he probably hadn't gotten any more sleep than the rest of us after what happened last night.

Mom and I sat facing each other across the map-of-Florida tablecloth. I was eating bacon and scrambled eggs and the best cold fresh-squeezed orange juice in the world—trust me, nobody could squeeze oranges like Mom.

"I still can't believe it." Mom shook her head. "How could she live in that awful basement apartment all that time?"

The chain of blame for Marilyn's disappearance went something like this: the police blamed Mom, Mom blamed me, I blamed Evil Aunt Suzie, and Evil Aunt Suzie blamed me back. But since Mom had made me orange juice, I figured she must have forgiven me.

"What I don't understand is why you screamed like that?" I said.

"Food kept disappearing from the Frigidaire, and when I heard a noise in the kitchen I tiptoed downstairs to catch the Boarder red-handed. But when I saw Marilyn's cute little face I was so shocked it scared the bejeezus out of me."

I took a few bites of eggs and a sip of orange juice.

"What I don't understand," Mom said, "is why the police didn't find her when they searched down there."

"Because when she heard them clomping down the inside stairs, she ran out the back door and hid in the vacant lot until they left."

"But why didn't she tell you she was there?"

"She says she kept creeping up to the hall, trying to catch me alone, but she never did."

"So the fruitcake, the cheese in the traps, the squeaks in the basement— "

"All Marilyn."

"So what are we waiting for?"

While Dad popped eyeballs into grinning skulls, Mom and I set forth on our pilgrimage to the sun.

We stopped for Marilyn.

"I have to stay home to protect Duchess," she said. "My mom's going to murder her because I ran away."

"WHAT? She promised not to punish you!"

"That didn't include Duchess."

And here I thought it was impossible to hate Evil Aunt Suzie any more than I already did.

"*I* know," I said, "let's take Duchess with us. Come on, Duchess. Good dog, want to go for a swim?"

Duchess started barking, running in circles, furiously snapping at her tail.

Mom put her hand on her throat and backed away.

"Will you get this damn mutt under control!" Suzie yelled at Marilyn.

Uncle Nat came wheeling in. "Calm down, girl." Duchess stopped barking and wagged her curlicue tail. "There's a good girl."

Suzie heaved a sigh.

"Okay, okay already. Get the hell out of here this minute and I won't strangle that goddamned stinking flea-bitten mongrel."

By now, the end of June, the rumble of backyard firecrackers (strictly illegal in New York City) in preparation for Independence Day was well under way and would get louder and louder until it reached eardrum-breaking intensity on the Fourth of July.

As we walked along Mom made me carry her cumbersome webbed lounge-chair, which kept popping open. Slung over her frail shoulder was her huge Welcome-to-Florida straw bag stuffed with towels and Coppertone.

After we walked under the el at Brighton Beach Avenue into the Land-of-Art-Deco-apartment-buildings Marilyn and I started singing "How much is that dog-gie in the window? Arf, arf." We passed the playground and kiddy rides, then the sand roses at the border of the Land-of-Sand. Here we went under the boardwalk and down a dark damp path between the comfort station and the cage for lost children—then bam! The sun smacked us in the face with a big white hello. Marilyn and I kicked off our flip-flops and ran toward the ocean, screaming "Ow! Ow! Ow!" past sunbathers roasting themselves with tri-fold reflectors until our burning feet hit the crusted sand at the high tide line.

When we came to a stop Marilyn and I shook out the blanket and Mom cracked open her lounge chair, establishing our turf. Before the sand had even settled she was running down to the water on her Tinkertoy legs, jumping in, and swimming out further and further until I lost sight of her.

By now Marilyn and I were bouncing up and down in the waves.

"Let's swim out to my mom," I said.

"What!"

"Let's swim out to where my mom is. I'm worried about her."

"We can't swim that far. I've never even swum past where I can stand, and neither have you."

"Yes I have. Lots of times."

"Anyway, the lifeguard can watch her. He'll blow his whistle if she goes out too far."

I looked at him up there on his stand, muscles glistening, surrounded by teenage girls, rat-tailed combs sticking out of their bikini bottoms. He was laughing, trying to kiss one of them who was pulling back while another planted a smooch on his cheek.

The beach was crowded today, Joanie galloping along the hard wet sand waving her cowboy hat, David trying to push Elaine in, Bernie in a Hawaiian shorts set hugging somebody, other kids on the block jumping up and down in the waves, elderly Yiddish ladies splashing themselves by the ropes and repeating "It's a mekhaye."

"Let's go play," Marilyn said. "Everyone's here."

"You play, I'm going out." And with that I just started swimming. I don't think I could have stopped myself if I tried. I felt as if I could swim forever.

"Wait!" I heard her calling. Soon she was at my side, somehow keeping up, swimming out further and further, way over our heads. I turned to her, treading water.

"Go back," I said. "You'll never make it."

"Neither will you."

"Yes I will." I started swimming as fast as I could, leaving her behind.

I couldn't see Mom yet, or anyone in the deep water, but I kept scanning the horizon. The lifeguard should have been blowing his whistle at her by now, at me too. Maybe he didn't see us, or maybe I just couldn't hear it from here. I looked behind me. Marilyn had disappeared. The swimmers near the shore looked really far away.

I could see why Mom loved it out here. I sucked in the salty air; it felt clean and fresh, alive. It was so peaceful, just the wind and the waves carrying me up and down, the wide open sky glowing blue-white, all that water under me, dark and unknowable, full of fishy monsters and starfish stars.

My arms and legs took on a life of their own, swimming, swimming, swimming.

Where was Mom? I should have reached her by now.

I looked toward the beach. I felt so tiny out here, the waves so big I could only see land from the top of the swells. This was as far as I could swim. I started swimming back, but the land didn't seem to be getting any closer.

"Mom!" I shouted as loud as I could, "Where are you?" She had to be here somewhere.

My arms weren't moving as fast any more. The wind and tide were against me, waves smacking me in the face, making me swallow water.

My love is always true... A smooth voice was all around, whispering on the wind. *I never ever lied...* It was Lenny, wooing me, drawing me further out, telling me, *Give up, don't fight the tide...*

I pushed him out of my head.

The water turned cold. I kept swimming and swimming, but the beach was looking further away with every stroke. Somehow I could still see the boardwalk, which looked magnified. There was Mississippi, waiting for me, strumming his guitar. I should have listened to him, been more careful. He looked up, saw me, waved me in.

And there I am. It feels so good to be back on land, back on the boardwalk. Here comes Cerbie, running at me, practically knocking me over, licking my face, my arms around his neck. Such thick fur, his amber eyes so happy. Mississippi singing:

> Oh-oh oh-oh oh-oh I missed you so
> Why did you swim out?
> Why did you go?

Cerbie runs circles around us, protecting us.
Then Lenny's walking our way, eyes on me. He starts singing:

> Swim as far as anyone dares
> Look around and see if anyone cares
> Just remember when you come downstairs
> You'll be seeing me.

"They *do* care!" I yell.

Don't they?

Then Cerbie runs between us, head high, fur bristling. His eyes are fixed on Lenny. He bares his teeth and gives a low throaty growl from deep inside.

"See?" I shout.

Lenny backs up. "Okay, mongrel," he says, "you win, but just for now."

He turns and walks away.

Smacked in the face by another wave, I swallowed more water. Too much water, more water than air. Water's like time, just flowing away, ungraspable, all of it part of one huge thing. It's the ocean of time. We're all drowning in it, yet there isn't enough of it. My shoulders ached. What's the use? The current's so strong, and I'm just a skinny kid. Nobody ever told me what it was like out this far.

All this water under me. It would be so easy to let go, sink down, breathe in. But then I'd miss my whole life. Never grow up. Never be a singer. And I'd never get to hang around with Marilyn again. I couldn't bear the thought.

The wind was kicking up, blowing harder. Angry green waves towered over me, frothing at the top. So tired. My whole body ached.

Would Mom and Dad miss me if I didn't make it back? Dad would. I already missed the good times we'd never have.

What about Mom? I knew one thing for sure—she'd be furious. And so would Marilyn.

Can't feel my arms and legs any more, but they keep on going. Funny how things keep going.

Bubbie's sitting across the dining room table. I can see her so clearly, the burgundy bow at her neck, the dip in her gray hair. Just the two of us. She's drinking strong European coffee with the milk cooked in, sewing another ruffle onto my red party dress, lengthening it. I'm getting so tall. Tall enough to swim out way over my head. It's real silk, my red dress. Not remnants, but yards and yards of silk taffeta off the roll. The most beautiful dress in the whole world. I love the way it feels, strong and stiff, the sound it makes when it rustles. "Don't spend so much on a growing kid." That's what Mom told her. *You are my grandchild, my only grandchild,* she sings as she sews the last stitches on my dress, smoothes it out. *You are my joy…* Keep moving, one arm in front of the other. Kick the water. "I don't know why," Bubbie says, "but I'm so sleepy." It's snowing on the other side of the window, a late-season dusting of powder, and poking through the snow on the ground are yellow crocuses. Bubbie puts her head down on the table, and then she—

"No!" I cry out. "DON'T!" But there's nothing out here, just sky and sea.

I should have called an ambulance, I know that now, instead of waiting, thinking she'd wake up, thinking she just put her head down because she was sleepy.

"I'm so scared," I tell Bubbie. "I can't swim any more." I feel numb.

There's a whisper in the wind. I strain, try to hear it: *...in every way...* It's Bubbie singing, part of nature now. And for the first time I'm glad I was with her when it happened, glad she didn't have to die alone. And now she can be with me when I...

Turn on your back, dear. You have to float here.

But if I float, the current will carry me out. It's a rip tide. It's stronger than me.

I've come to tell you, it's the only way...

I roll over on my back, thrust my chin up to the sky, and... I'm floating, not struggling, just letting the sea carry me out, rocking me up and down, up and down.

Sixteen

Mom's nerves were totally shot—my fault for almost drowning. I don't know why she cared since she didn't want me around, just sat in her room staring in the mirror. I was alarmed to see the kitchen shears on her vanity, worried she'd come into my room when I was sleeping and cut off all my hair. She snapped the shears open and closed, then snipped a little curl off her left side. She scrutinized her reflection this way and that, snipped one off on the right side, then banged the shears down.

"I'm going over to Marilyn's," I said through the open door.

My shoulders ached and my arms felt as if they'd fall off, but I had to get out of the house.

"Stay there," she said without turning around. "Let someone else deal with you a while."

When Marilyn came to the door she wouldn't let me in.

"You abandoned me!" she shouted. Then she scrunched up her face and gave me a look so murderous I could see her mother in it.

"You abandoned me, too," I said. "When you ran away without telling me where you were going."

"It's not the same. *You* were the one who told me to run away, but *I* begged you not to swim out. And when I tried to get the lifeguard to save you he recognized me as the kid everyone had been looking for and didn't believe me...." Her words were shooting out so fast she had to catch her breath here. "And if I hadn't started crying and begging and if one of the girls sitting up there on the lifeguard stand hadn't felt sorry for me and grabbed his binoculars and spotted you way out there and told him you were caught in the undertow so he had to get the inflatable dingy and save you, you would have *drowned*."

Then she slammed the door in my face.

The next morning Mom seemed to be feeling better, or at least she was more animated. From the kitchen where I was eating breakfast I could hear her on the living room phone talking to her friends. One after the other she called them, to complain about me, about how out of control I was and how it was all Bubbie's fault for passing away and leaving everything on her, and she just couldn't handle it. More than once I heard her say why couldn't I be more like Marilyn, which was crazy considering what Marilyn had done.

I finished breakfast and ran back up to my room.

I spent the rest of the morning making up a blues song. I'd learned a few basic rules from Mississippi: first you sing a line, then repeat it, then another line—the more depressing the better. And every blues song tells a story.

I started singing mine:

She put her head down and then she closed her weary eyes
She put her head down and then she closed her weary eyes...

I couldn't believe it. I actually said the words. Somehow it hurt less when I was singing it.

And then she—

There was a rappa-tap-tap on the frame of my open door. I looked up and there was the great-great-grandmother killer, all four feet three of her.

"Yoo hoo!" A little wave and a big grin. "You should excuse my bothering you, but I just wanted to tell you I wouldn't stop you."

"From doing what?"

"Since you can't help yourself, what can I do?" She shrugged. "Stick tape over your mouth?"

"What can't I help myself from doing?"

"What's not to understand?" She poked a finger into her knotted clumps of white hair and scratched her head. "It would be better for you not to take no for an answer."

"Not to take no for what answer?"

"Okay, okay already. Stop with the twisting of my arm. You can call me grandma. With the great-greats."

"I only wanted to call you grandma because I thought you *were* my grandma. Instead you're some creepy old lady who tricked my real great-great-grandmother and made her die."

"You like my stories, I tell you stories." She shrugged. "So I'll change the story a little. This time I really am your great-great-grandmother. I came to America when your grandma Lena sent for me." She flung her arms out. "And here I am."

"You can't just change the story! Not if it's true." I heaved a dramatic sigh. "And don't let Mom see you talking to me. You can get me in big trouble."

"One more thing," she said, "you never brought to me the playing cards. Remember? I want you should teach me to play poker."

"Poker! You killed my ancestor!" With that I pushed around her and ran downstairs.

I made myself lunch, then walked to Brighton Beach Avenue and followed it toward the amusement area. As I was crossing Ocean Parkway I saw Negro families walking on the other side of the street, passing the Tuxedo Theater. They looked so nice, all dressed up. Then I spotted Mrs. Jones, arm in arm with a tall man. Clarence and Edgar were following behind, horsing around. Then my heart started skipping—there was Mississippi! I'd never seen him like this before, wearing a suit and not carrying his guitar. He was talking to another elderly gentleman. I ran over.

"Hi!" I shouted.

"Well, hello, Little Sugar." He gave me a big smile. "This here is Mr. Washington, Mrs. Jones's daddy."

We said hello and I tagged along.

"Did you run away the other day because of the new policeman?" I said.

Mississippi nodded. "He talked to me the day before, don't want me playing on the boardwalk no more. Said he had complaints."

"Complaints!" There were lots of other musicians on the boardwalk, mostly of the accordion-playing type, and nobody complained about *them*.

"I reckon it was your uncle," he said. "Don't want no competition."

I felt blood rush to my face. Uncle Max, that rat! He'd be hearing from me.

"So you can't play on the boardwalk any more?"

"I don't want to end up in no New York jail."

"Don't worry, they won't arrest you," I said though I felt a flicker of doubt. "I think they'll just ask you to leave."

"I reckon I could give it another try. Long as I keep my eyes open it might be okay."

"Are you going to try this afternoon? I'm dying to hear the blues."

"Lord, no. I wouldn't never play for no money on a Sunday, just go to church, then sit me down on the back porch afterwards and strum."

By this time we'd turned the corner under the el and were walking along the front of the shanty town. The shacks were close together, striped with shadows from the overhead tracks. They were the opposite of our house: totally simple. You looked in the front window and saw out the back.

"You live here?" I asked.

"I sure enough do."

"Can I come to your house?"

"I don't reckon that would be such a good idea, me living alone and all."

"Come on over to our place." Mr. Washington gave me the warmest of smiles. "I was aiming to invite Mr. Mississippi over anyway."

"Really?" I couldn't believe my good luck. "That would be great—I could sing you the song I made up."

Mississippi stopped at a dilapidated door.

"I'll just get my guitar," he said.

The Jones family went into the shack next door and I waited there with Mr. Washington until Mississippi came out carrying his guitar.

"Let's go round back," Mr. Washington said, and we followed him down a narrow path between the two shacks. When we got there I found out theirs was the one with the goat in the yard. It was tied to a dead tree that had bottles stuck on the ends of its branches.

We climbed onto the back porch, which was covered with a corrugated tin roof. Mississippi and Mr. Washington sat down on the two rocking chairs and I pulled up a milk crate.

"Want to hear my song?" I asked. "I mean, the beginning of it, that's all I've got so far."

"Why, sure," Mississippi said.

> She put her head down, and closed her weary eyes.
> She put her head down, and closed her weary eyes...

"That there's a good start on singing from the inside," Mississippi said, "but you can go more deep." He started twanging away on his guitar, putting in extra beats, singing my words but with some oh, oh, oh's thrown in. Somehow he wrestled a haunting tune out of it. Mr. Washington plucked his harmonica off the window sill and jointed in.

Then Mr. Jones, Edgar, and Clarence came through the screen door and started tapping their toes and clapping with the rhythm. Mississippi waved me in as he sang, so I started singing too, loud and clear. Then he stopped singing—gave me a solo:

> She put her head down, and closed her weary eyes
> She put her head down, and closed her weary eyes
> And then I waited and waited...

I felt like it needed an "oh Lord," so I stuck one in.

> Oh Lord, for her to rise.

My voice sounded different—deeper, more layered, like it wasn't even mine.

"That's there's a fine song," Mr. Washington said when we finished. "And you got a mighty fine voice for a…" he thought for a second, "little girl." That made me smile so big I thought my face would break.

The boys ran over to Mississippi and started singing him songs they'd made up. Mississippi was smiling, laughing, singing their songs, showing them how to play the guitar.

I couldn't help but feel a little jealous.

The aroma of something mouth-watering wafted through the screen door and I was suddenly starving. Mrs. Jones pushed the door open with her hip. She was wearing a white apron and carrying a big tray of rolls, which she offered around.

"Thank you so much," I said after I took a bite. "These are about the best rolls I ever had." For some reason this sent them into convulsions of laughter.

"These ain't rolls," Mrs. Jones finally managed to say. "These here are biscuits."

I was sure glad Mississippi had these nice neighbors. They could look out for him when I wasn't there, and if I couldn't find him I could always ask them where he was.

Then Mr. Jones stood up. "I got an important announcement to—" All of a sudden there was a loud banging, clanking noise, the whole house shaking. But it was only the train passing overhead, slowing down, hissing to a stop at Ocean Parkway.

"I can't stand that train another minute," Mr. Washington said, then turned back to Mr. Jones. "What were you saying?"

"We finally found us an apartment."

"Hooray!" the boys shouted and started running all over, cheering, hugging everybody.

"It's near to where I work," Mr. Jones went on. "Got separate bedrooms, running water, 'lectricity."

"That's great," Mr. Washington said. "When can we move in?"

"Lease starts July first."

"But that's today!" I cried. I was very aware of the date because of its closeness to the Fourth of July, Coney Island's biggest day of the year.

"Come on, boys." Mrs. Jones waved them toward the door. "Best we start packing if we want to move in by suppertime."

"Wait a second," I said. "How can you pack up everything and move in that fast?"

"Because we don't got two sticks to rub together," Clarence said with a big grin.

"What about the goat?"

"Oh, the goat ain't ours," Mrs. Jones said. "It comes with the house. Now, let's go, boys. I don't aim to spend another night in this miserable shack."

"Be in shortly," Mr. Washington said, then turned to Mississippi as soon as the rest of the family filed inside. "I want you to come over for dinner. Next Sunday. See that new place of ours."

"I sure enough would enjoy that."

Mr. Washington went inside. I heard pots and pans banging, the boys laughing.

"Is it all right for us to be alone on the porch?" I asked Mississippi.

He smiled his kind smile, which reminded me of Bubbie's.

"Long as that door stays open."

I got up off the milk crate and sat in on the rocking chair. It felt gigantic.

"I bet Edgar and Clarence will miss you after they move away."

"I don't reckon they will. They got their real granddaddy."

"You're not going to move away too, are you?"

"Can't never leave till I find that dog of mine." He sighed. "I went back to the pound yesterday, but he wasn't there. Brooklyn's a mighty big place, they told me, a dog could go anywhere, find himself a new home."

"Does Cerbie have tags?"

"I don't know what you mean."

"Tags on his collar?" Then I remembered he didn't have a collar. "They, um, have a dog's name, address, and proof he had rabies shots."

"Cerbie and me, we hardly never had no address. And even when we did, I wouldn't never write it down on no collar. I'm a man on the run."

I thought of what might happen if the dogcatcher picked him up and saw he didn't have tags. I didn't say anything, but Mississippi saw my face and put his hands over his for a minute.

"I best be going back first thing in the morning and explain about the tags."

"If you want you can give them my telephone number, and I'll bring you a message if they call."

"That's real kind of you, Little Sugar, but I don't want to leave no trail." He started strumming.

"Do you rent your house?" I asked.

He stopped strumming and looked at me.

"Why, I sure enough do. Day to day, fifteen cents a day. Man at the end of the block owns most of them. Why you asking?"

"I don't know, just curious."

He went back to strumming.

"Mississippi?"

He stopped playing and frowned at me.

"So if you're renting by the day, and when you find Cerbie you can leave without a moment's notice?"

"Might have to. I sure wish I could stay right here. I'm so weary of running, but there's a hellhound on my trail."

He started strumming again. I wanted to ask him how he knew the meat-faced sheriff was still after him after all these years, but I managed to restrain myself, until—

"I know where he might have gone," I couldn't help blurting, then I clamped my hand over my mouth.

Mississippi put his guitar down.

"You mean Cerbie?"

"Yeah. I was just thinking of the Jamaica Bay Wildlife Refuge. He might have joined a wild dog pack there."

"Where's that?"

"It's not far from here, just a few miles up the coast. It's gigantic, about ten thousand acres. It has marshes and islands and wilderness. We did a boat tour of it, the guide said there were packs of wild dogs on some of the islands."

"Cerbie wouldn't never leave me for no pack of wild dogs. He's been my best friend for forty or fifty years."

"But dogs don't live that long." I did the math. "If he's forty, that would make him... two hundred and eighty human years old."

"Well, Cerbie ain't no ordinary dog. He ain't never got sick nor aged a single day. I have this feeling Cerbie will live forever."

"So he's an immortal being?"

"That's what I reckon."

"Where'd you get him?"

"I can't rightly say I got him at all. More like he got me."

"What do you mean?"

"It's a mighty strange story," he said. "It was real dark that day, sky just about to burst with storm clouds. I was walking along somewhere in Arkansas when I reached a fork in a dirt road. Weren't much there, no houses, no farms, just trees and brush. There was a signpost at the fork, but weather'd worn away the words. I was just standing there like

I was stuck in mud. Don't know why, but it seemed real important I pick the right fork to walk down."

"Just put your stuff in the sack!" Mr. Jones shouted from the house. "It ain't that hard. No, you can't take that, it ain't nothing but trash."

"Calm down!" I heard Mrs. Jones say, and the voices dropped back to normal.

"Thunder was starting to rumble," Mississippi went on. "I looked down one fork for the longest time, same with the other, when out of the blue, Crack! A bolt of lightning hit the signpost, left it burnt and charred. Before I could even catch my breath this here dog comes crashing out of the underbrush, running right at me. Big as a wolf. I look back down the other fork and that's when I get the shock of my life, because there was that meat-faced sheriff lumbering toward me, swinging his shotgun."

"Oh, my God," I said.

"The dog stops dead at my feet and locks its burning eyes on mine, and I'm just about as scared as a man can get." He rubbed his face. "But then the dog takes off again, running straight at the sheriff. The sheriff lifts his shotgun, takes aim, and shoots. I don't reckon he could of missed, not that close up, but the dog keeps charging. The sheriff takes aim and shoots again, weren't no way he could of missed that time, but the dog don't even slow down."

"So bullets can't kill him?" I cried out.

He nodded. "Sure enough looks that way."

"Then what happened?"

"The sheriff raises his shotgun a third time, but the dog lunges at him, bites his arm. He screams, drops his shotgun, and takes off running."

"Oh! So now *he* had a hellhound on *his* trail!"

"He sure enough did."

"Then what happened?" I could hardly wait.

"Then the dog turns and runs at me, but something in my gut told me what to do. I grab hold of my guitar and just start strumming. I can hear a song coming out of my mouth." He started singing:

> I hate to see the settin' sun go down
> Oh, I hate to see the settin' sun go down
> 'Cause it means I got to quit this here town…

"My throat was dry like dust, but somehow I sung sweeter than tupelo honey. The dog starts dancing around, then give me the widest grin I ever did see, those eyes of his slanting back. He starts running down one fork, back and forth like I should follow, and I knew right then he'd stick with me the rest of my life."

"But I don't understand. How come Cerbie didn't get killed?"

"It don't make a lick of sense, but there weren't a mark on him."

"So maybe Cerbie really *is* a hellhound." This made perfect sense to me.

"Naw," Mississippi said. "He's too nice to be a hellhound."

"But maybe he's a good hellhound who only bites *bad* people and sends them to hell."

He smiled. "That there's an idea I never had."

"Why'd you name him Cerbie?"

"It just popped into my head."

"What about the meat-faced sheriff?"

"We ain't never stuck around long enough for him to catch up with us. This is the longest I ever stayed in one spot."

"What if he shows up and Cerbie's not here to protect you?"

"If he finds me here I'll just have to…" His voice trailed off.

"You know what, Mississippi? I think Cerbie's protecting *me*!"

I told him about my latest brush with death.

"Good Lord!" He look so worried I was sorry I'd told him. "You got to be *real* careful from now on."

"My mom doesn't believe me about the secret messages and Cerbie protecting me." I bit my lip.

"You know what? You probably the only one who believes *my* story too."

Clarence came banging through the screen door.

"I don't want to go!" he yelled. Mrs. Jones came out as Clarence ran over to Mississippi and grabbed his arm. "Don't let them take me—I want to stay here with you."

"Don't pay him no mind," Mrs. Jones said. "This happens every time we have to move. He just needs to settle down." Then, to Clarence, "You leave Mr. Mississippi alone or we really will leave you here." And with that she pried him loose and dragged him back into the house.

I glanced at my Mickey Mouse wristwatch.

"Oh, no," I said. "It's almost three o'clock. I'll be late for my milk-drinking-torture. Can I come back? I only live about four blocks away."

"Not now, Little Sugar, I got to go back to my place."

"Can't we sit on your back porch?"

"That wouldn't be a good idea. Besides, I reckon I'll have me a rest inside."

"When can I see you again?"

"I'll give the boardwalk another try tomorrow."

"Can I pick you up on my way there?"

He frowned and shook his head.

"I already told you, I don't want you coming by my place."

"But—"

"You ain't listening to me, Little Sugar." He sounded really serious.

"You got to listen when I tell you to be careful, listen when I tell you don't never come by my house. Do you promise?"

"Do I have to?"

"You sure enough do."

I promised.

Seventeen

I came up with a plan to make amends to Marilyn.

I went up to my room, took out my paint set, and painted a piece of paper. Then I walked next door, rang the doorbell, and waited. Finally it opened, and there stood Marilyn, wearing pedal-pushers and a pajama top, a toothbrush in her hand. Glaring at me.

"Can I come in?" I asked.

For some reason, or more likely no reason, the hall was littered with pots and pans today. Doors banged on the second floor, followed by loud voices and laughter. A group of teenage boys in bathing suits came thundering down the stairs, grabbing towels off the banister. We jumped out of their way as they rushed past us, down the stoop, and into the street.

"Go away!" Marilyn said.

From another room came Evil Aunt Suzie's much angrier voice.

"I'm leaving you and this stinking dump forever!" she yelled. "It's like I'm dead living here."

Then Uncle Nat's voice: "Can't you leave me alone for five minutes?"

"Didn't you hear me? I'm leaving!"

I heard banging and slamming noises from their bedroom, then

Suzie came stomping through the hall, kicking pots out of her way, swinging a suitcase with clothes sticking out of it. We stepped back as she marched out the front door, down the steps, and into the world.

"I love it when she leaves," Marilyn said.

"Where's she going?"

"Who knows?"

"She looks like she slept in her dress."

"She did."

"Who's going to take care of the boarding house?"

"No one. It's better that way."

"Think she'll come back?"

"What is this, twenty questions?" She was back to glaring. "What do you want?"

I pulled out the painted paper.

"Let's become blood sisters. You saved my life! We can share everything."

"Will you take half my mom?"

"Sure. Will you take half mine?"

She thought about this.

"Okay." She grabbed me in a bear hug. "I hate it when we fight." A tear slid down her rosy cheeks.

So we ran up the littered stairs to her room and sat down on the floor leaning against her white canopy bed. She tucked her shiny hair behind her ears and I handed her the piece of paper. "Blood Sisters," I had painted on it in dripping red letters. Under that I'd painted a blue daisy with our names on either side of it.

We pricked our fingers with a needle and touched the blood to the daisy's center.

"Where is everybody?" I said. "I haven't seen anyone for days."

"Don't you know? They're all quarantined. Mono."

I wondered if one of *them* was the one who was supposed to die.

"Okay, blood sister," I said. "Let's go look for Mississippi."

For variety, we took the back path through Seaside Park, past the old men playing chess at marble tables, through the little playground, then across the street, past the handball courts, and up the stairs to the boardwalk.

It was late morning by now, a sunny day, the ocean calm, the beach filling up.

We passed the penny arcades and hot dog stands. The Wonder Wheel turned, the Cyclone plummeted, and passengers screamed, all to a random background beat of firecrackers.

We got to Jones Walk, but Mississippi wasn't in his usual spot.

"Let's try again later," I said. "Maybe he's at the dog pound."

"What do you want to do now?"

"Uncle Max's?"

"What is it with you and that place?"

"I have to ask him to stop complaining about Mississippi."

When we got there Lenny was standing at the wide-open accordion doors talking to Uncle Max, who was sitting at the bar, tapping his cigar into an ashtray.

"Look, I'm sorry," Lenny said. Though he didn't sound sorry. "But I got a better offer."

"Go to hell," Uncle Max said. "Don't come crawling back here."

Lenny turned and walked out.

"Stay away from my mom!" I yelled at him.

He didn't even look at me. He cracked his knuckles and put on sunglasses.

"And stop trying to kill me!" I added.

His head jerked to face me.

"You are one nutso kid," he said, then continued on his way.

I looked into the saloon, watched Uncle Max pick up the phone. He thought for a minute, then slammed it down. Let out a huff and picked it up again.

To my surprise, Marilyn called out, "Hi, Uncle Max!" and waved at him when he looked up. He hung up the phone again.

"Excuse me," I called out. "May I talk to you a minute, please?" I stepped over the threshold onto the stained red carpet.

"Hey!" he yelled.

I jumped back onto the boardwalk.

"Don't ever step foot in here again! Next time, no more Mr. Nice Guy. Now what do you want? I'm busy."

"You don't look busy," Marilyn said.

He let out an exaggerated huff, got up, and walked outside to where we were standing.

"Just get to the point."

I looked into his icy blue eyes and concentrated on making mine icy too.

"I don't know why you have to complain about Mississippi playing on the boardwalk. It's just not fair!"

"Who?"

"Mississippi. The singer you fired even though— "

"Oh, the bluesman. I never complained about him. Didn't even know he was still in town."

"The new cop on the beat told him there were complaints."

Uncle Max laughed. "He just wants a kickback. Doesn't your bluesman know anything?"

"How much does he want?"

"About fifteen bucks for the season."

"Fifteen dollars! That's a lot of money." I had seven dollars in my cigar box I'd been saving for what seemed like years. Maybe I could get the rest by hoarding the money Mom gave me for lunches, just not eat them.

"It's all your fault," I said. "You should never have fired him."

"You know something? You're right, he's a great singer." He looked up for a few seconds, reached into his pocket, pulled out two bills, and handed us one each.

"Fifty dollars!" we both cried.

"What's this for?" I asked.

"Buy some candy or something."

"No, I mean why are you giving it to us?"

"You just gave me an idea."

"But Uncle Max, this is so much money," Marilyn said. "I never saw so much."

"Not to me it's not," he said.

"You're not going to tell our parents, are you?" I asked him.

"Nah. It's just for you to spend however you want. Now scram."

Eighteen

I looked at the green fluorescent hands of my bedside clock—2:05 in the morning. I turned over, then turned back again facing the clock—2:06. It was so hot in my room, it was hard to breathe. I turned over on my belly. Too uncomfortable, flipped over on my back. Then my side. The clock seemed to have stopped at 2:06. I put the pillow over my head, tried to shut out the firecrackers bombarding the neighborhood. *The Molech could be in the room right now staring down at me, but I wouldn't see him.*

I couldn't stand it a minute longer.

Sometimes when I can't sleep I go downstairs and watch the late movie. I liked *Sunset Boulevard* and *The Big Heat* and especially *Imitation of Life*, because the first scene takes place right here on the beach with the Parachute Jump in the background.

But it was too late for the late show, so I crept into the hall and tried the Boarder's door. I was still angry at her for killing my ancestor, but if there was one place I might be safe from the Molech it was with her.

The door opened. I entered the trash-walled vestibule and flipped on the light, scattering a carpet of cockroaches. It was hot and stuffy, the smell of mildew stronger than ever. I took the path I'd taken before, turning this way and that, around the bend and into her den.

"Oy vey iz mir!" She threw up her arms.

The golden glow of the milk-glass lamp lit the room, and the little television was sending out its own flickering blue light. I sat down on the ottoman. With her in a ratty chenille robe and me in my baby-doll pajamas it felt like a slumber party.

"What are you doing here?" she asked. "I thought you mortals had to sleep at night."

"I couldn't sleep. I hope you don't mind."

"Mind? Why would I mind? This television program is for the birds."

There was a picture on the screen of what looked like five propellers and an Indian wearing a feather headdress.

"That's the test pattern," I said.

"The what?"

"The test pattern. They put it up when there aren't any shows on. It never changes."

"So why am I watching it?" She went over and turned it off. The screen turned to snow, which condensed into a white dot, then blinked out.

"You call this a city! New York-shmew York, there's nothing here to do at night."

"I bet Uncle Max's is open."

"Oy! That's the sort of place the Molech loves."

I started to tell her about how I almost drowned, but she stopped me.

"This I know already." She wagged a finger in my face. "You shouldn't take for yourself any chances. Next time you want you should take a chance? Clear it with me first."

"Um… okay. Can I ask you a question?"

"Go ahead, ask already."

"You said you wanted my real great-great-grandmother to rest in peace and stop kvetching. If you *did* take her passport, and the Molech *did* kill her, and she *is* kvetching, does that mean she's in the Place-between-Life-and-Death?"

She shrugged. "Could be."

"But she's dead, right?"

"Dead like a stone, but she refuses to move on. She's angry I cheated her. Wants to push me out and come back to life, move in here with you."

"How do you know? Did she tell you?"

"What are you, crazy? To me she wouldn't talk. The Molech, he told me."

"So the Angel of Death finally caught up with you?"

"Of course." She flung her hands out. "How else could he tell me?"

"Then why are you still alive?"

"You want I should tell you why I'm alive? This you want to know? Okay, okay already, but first how's about a little drink of schnapps?"

"Sure," I said.

She hopped off her chair, took out the bottle, and placed it on the table. Then she hoisted herself back onto her seat and poured us each a drink.

"L'chaim," we toasted.

"So how come you're still alive?"

"After your grandparents picked me up at Ellis Island we went back to the railroad flat on Norfolk Street. They gave to me in the kitchen an armchair, and there I sat night and day because I never slept any more."

"Is that when the Molech caught up with you?"

"This I'm getting to. Your grandmother, may she rest in peace, she was strong like an ox. She kept making babies, shopping and schlepping, stuffing the husband, stuffing the babies. She had this big pot of stew always cooking on the stove. Just kept throwing things in. Dried up cabbage leaves, chicken skin, gristle, whatever was left over from the butcher shop. Feh. I wouldn't eat it, garbage it was. And the rugelech? Not enough with the walnuts. But did she make stuffed cabbage! Out of this world. She was a regular balebosteh."

"So how come you're not dead?"

"Stop changing of the subject already and I'll tell you. So, finally I had the time to read the greatisha books—"

"Mom says her great-grandmother was a hundred years old, so if she thinks you're her, then you must be—"

"Oy! Oy! Oy!" Guffaw, guffaw, cough, cough, cough. "The hundred-year-old-lady schtick. I forgot all about that." She waved her hand.

"Can I have another drink?" I seemed to have finished my schnapps.

"Why not?" She poured me a little more.

"Somehow…" She winked at me. "A rumor got started that I was a hundred years old. Then each year, also somehow, I got five years older. I must be two hundred and fifty years old by now. Anyway…" She grinned. "What with the not sleeping and the no housework, I had for myself plenty of time to start on my reading."

"What'd you find out?"

"About what?"

"The meaning of life. Did you find out what it is by reading the great books?"

"Ay-yay-yay, I couldn't even get started because of that farkockter beagle. Like an angry dybbuk it howled. I would scream at it, 'shah! shah! shah!' but that just made it bark worse.

"What's a dybbuk?" I asked.

"A dybbuk? About this you have to ask?"

"My mom said it was a demon or something, but I don't think she knows."

"Oy! A demon!" She laughed. "A dybbuk," she pointed up, "it's a ghost from a dead person who can't let go of the world. Sometimes they jump into someone and can't get out. Like in prison they are. Then you have an angry dybbuk."

"Ohhh. So then what happened?"

"Psssh. About then a certain Molech starts turning up in the hallway, only now he's not a fiddler. He's carrying a banjo and wearing a white suit. Also he shaved off his beard."

"You didn't tell me he could look different."

"Of course. He can look how he wants, to whomever he wants. Everyone can see him differently or the same, it's up to him."

"Oh my God." I went cold inside. "Other people can see him?"

"Of course. When he's not collecting souls he likes to sing on the stage. All the big shots in the afterlife do. Showoffs they are."

"But it doesn't make sense," I said. "How can the Molech spend so much time singing on stage *and* collecting souls? Lots of people die every day. He'd have to be in different places at the same time, all over the world."

"He is," she said. "That's because Molech ha-Movess? He can send out as many emanations of himself as he wants. And they can all act independently, so he can be in millions of places at once."

"Oh, noooooo...."

"What?"

"I just realized that since you can see the Molech when he doesn't want to be seen, and I can hear Lenny's thoughts when he doesn't want them to be heard, but only when he's singing, it must mean..."

"Do you think..." Her eyes widened.

"*Lenny's* the Molech!"

Nineteen

Finally, the Fourth of July.

It was a glorious day, dads bouncing toddlers on their shoulders, lovers arm in arm, kids wild with excitement, barkers shouting, calliope music. Marilyn and I were weaving through it all, passing booths of Shoot the Ducks, Hit the Clown, walking alongside Spook-a-Rama.

A man bumped into us, spilling his orange drink on our sneakers. "Oops," he said, then disappeared into the crowd.

"Great," Marilyn said. "Now our shoes'll be sticky all day."

"Let's call all our aunts and uncles. Someone must know where your mom is."

"Don't you dare."

At the Wonder Wheel's red THRILLS arrow, we turned onto the midway and merged into its flow.

"What about the Place-between-Life-and-Death?" I said. "You think it's an invisible world right on top of this one?"

"You come up with the weirdest ideas."

"That one's nothing compared with the fact that Lenny's an emanation of the Molech who can be seen only when he wants to be, except by the Boarder, and heard only when he wants to be, except by me."

"What about Mississippi's secret messages?"

"I don't know where they're coming from and neither does he."

"So where are we headed?" Marilyn said.

I sighed. "Want to go on the bumper cars?"

There was a huge bumper car ride just past Schweickerts Walk with Elvis blasting, sparks exploding, everyone crashing into everyone else.

"Too much like home." She smiled at last. "Let's go on the Magic Carpet ride. We haven't been on it all summer."

"Sure." I hadn't cleared this ride with Dad, but it was just a walk-through.

Dad had left this morning at the break of dawn, as usual. Today would be a killer day for him. The most pressing worry was the toboggans on the Bobsled getting stuck, which could cause a nasty collision.

On we walked, past the World in Wax Musee, the Haunted House, Thirteen Ghosts, and the House of Madness, which was under the Tornado. We crossed Stillwell Avenue. The Bobsled seemed to be running at full speed, which was good since there was a line around the block. Then I noticed a standing sandwich-board sign, crudely painted in bright pink, chartreuse, and purple.

"Look." I pointed. "Madame Clarissa put up a sign, like I told her to."

"How come whenever I'm not around you meet so many interesting people and then the minute I get back they all disappear?"

"Madame Clarissa didn't disappear, she's right around the corner. Come on, I'll introduce you."

We turned onto Schweickerts Walk. This dark little walk was usually deserted, but today there was a line coming out of the Dunes Hotel's side door.

"Is this a line to see Madame Clarissa?" I asked the last person standing there.

She was wearing a harsh shade of red lipstick, and her makeup was too thick and too pink, like a plastic mask. Mom could have given her a few tips.

"Wait your turn like everyone else." She frowned at us. "I've been here for a half-hour and the line hasn't budged."

"Let's go." Marilyn pulled on my arm.

"Just a minute, I want to ask this lady something." I turned to her. "We're not getting in line or anything, but I was just wondering why so many people are waiting to see her."

"Haven't you heard? She was the one who found that awful little girl, the one who ran away and hid in someone's basement. Up to me, I'd take that kid and lock her up in reform school."

That evening Marilyn and I went to the boardwalk for the Fourth of July fireworks with Uncle Nat and a few of Suzie's boarders. Mom couldn't make it. She said she was having a nervous breakdown from the noise.

The sky was a Technicolor wash of scarlet and orange, the light of day fading. We'd gotten here early so Uncle Nat could get up the ramp and park his wheelchair near the railing before hordes of people streamed onto the boardwalk. The kids from our block were still quarantined, but I saw a few grownups I knew.

"We're going down to the pier to get a better view," Marilyn told her dad, and off we ran. I felt so free, just the two of us loose on the boardwalk. By the time we got to the penny arcades and hot dog stands the crowd had thickened, the sky was dark, and the amusement area glowed with neon and incandescent light.

"I sure hope Mississippi's here," I said. "This is the perfect night for him, there must be a million people." I found out later there were a record-breaking million-and-a-half visitors that Fourth of July.

We walked along the beach side of the boardwalk so we could see Mississippi if he was playing in his old spot. As we approached the Wonder Wheel revolving high above Jones Walk, my hopes took a swan dive. His usual place was filled with boys leaning on the railing, laughing, snickering, and shoving each other under the light of the streetlamp.

"I was so sure he'd be here," I said.

"Come on." Marilyn tugged my arm. "We have to get to the pier before the fireworks start."

We started weaving through the crowd on the boardwalk, excusing ourselves, pushing our way to the middle, where we joined a lane of traffic heading toward the pier—

I thought I heard Mississippi's voice.

"Why are you stopping?" Marilyn said. "Come *on*."

"I can hear Mississippi, he's somewhere up ahead."

> Such a pooooor boy, a long way from home
> I'm just a…

I grabbed Marilyn's hand and pulled her, zigzagging crossways through the crowd.

> Oh, no, no, why did I ever leave my home.

In no time we were standing in the crimson glow of Uncle Max's neon sign, looking in. The place was packed—ladies in low-cut dresses, men slouched against the bar, silent, frozen, all eyes fixed on Mississippi singing, strumming his guitar, standing behind the microphone on the raised stage.

"He's—"

"Quiet," I said.

"Oooooh, no, no, no…" The spotlight seared through the smoke, framing him in a pale cone of light, magnifying him, making him more vivid than life. I longed to go in.

"Got no home of my—"

Boom!

We turned. A chrysanthemum of white fire bloomed in the black sky.

"Come on." Marilyn grabbed my arm and tried to pull me. "We have to go."

Mississippi stopped singing, drinkers at the bar hopped off their stools, and gradually the whole place emptied. Patrons walked out to the boardwalk and turned their faces toward the fireworks, martini glasses still in hand.

"You go," I said. "I have to talk to Mississippi."

Boom!

"But what about Uncle Max?"

"I don't see him. Don't worry, I'll be here when you get back."

"Promise?"

"Cross my heart."

She slipped into the crowd.

Mississippi climbed off the stage and took a seat at a table in the back littered with glasses. He picked up a half-filled shot glass and slugged it down.

I'd never gone into the saloon at night before. It seemed more dangerous, more forbidden, more thrilling. I looked around again for Uncle Max, my heart flapping like a blown-out tire on a dirt road. I put one foot over the threshold, then the other—and there I was, running over to Mississippi, plopping down in the seat across from him.

He frowned at me for a moment, then his face broke into the gentlest of smiles.

"Little Sugar, your Uncle Max will be mighty angry if he catches you in here."

"I know, but…" I looked around. The fireworks kept booming, the crowd kept ooooohing. "Do you know where he is?"

"He stepped out with that blond gal who's always hanging around."

"Where've you been?" My voice sounded whiny, but I couldn't help it. "Marilyn and I have been looking high and low for you."

"I'm sorry, but you got to stop that. I told you a long time ago not to count on me."

"But—"

"Now I reckon you best be running along, before your uncle gets back."

"Don't worry, I have a plan. If he shows up, I'll just run out the fire exit." So what if it set off the fire alarm. "How'd you end up playing here?"

"Lenny was supposed to perform tonight but he canceled. Got a better offer in Manhattan. Your uncle was mighty angry, didn't think he could get another singer at such sort notice. Then you came along and recommended me. He said he paid you a commission."

"So that's why he gave us all that money."

I had put it in my cigar box with my other treasures. One thing I wanted to do was buy some Ethel Waters records. She's a girl blues singer like me. There was no record store in the neighborhood, so I'd have to talk Mom into driving me to Kings Highway.

"Did he tell you about giving a kickback to the cop on the beat if you want to play on the boardwalk?"

"He sure did."

"I can pay it for you—I'm rolling in dough."

"Why, that's mighty kind of you, but there ain't no need. That uncle of yours, he booked me for every Tuesday-night fireworks. I can play here till the end of summer, so I'll finally have me a few bucks."

"Tuesday night fireworks! That's the best night—it's Lenny's night." I was almost giddy with relief. "Does that mean he's not coming back?"

"I don't rightly know."

"I think Lenny's the Angel of Death."

"The Angel of Death! What makes you think a thing like that, Little Sugar?"

"Because of the secret messages."

"But you hear messages in my songs too. And I still don't know why or what all they might mean."

"Yeah, but yours are warnings, not threats. You're much too nice to kill anybody."

"That's mighty kind of you, but..."

"Will you be my godfather?" I blurted out. "Then I'll feel safer."

He gave me his wonderful smile.

"I'd sure like that, Little Sugar. It's a sorry thing to leave this world without a trace like you ain't never been here."

BOOM! A series of fireworks exploded, too loud for us to talk for a minute.

"Would you show me again where you put your fingers on the guitar?" I asked.

"Okay, but soon as them fireworks is over, I got to play another set. You pay attention now." He pressed the strings down with his left hand and started strumming with the finger pick on his right. Oh, my goodness—he was playing my song.

"She put her head down," I sang out loud and clear, "and then she—"

Boom! Boom! Boom! Boom! Boom! The grand finale, followed by the ship's horn. People started ambling back into the saloon, chatting, sitting back down.

Then Marilyn came running in, right over to our table.

"You missed it!" she cried. "The grand finale—it was great!"

"I got to go," Mississippi said. He picked up his guitar and climbed back on stage. Someone flipped the spotlight on. Mississippi stood there waiting for everyone to be seated. I don't know what got into us, but Marilyn and I pulled up a pair of stools at the counter, near the stage.

Mississippi tapped the mike.

"Listen up, please."

The noise died down, faces turned toward him.

"This song was made up by a sassy little gal name of Brooklyn." A thrill shot through me. "And here she is to sing it herself."

Oh, my God! He was waving me on stage.

Everyone turned and looked at me. I shook my head, but they started applauding and whistling, and before I knew it, Marilyn was pushing me up the stairs, and there I stood in the spotlight—a messy-haired kid in red Keds sneakers and pedal-pushers, staring out at an ocean of grownups.

Mississippi sat down and I took hold of the microphone on its stand.

"Hi," I said. My voice boomed. "Hi," I said again a little lower. I turned to Mississippi. "Go ahead. You start and I'll come in."

He started strumming. The cone of light isolated us, protected us from the real world. I sang out:

> She put her head down, and she closed her weary eyes
> Oh, oh, she put her head down, and she closed her weary eyes
> And then I waited and waited, oh Lord, for her to rise…

My voice was coming from some place I didn't know existed, loud and rough, sweet and sad, the guitar lifting it up, bouncing it on its shoulders, carrying it along without missing a beat. And me? I turned into a little Billie Holiday up there, flinging my arms out, grabbing the microphone off the stand, belting my guts out. I couldn't help it, it felt so good, the burden lifted at last, the grief flowing out of me and into the audience, all those people taking it in, wanting more. And I gave them everything I had.

> I tried to wake her, oh Lord, I surely did
> Oh, oh I tried to wake her, oh Lord I surely did
> But I couldn't, no I couldn't, oh Lord, I'm just a kid…

Oh no! A man with a scarlet face and straight black hair was working his way through the crowd. Uncle Max.

> I miss my bubbie, oh Lord, I'm all alone

He was coming around the bar, Marilyn sticking her arms out, trying to block him, he pushing her aside, but would I stop? Would I even look his way?

> Oh, oh, I miss my bubbie, oh Lord, I'm all alone

Flashbulbs going off, the audience going wild, applauding like crazy, calling for more, then quieting down while I gave it to them.

> Because the Angel of Death, oh Lord, he took her home.

Twenty

Three days had gone by since Uncle Max yanked me off the stage even though the audience loved me. When he let go I tried to run back on, but he grabbed my arm.

"Quit while you're ahead, kid," he said.

"But I just want to—"

"Get out of here before somebody reports you. You could get me in big trouble."

"Did I break the law?"

"The law?" He laughed. "It's your mother I'm worried about. You never know what she's going to do."

The telephone rang, interrupting my daydreaming. I picked up.

"Collect call from Suzie Schorr," a nasal voice said. "Will you accept the charges?"

"Ummm…"

"Girlie, you still there? Will you accept the charges?"

My curiosity won out. "Yeah," I said.

"Put your mother on!" Suzie screamed in my ear.

"Where are you?"

"Didn't you hear me? Put your mother on this minute!"

"I can't, she went to the beauty parlor. Where've you been? It's been days."

"Just tell her to drive over to the police station as soon as she gets in. They won't let me go until she brings me my—" We got disconnected.

I put on my sneakers and ran next door. Marilyn was standing in front of her house, snapping a pair of scissors open and closed.

"Don't tell me," she said before I even reached her. "My mom called, right?"

"How'd you know?"

"Come on in."

We ran into the house, through the hall, and into the living room. I hardly recognized the place—that's because Uncle Nat had hired a cleaning lady and handyman, a married couple who'd cleaned and fixed up the whole first floor. Then he'd laid down the law to the boarders about picking up their things. Now he was a lot happier because he could finally get around in his wheelchair. And with Aunt Suzie out of the house he could finally do his accounting work in peace.

We plopped down on the cracked plastic slipcovers encasing the couch. Mmmmm, nice and crunchy.

"Isn't this terrific?" Marilyn said once she explained. "Everything looks so nice."

The couple Uncle Nat hired had done a great job. They'd stored all the extra cots, dressers, and odds and ends in the garage, so now I could see features of the living room I never even knew existed. For instance, they'd pulled up the gray threadbare carpeting patched with duct tape to reveal a shiny unmarked parquet floor, and they'd washed the windows so the whole room sparkled with sunshine.

"How'd you know your mom called?" I asked.

"She called here first, but I hung up. Then she called again collect, but I wouldn't accept the charges."

"What's she doing at the police station?"

"She's at the police station?"

"She wants my mom to drive there and bring her something, but I don't know what, because we got disconnected."

"Don't tell anybody," Marilyn said. "Just let her stay there and rot."

"She'll just keep calling until my mom answers, or she'll call here until someone else picks up. I'm surprised she hasn't called back yet."

"She can't."

"Why?"

"I'd say…" A little grin started across her face. "Someone cut the wire."

"You didn't!" The grin got bigger. "But Marilyn, now nobody in your whole house will be able to get phone calls."

"Good. I'm tired of taking messages."

"But she'll just call *my* house."

"I thought of that."

"Oh no, you don't— Mom will kill me."

"Just say I did it." She was awfully cheerful about this.

"You actually cut the phone line to my house?"

"It was easy. The wire comes in from the outside, right next to the patio."

She was right. I could see it running down the white stucco, snaking under the window and through a little hole in the green window frame.

"But she'll put you under lockdown for the rest of your life!"

"She can't—the police told her she wasn't allowed do that, they said it was child cruelty and she could go to jail."

"Then she'll punish you some other way."

"If she ever comes back." She shrugged. "What do you want to do now? I'm tired of playing. Let's do something different."

I looked at her—my blood sister, all happy and grinning. If *I* had Evil Aunt Suzie for a mom, I'd probably do the same thing.

"I have an idea," I said. "My mom's not home, so...just follow me."

"You want now I should tell you the meaning of life?" the Boarder asked from her ratty old armchair.

There we were, Marilyn and I, sharing the ottoman in the Boarder's trash-walled den.

"No thanks," I said. "Tell us why the Molech didn't get you when he finally showed up."

"This you want to hear? Okay." She settled back in her chair. "I always knew this could happen, but I was hoping maybe I could grab in first a little reading. So there he is, at your grandparents' railroad flat, pacing back and forth in the hallway, looking at his ledger, rubbing his chin. He slams it shut, flings it open, sticks his face into it, then with the finger down the page. Suddenly he stops at the door and stares right at me. He slams the ledger shut again and scratches his head, then he goes back to pacing. He keeps doing this, night after night.

"It's getting on my nerves, so I start locking the door. Then one chilly night I'm sitting in my armchair with a fluffy feather bed wrapped around me, trying to read about the illusion of time, when..."

I reached for the bottle of schnapps on the table, but she slapped my hand.

"Don't take without asking." She poured us each a little.

"All of a sudden there he is, walking through the closed door. He plays a little ditty on the banjo. He doesn't even bother to sing, like I'm not worth the trouble. Then he puts the banjo down and saunters over to my armchair. He takes out the eyeglasses from the case, but now no more with the pince-nez. *Now* he has horn-rimmed. He puts them on his gorgeous nose, but even with the eyeglasses he's still squinting at me. The wrong prescription maybe? He runs his index finger down a page in his ledger and stops near the bottom. Then he reaches out to touch my forehead.

"'Wait!' I shout at him.

"'What?' He looks goggle-eyed. 'You can see me?' He speaks Hinglish like a regular New Yorker.

"'You have for yourself the wrong dead lady.' I tell him. 'Is it Mrs. Morganstern for whom you are looking?'

"'Of course not. She's healthy as a horse.'

"'Good, because that's me, Mrs. Morganstern. The first name's maybe Ida.'

"'No, you're not. Mrs. Morganstern lives next door. You're Riva Greenhouse.'

"'Aha!' I yell in his face. 'In which case, I'm already dead!' And I tell to him the whole meshuga story.

"Hau boy, is he tsedreyt. 'I thought there was something odd about you,' he says, 'that's why it took me so long to come in. But…' He slaps his head. 'Jumping hellhounds! That's where the discrepancy is.' He squints at me. 'It's you, isn't it? You're the Malky Levine who should have died.'

"'That is correct.'

"'You know what this means?' He shakes his finger in my face. 'Do you have any idea what you've done?'

"'Farpotschket with life and death?'

"'Go ahead, gloat. Now everything's a mess. One little mistake and the whole space-time continuum gets out of whack.'

"'Oy-yoy-yoy, and this would be two little mistakes. So tell me, nobody ever did this before?'

"'About two thousand years ago,' he said, 'and I'm still cleaning that mess up.'

"So I say to him, 'Why not make like it didn't happen? Or better yet, just erase the name. Riva Greenhouse, only fourteen letters, even fewer in Yiddish. She's dead anyway. And me? I wouldn't tell a soul.'

"At this he frowns.

"'But if you do kill me,' I said, 'I wouldn't count on me not telling anyone on the other side.'

"'Are you blackmailing me?'

"'I'm just saying I maybe couldn't keep my mouth shut.'

"'The best I can do is give you a little more time." He looks in his book. "Depending on availability.'"

"So he could show up any time and take you away?" I asked.

"What have I been telling you?"

"But it's been so many years since you were supposed to die. Why hasn't he come yet?"

"Could be he forgot about me," she said. "Just then, that farkockter beagle starts howling so loud it's like there's fifty of him. The Molech's eyes practically pop out of his head. 'How do you stand it?' he shouts. 'I'd rather die than listen to this.'

"'So maybe you could do for me a little favor,' I say, 'and get rid of the doggy. Give to it some doggy disease.' He says okay."

"You killed the poor dog?" Marilyn said. "That's horrible."

I glared at the Boarder. "What did you give him in return?"

She gave me a sheepish grin, and a horrible thought occurred to me.

"Oh, no," I whispered. "Not your *soul*."

"For what reason do I need a soul?" She waved her hand. "You mortals, you think everybody's trying to steal your precious souls, like every schmegegge doesn't have one? I even knew a gentleman who had two, but one of them was a dybbuk. And why would the Molech want a soul? He wasn't the devil."

"Then what?"

"He didn't want anything." She shrugged. "He said getting rid of the doggy was something he had to do anyway, to fix up the mess I made."

"So what happened?" I said.

"For a while everything was the same, except the doggy got friendlier. This made me worry, so I warned your mama about it. Then one day the doggy goes crazy and bites Suzileh on the ankle. For this your grandma kills him with a frying pan."

"*You* killed little Suzie!" I cried.

"What?"

"The first Little Suzie died because you asked the Angel of Death to give Prince rabies."

"He told me it was just the doggy," she said. "Did I yell and scream! But he didn't care. Never trust the Molech. He's a Farschtinkener liar."

"But why did he do it?" Marilyn asked.

"Something about a smallisha tear to the cosmic structure, and for this he blames me. He says I was such a pain in the neck your grandparents would lock themselves in the bedroom, which made the first Suzileh get born too soon."

"But… it's still your fault she died," I said, "because of the mess you made."

"Noooo. Because Suzileh didn't stay dead, she got born again—but this time at the right time."

"So the dog was gone and the Molech left you alone," I said. "Did you figure out the meaning of life then?"

"I couldn't read a word. After your grandma killed the doggy, the walls started shaking and making such a racket I couldn't even hear myself think. 'It's just the wind,' your grandma kept saying. Wind? Wind in the walls? More like cats whooping it up on New Year's Eve.

"Then Suzileh was born again and, pssh, the wind stops. But the minute it stops, the baby starts to shriek. Did she scream and howl! Not crying, not like a normal baby, but like she's—"

Suddenly she jumped up on her chair, both hands cupping her face.

"Gotenyu," she whispered. "You don't think Suzileh is possessed by…"

"A dybbuk!" we all cried out.

Twenty-One

When we went outside we saw Evil Aunt Suzie was back, pulling weeds out of her rose garden. She had a black eye and was wearing the same dress she'd run off in. She had on her hearing aid, the batteries tied to her belt. She looked peaceful, like she always did among her roses.

"Let's get out of here before she sees us," Marilyn said.

"No, wait, I'm dying to find out where she went." I pulled Marilyn along the sidewalk towards her house until we got to the gate in the chain-link fence.

"Aunt Suzie!" I called out. She looked up, and her face turned furious.

"What do *you* want?"

"Where have you been all this time?" I asked.

"What do you care?" She stood up, dropped the weeds she was holding, and put her hands on her hips. "First you tear out my carpeting, then you cut the phone lines—"

"Dad had the carpeting pulled up," Marilyn said, "all I did was cut the phone lines."

"Who gave you the black eye?" I said, and the whole story poured out.

Turns out she'd been staying in Far Rockaway with her sweet-natured blind adopted sister Leah. They got into an argument about Suzie leaving things on the floor. Here the story got a little fuzzy, but blows were struck, police were called, and Auntie Leah ended up in the emergency room with a broken arm. For this the police arrested Suzie, which is why she wanted Mom to come to the police station—so she could make bail. But Auntie Leah dropped the charges, and that was that.

"Okay, so now you know," Marilyn said. "Can we leave now?"

"Hold on a second." Suzie glared at Marilyn. "If you think you're going to get away with this, think again."

Marilyn turned to me. "If she tries to put me in lockdown, call the police. They'll put *her* in lockdown."

"Oh, don't you worry," Suzie said. "What I'm going to do to you will be much, much worse."

Two days later I came clopping down the stairs and into the kitchen. Mom was having a cigarette and a cup of instant coffee, a *Glamour* magazine upside down on the table.

"I'm going to Marilyn's," I said. We were going to the boardwalk to look for Mississippi. We hadn't been able to find him since the Fourth of July, almost a week ago, and I was getting worried.

"We could go for a drive after lunch," Mom said.

Her anxiety seemed to vanish behind the steering wheel. The sleek cherry-red Buick with its big-toothed chrome grin was her car. She loved that it was the deluxe model with automatic gear shift, a new thing you had to pay extra for. The beat-up black pickup was Dad's.

She didn't like him parking it in front of the house, but he didn't have anywhere else to park it.

There were days, before she stopped eating, when we'd climb into the front seat of her car with its wonderful smell of vinyl and smoke, and she'd drive us around and tell me all about driving. I still remember the first time, how thrilled I was.

"This is the speedometer, and here in the middle is the odometer, see it moving? The most important thing is the brake." She waved at it with her cigarette, then took a long drag, the tip brightening to red. "Never forget where the brake is. And whatever else you do, never drive like…" and from there she went on about various friends of hers and how they should be banned from the road.

When we got home she turned the car around and backed into the garage so it would be facing the street for next time. She always did that.

"Not everyone can back up this good," she said. "Even your dad has trouble."

At this point, on days when she was in a really good mood, she'd let me sit behind the steering wheel and try everything out, especially the brakes.

Mom didn't know that sometimes, when she wasn't home, I lifted the car key from the box near the side door, went into the garage, and got in the Buick. I'd take Mom's back cushion and sit on it to make me taller, then with a quick turn of the key I made the engine spring to life and practiced braking and steering. I never gave it any gas or shifted it out of park, just imagined myself driving down the Belt Parkway, shooting ahead of all the other cars. I couldn't wait to grow up and really drive.

"By the way," Mom said. "Do you know someone named… it's a state, I think… maybe Tennessee?"

"Mississippi!"

"That's it."

"Yeah," I said. "He sings on the boardwalk. Why?"

"I just remembered, the other day someone came looking for him. I told him he must have the wrong address."

Oh, no.

"Was he a sheriff?"

"A sheriff!" She laughed. "You watch too many cowboy shows."

"But who was he? Did he leave a name?"

"Not that I remember."

"Why didn't you tell me sooner?"

"Why are you so interested?"

"Because... I just am. What did he look like?"

"If you must know, he was a big fella with a southern accent. Very polite. That's it, everything I know about him. You happy now?"

No, I was *not* happy.

"See you later." I ran out the door.

"So that's why we *have* to find him," I told Marilyn as I dragged her out of her house.

"Could you just hold up a second?" She stopped on the stoop to tie the laces on her sneakers. The day was clear and shiny as a marble, but I felt heavy and jumpy at the same time.

"Don't worry," she said. "If he's not on the boardwalk, we can always try his house, right?"

"But I promised never to go there."

"I could go. I didn't promise."

Marilyn was a fast walker and I tended to drift along, but today I was practically running. We emerged from the Land-of-the Semi-detached into the shadow of the el and turned right on Brighton Beach Avenue. I could see right away something was wrong, but it took me a minute to piece it together. And just then a train pulled out of the station, clacking and clanking so loud I had to shout in Marilyn's ear.

"Look!" I pointed.

"I don't believe it," she said. "What *happened* to it?"

The shanty town had been there as long as I could remember, but now its splintered walls, back porches, and farm animals were all gone. We crossed Ocean Parkway and looked at the empty lot. The only thing left was some debris on the ground. Even the bottle-tree had vanished. I picked up a piece of tarpaper brick and stared at it.

"Come on." Marilyn took my arm and pulled me away. "We have to look for Mississippi on the boardwalk."

That evening was Tuesday, fireworks night, and Marilyn and I were standing in front of my favorite saloon. The blood-orange sky was darkening. Streetlamps and neon signs were all blinking on, the crowd thickening.

Uncle Max was sitting at a table, tapping his cigar into an ashtray. Most of the tables were empty, just a few regulars leaning against the counter.

"Uncle Max!" I called to him from the boardwalk.

He looked up, let out a snort of laughter, then walked out to us.

"You two again? Next you'll be camping out here."

"What time is Mississippi supposed to show up? We have to find him, it's an emergency."

"Let's see now." He looked at his watch. "That would be about an hour ago. He was supposed to be here early to pull in customers before the fireworks. Now what am I supposed to do?"

"Where do you think he is?" Marilyn asked.

"If I knew, you think I'd be standing here waiting for him?"

"We've been looking for him all day," she said.

"Well, if you find him, tell him he's late for work." He gave a grunt of frustration. "Damn. Now I'll have to call Lenny again. It's like I can't get rid of the guy."

Oh my God. Mississippi not showing up for work, Lenny coming back, the sheriff coming to my house…

"Uncle Max," Marilyn said, "did you know the shanty town was torn down?"

"Everybody knows that. The Tuxedo's putting in a parking lot."

"But where'd all the tenants go?"

"I'd say by now they've found some other slum to live in."

"Maybe that's where Mississippi is," Marilyn said, "looking for a place."

Another disturbing thought came into my mind.

"Uncle Max? Did a man come around here a few days ago looking for Mississippi?"

"Big fella with a southern accent?"

My throat went dry. "Was he a sheriff? Did he leave a name?"

"A sheriff?" He laughed. "All I know is, every time I find a great performer, some other club owner tries to steal them away."

"What did you tell him?"

"Get lost! Find your own damn bluesman."

Twenty-Two

Mississippi never did show up at Uncle Max's Tuesday night. Now more than a week had gone by and still no sign of him.

I rang Marilyn's doorbell.

"Who's there?" Evil Aunt Suzie's sour voice.

"It's me," I said.

She cracked the door open on the chain-lock.

"What do you want?"

"Can Marilyn come out to play?"

"She's not here."

"Where is she?"

Bang! She slammed the door in my face. I heard the deadbolt turn.

I pounded the door as hard as I could.

"Go away!" she shouted from the other side.

"Where is she?" I shouted back.

"She's visiting relatives!"

"What relatives?"

"Drop dead!"

I ran home, up the front steps and into the hall, practically crashing into Mom, who was headed out.

"Mom!" I cried. "You have to help me!"

"Can't this wait? I was just on my way to—"

"It's Marilyn. She's gone."

"Oh, no, not this again—"

"No, it's not like that." I told her what just happened.

"All right." She gave a weary sigh. "I'll call that lunatic sister of mine. But don't expect anything." She went into the kitchen and dialed.

"Suzie…? Yeah, she just told me… *What*! How could you *do* that?…. I don't care, it's child torture!" She slammed down the receiver.

"What did she say?"

Mom sat down at the kitchen table, so I did too.

"You don't want to know." She rubbed her eyes, then sat there shaking her head.

"Mom, you have to tell me!"

"She sent her to Anna."

I couldn't believe I was hearing this.

"Aunt Anna's a slave driver! She ruined your childhood!"

"She says Marilyn's out of control. Says it's your fault, that you're a bad influence."

"Why would Aunt Anna even want Marilyn? You're always saying how snotty she is."

"She probably wants Marilyn to take care of that spoiled grandson of hers. And be her servant."

I could just see Marilyn scrubbing the floor, looking up—hurt—because we abandoned her.

"They're in Budd Lake for the summer," Mom said.

"We have to get her."

"What?"

"We have to get in the car and go free Marilyn!"

"Are you crazy?"

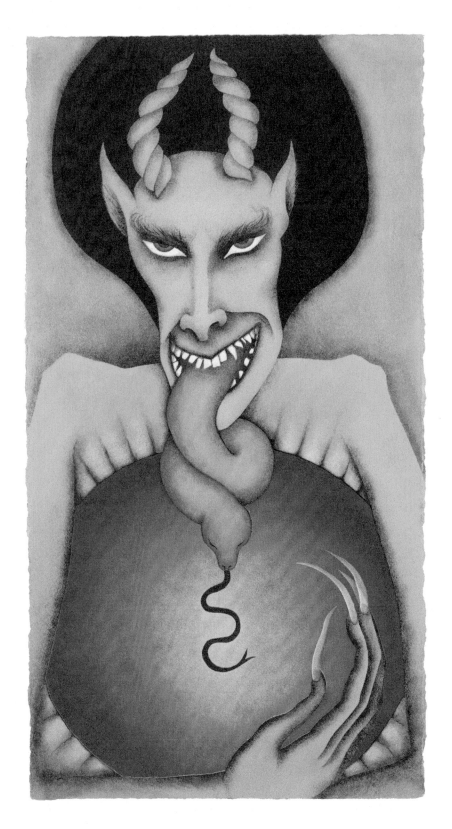

"We can't just leave her there! Please, Mom."

"I don't want to get involved."

"But Mom, we *are* involved. Marilyn's my blood sister. She saved my life, now we have to save hers."

"Nobody rescued me."

"All the more reason to rescue Marilyn."

"Nobody lifted a finger to help *me*. I never cut any phone wires. I never ran away from home. I was a good girl." She slammed her fist on the table. "I had seven brothers and sisters and no one even missed me." Then she jumped up, ran into the bathroom, and banged the door shut.

I walked over. I could hear pills scattering on the tile floor.

"Mom, are you all right?" I called through the door.

"Leave me alone! I'm not going to kidnap Marilyn. Suzie's right, she's out of control. And you *are* a bad influence."

"Mom, could you come out, please?"

"Go away. You ruined everything. I used to be happy."

"I hate you!"

I ran up to my room and slammed the door. When I came out, Mom had shut herself in her room. I decided to try again, knocked.

No answer.

"Mom?" I called out.

Silence.

"Mom! Are you okay? Please just answer me. I won't bother you again if you answer."

Silence.

I grabbed hold of the knob—my hand shaking—turned, and pushed.

She was sitting in front of the mirror as usual, but this time stripped down to bra and panties. I could see her ribs pushing against her skin.

She was staring at the sewing shears in her hand. She turned. I could almost hear bones cracking.

"What do you want!" she yelled weakly. "Can't I have any privacy?"

"I was—"

"Just leave me alone for crying out loud!"

I closed the door.

Twenty-Three

The fluorescent dials pointed at midnight. I turned on my stomach. The air in the room was hot and suffocating. I couldn't keep my legs still — or my mind, which kept imagining Lenny slouched against my ballerina wallpaper, flashing his white teeth at me.

I slipped out of bed, opened the door, and stepped into the hall. I heard faraway shouting. A cry of pain.

I ran downstairs.

There was Dad, slumped over on the couch, eyes closed. His red hair looked dark in the flickering blue light. I ran over, sat down next to him, and tugged on his pajama sleeve.

"Dad?"

He jerked awake with a start, blinked, and focused his eyes.

"Princess." His goofy grin transformed his freckled face. "What are you doing up?"

"I couldn't sleep."

"Join the club. I was so tired I couldn't sleep either. Thought I'd come down here, watch some TV, unwind."

The ballet-dancing wrestler Ricki Starr, my favorite, was twirling

and leaping around a pig-faced opponent with a bald head. He kicked
the man in his big chin. The audience applauded.

Dad wrestled too, at the Y, but not during the busy season.

"Can I stay up and watch with you?"

"Sure." He yawned, which made me yawn too. "Whatever you want."

I couldn't believe my good luck. This was the first time I'd seen him
alone all summer.

"You know what, Dad?"

"Not unless you tell me."

"I wish I could see you more."

"I know, Princess. I wish I could see you more too, but I have to
make the rides safe. People's lives depend on it."

"But this summer you've been working much, much more. Even
before the busy season. Ever since Bubbie…"

"Maybe I've been throwing myself into it too much." He yawned,
sighed. "After Labor Day I'll have plenty of time for you and your
mother."

Labor Day! It was eons away.

We were quiet for a couple of minutes watching Ricki pirouette in
his pink tights.

"Dad?"

"Yes?"

"Mom won't drive me to Aunt Anna's to save Marilyn."

He frowned, sucked in a deep breath, and let it out slow.

"You know what, Princess?" he said. "I think it's best that way. Let
everyone cool down."

They'd never cool down, why couldn't he see that? Because he was
never here, that's why. And he always took Mom's side.

"But Aunt Anna's a slave driver," I said. "Mom said so. She's worse
than Aunt Suzie."

He gave a sad laugh, shook his head.

"I'm worried about your mother," he said. "The things she says… and she's lost so much weight. Could you keep an eye on her for me?"

"What about Marilyn?" What about me?

"Your mother's not like us," he said.

"What do you mean?"

"She's just… I don't know, I'm too tired to think."

"Okay, I'll try. But she never listens to me." It struck me that this was the very same complaint she had about me.

"We'll talk about it some other time, okay? Right now I can't stay awake another minute."

He got up, kissed me on the forehead, then abandoned me in the flickering blue light of the TV.

Twenty-four

I really wanted to do what Dad asked me to do and keep an eye on Mom, but she wouldn't let me. She had a sliding bolt installed on her door and literally locked me out. My dad had dropped this on me, then disappeared back into the machinery.

But I still had to save Marilyn, so after lunch I headed to the board-walk. When I got there the accordion doors were open and Uncle Max was sitting at a table in front, chomping on a cigar.

"Well look who's here, the Bessie Smith of the sixth grade." I think he was warming up to me.

"Can I come in?" I said. "I have to ask you something important."

"Don't push your luck, kid, ask from there."

I told him how Evil Aunt Suzie sent Marilyn to be a slave for Aunt Anna.

"So I need you to drive me there and save her," I said.

He laughed and shook his head.

"I'm *serious*, Uncle Max. We could visit Anna—she's your sister, after all."

"If it were up to me I'd build an insane asylum around the whole lot of those sisters of mine. Now scram."

I scrammed.

When I got home I went to the garage and got the map of New Jersey out of the Buick's glove box. I took it up to my room, laid it out on my desk, and circled Budd Lake, then started penciling in a route. I've always been good with maps, much better than Mom, so Dad lets me navigate family trips. I was happy to see we could take the Brooklyn/Staten Island ferry and was pulling my pencil across Staten Island when I heard the doorbell ring. A few seconds later Mom called up the stairwell.

"Brooklyn! That southern fella's here again!"

I ran down the stairs two at a time, right up to Mom standing at the front door, her arms crossed.

Out on the stoop was Burl Ives—well, not really, but he looked just like him: large, reddish hair, a goatee. He was wearing a white three-piece suit with a black string bow tie. Nothing meat-faced about him.

"May I come in, ma'am?" he said, slow as rush-hour traffic.

"Who'd you say you were again?" Mom asked.

He pulled a business card out of his breast pocket and handed it to her. She squinted at it and read it out loud.

"Doc Markowitz, folklorist, anthropologist, writer, record producer, radio producer, and field recordist." She shrugged and handed the card back to him. "None of this makes any sense to me. What is it you want?"

He craned his head around her and smiled at me.

"Well, ma'am, it's actually the little miss I came to see. I'm trying to hunt down an acquaintance of hers."

"It figures." Mom let out a huff. "You may as well come in."

We followed her into the kitchen.

"Have a seat." She waved at the red vinyl chairs and we all sat down.

"Are you a sheriff?" I said.

"Sheriff!" He burst into a jolly laugh. "I'm sorry, I don't mean to be rude, but I'm the furthest thing there is from a sheriff. I'm an ethnomusicologist—means I study music from different cultures. I'm looking for Mississippi Charles Yates. I believe you know him?"

"Why are you looking for him?" I asked.

"I would very much like to record his voice for posterity. If you could tell me where I can find him I'd be mighty grateful."

"What makes you think my daughter knows where he is?" Mom asked.

"Why, ma'am, it's this." He pulled something out of an inner pocket and spread it out on the table. "Bulletin of the Blues," its banner read, and under that was a photograph of me, arms flung wide, belting out my song on Uncle Max's stage. I remembered flashbulbs going off while I sang.

"What in the…" Mom was frowning at it.

"I'll explain later," I said. Then she surprised me.

"Can I have a copy of this for my scrapbook, Mr.… Markowitz?"

"It would be my pleasure, ma'am. Y'all can have this one." He pushed it in front of her. "This is the bluesman I'm looking for." He pointed to Mississippi sitting off to my left, playing his guitar. "He's a blues legend. A blues fan on the boardwalk took this picture and sent it to the newsletter, which is what led me here. Been hunting Mississippi down for ten years now. Truth be told, he's got to be the most skittish bluesman that ever did live. Every time I get close, he and that big dog of his take off."

"That's because the meat-faced sheriff's trying to kill him," I said. Didn't he know *anything*?

He smiled. "So you heard that story too?"

"Of course. He told it to me."

"Don't you worry yourself," he said. "There's not a speck of truth in it."

"Are you really a doctor?" Mom said.

"Well, yes, ma'am. Got my degree from Tulane University, but I'm not—"

"Are you married?"

"Beg your pardon?"

"You know, do you have a wife?"

"Why, no, ma'am. I'm so busy you might say I'm married to my work."

"I have a nice niece," she said, "very attractive. She goes to college." The word college brought out a note of awe in her voice. "I could show you a picture."

"That's very kind of you, ma'am, but if I don't get a lead on Mississippi I'm afraid I'm going to have to head back to Memphis."

"You wouldn't even give her picture a little peek?"

"I'm sorry, ma'am, but all I want here is to find Mississippi, and I was hoping the little miss could tell me where to look."

Mom got up and walked out, just like that.

"I haven't seen him since the Fourth of July," I said, "when that picture was taken. I've been looking high and low for him myself. He didn't show up at my Uncle Max's saloon the next Tuesday night when he was supposed to play, and nobody's seen him since. Maybe he heard you were looking for him, thought you were the sheriff, and ran off."

"I have a feeling he's still in the area, hiding out."

There was something else I had to tell him.

"There's a singer named Lenny. I think he kidnapped Mississippi's dog."

"Mississippi's dog is missing too?"

"He just disappeared off the boardwalk."

"Do you think I should question this Lenny fellow?"

"He might be there for Tuesday night fireworks. But be careful, he's very dangerous."

"Don't you worry yourself, I've been up against some very rough characters." He scribbled in his notebook. "Is there anything else you can think of?"

"Yes, but…" Something had been knocking around in the back of my head. Something about the first song Mississippi taught me. "I'm sorry, I can't remember what."

"If it comes to you, could you call me?" He took out one of his business cards and wrote something on the back. "Here's a local number, my hotel."

"Sure. And if you find out anything could you call me? I'm very worried about him."

"I sure enough will."

Mom came back and opened our wood-covered family album on the table in front of him.

"If you don't like her," she said, "I have other nieces. Here she is—Linda."

"She looks real nice, ma'am." He took a gold pocket watch out of his vest and looked at it. "I'm sorry, but I have to be going now."

"You wouldn't stay for a cup of coffee? I could make percolated."

"I do apologize, ma'am, but I have blues legends to track down."

Just then a song started playing in my head: *You will eat, bye and bye…*

I realized with a start what it was—the first song Mississippi taught me.

Mom slammed the photo album shut. Doc Markowitz got up and stuck his notebook in his inside jacket pocket.

"I'm mighty grateful for your hospitality. And I'll be following up that lead Miss Brooklyn gave me."

Just then it came to me.

"Wait," I said. "Does the name Woody mean anything to you? Woody on Mermaid Avenue? Mississippi taught me one of his songs."

"Good Lord!" he said. "I should have thought of that."

"Thought of what?"

"Woody Guthrie's a famous folk singer. I forgot he lived in Coney Island. I'm going to call my office straightaway and see if they can track down his address. Maybe Mississippi's in contact with him."

"You can call from here." Mom pointed to the telephone.

"That's very kind of you, ma'am, but it's long distance." And with that he left.

"What was that all about?" Mom asked.

"You heard him. He's tracking down blues legends."

"No, I mean your picture in this bulletin thing." She pointed to it. "Where was it taken?"

"Um… well, uh… Uncle Max's. But I couldn't help it, Mississippi waved me on, then everyone was clapping and whistling until there I was, singing on stage."

"Why were you even there in the first place? You know you're not allowed in there. The one place I ask you not to go, the minute my back is turned, you go there anyway."

"Sorry, it just pulls me in."

"When did this singing thing start?"

"I've been singing all my life."

"Call that singing?" She gave an exaggerated shudder. "It's like a funeral dirge. Why can't you sing something cheerful."

"But—"

"Que sera sera!" she sang out so loud her voice cracked. "Whatever will be, will be. The future's not DA da DA…"

"But the people at Uncle Max's liked the way I sing," I said when she paused for breath. "They clapped and cheered and—"

"Bunch of drunkards. I can't believe that gangster brother of mine actually let you in. He did it for the attention, that's why he does these things."

"It wasn't his fault, he wasn't even there." Just then I had a brainstorm. "Punish me."

"What?"

"Punish me."

"Why? It never helps. I'm hoarse from screaming at you. If I get throat cancer it'll be on your head. And that father of yours? He's never here. And when he is, he refuses to hit you."

"Give me the worst punishment there is. Send me to Aunt Anna."

She sucked in a breath, then started laughing.

"You're kidding, right?" she said. "I wouldn't do that to a dog."

"But I want you to. I can help Marilyn take care of Eric, and Aunt Anna can whip us both into shape."

She sighed and shook her head.

"I don't know what I'm going to do with you."

"If you don't know what to do with me why not let Aunt Anna whip me into shape?"

"Weren't you listening? She treats us like dirt. Anyway, it's no punishment if you want it. Now go to your room or something. And don't ever go into that saloon again or I'll… I don't know what."

Twenty-five

The next morning I was sitting at my desk in my Bermuda shorts, legs sticking to the chair in the heat, going over the route to Budd Lake on the map again—even though I still hadn't figured out a way to get there.

"Come on!"

I looked up and there was Mom, standing in the crooked door jamb, wearing a too-big beach outfit. Even her new Lastex bathing suit seemed to sag. But not her spirits. It was unpredictable these days: up-down, down-up. Today she was grinning.

"Let's go to the beach!"

"No, thanks." I let out an operatic sigh. "It's no fun without Marilyn."

"Ask some of the girls." Oh, no, not this again. "What happened to Maureen, Elaine, Linda? You used to have such nice friends. Now it's just Marilyn this, Marilyn that."

"They're still my friends, but I can't enjoy myself while Marilyn's scrubbing floors like Cinderella."

"Forget about Marilyn. You're a bad influence."

"No, I'm not." My face got hot. "She's my blood sister."

"What are you doing with that map?" She came in, kicked off her mules, and sank onto the unmade bed, proving there's a first time for everything.

"I'm going over the route to Budd Lake so we can drive there and rescue Marilyn."

"We can't go there, she'll..." She blinked at me, biting her lip.

"Mom, you don't have to be afraid of her anymore. You're a grownup now."

She headed for the door.

"I'm going to the beach with Sadie and some of the other girls."

She walked out the door and headed toward the stairs, then turned around.

"If I'm not back by three, drink your milk." She walked a few more steps, then turned again. "Or else." That, finally, was it— she clopped down the stairs, then I heard the front door slam shut.

I grabbed the map, ran to the Boarder's door, pushed it open, and scrambled through the main mildewed trail, armies of cockroaches parting before me like the Red Sea. It seemed darker than usual, and I started hearing a noise that sounded like three or four people laughing off and on, but the laughs sounded weird.

I turned a corner and ran into a tumble of moldering books, orange and blue clown wigs, straw hats, shoes with the soles flapping open, all blocking the main corridor. I doubled back and plunged into an unfamiliar tunnel, but as I walked it got narrower and narrower, and darker and darker, until after a while it got so dark I had to feel my way along the walls, which were fuzzy, hard, bumpy—ouch! Before long I was squeezing through, knocking things down with my shoulders, the weird laughter coming and going, the trail forking, turning this way and that, until I was as lost as lost can get. How could one tunnel be so complicated?

Finally I just stopped, squashed between stacks of who-knows-what, feeling a little dizzy, the smell of mold stronger than ever, roachy things skittering across my feet. Worst of all was the creepy laughter getting louder and louder, hitting a crescendo, stopping, then bursting out again. The map of New Jersey crumpled in my fist seemed my only connection to the outside world.

"Hello!" I called out. "Anybody home?"

Laughter shook my junk-filled tomb. I decided my best bet was to aim in its direction. I crept along, pushing between the stacks. After a while the trail widened, split, then widened and split again. I saw a soft amber glow at the end of the tunnel—I ran toward it, turned a corner, and entered the Boarder's den through a back entrance. The milk-glass lamp bathed the room with golden light. There she was, in her ratty old housedress, white hair a mess, looking more like a wrinkled troll than ever. She was standing on her armchair, waving a cracker.

"Excuse me," I said. "May I come in?"

"Could you come in? Could you come in? Why couldn't you come in? Come in already."

"It's just that it sounded like you had company, but… where are they?"

"Of course I have company." She pointed at the parrot, now perched on poor Goldie's birdcage, which was perched on a wooden milk crate. The parrot had bright red feathers on his head and his wings were blue and green with a few random yellow feathers sticking out. Like everything else in the room, including me and the Boarder, he was disheveled. He was swiping his black beak on the bars, making a metallic clicking sound.

"I heard people laughing."

"What can I say? Birdchik, kayne horeh, he likes a good joke. I tell him your grandpa's old jokes and he laughs like a whole audience. Sit already. Don't be a stranger."

I plopped down on the ottoman.

"Did you know you had a cave-in on the main hallway?" I said.

"Did I know? How could I not know? It almost buried me alive." She pointed at the parrot, who fluffed up his feathers, shook them out, turned his head sideways, and sized me up through one pale blue eye set in a puckered patch of white skin. "Birdchik was a bad boy," she said. She scratched the top of his huge head as he moved it around. "Weren't you, Birdchik?"

"Oy-yoy-yoy," the parrot called out. "Birdchik bad boy," this punctuated by an ear-piercing squawk.

"See! See how smart he is? He speaks Yiddish already."

"Will I be able to find my way out of here when I leave?"

"You worry too much. Nobody ever starved to death looking for the door. You want maybe a nosh? Some home-baked rugelech?"

"Not right now," I said. "There's something I'm very worried about." I told her how Aunt Suzie had delivered Marilyn unto slavery.

"So I need you to help me rescue her."

"Take the bus, why don't you?"

"The bus doesn't go there. The bungalow's on a country road. They don't even have a phone. It's Aunt Anna's summer retreat while Uncle Ben stays in the city and works."

"Your Aunt Anna?" She shook her head. "Worse than Suzileh."

"That's why you've got to help me. Can you?"

"Of course."

I was so grateful I wanted to hug her.

"So how do we get there, Brookileh?"

"Here." I smoothed out the map of New Jersey on the table. "All we need now is a driver and a car."

"So?" She flung her arms out. "What are we waiting for?"

"You know how to drive?"

"What's to know? You step on one pedal, the car moves forward, you step on the other pedal, it stops."

"You have to turn the steering wheel, too," I said.

"It's like riding a bicycle."

"Or a bumper car."

"You're right, more like a bumper car." She was nodding, a big grin plastered on her pruny little face, green eyes twinkling. "I should know. I'm so good with the bumper cars, I won first prize in a contest."

"So you can drive me to Budd Lake?"

"Of course!" Her eyebrows shot up and she pounded the arms of her chair. "Every schmegegge drives," she said. "Why not me?"

"Now all we need is a car."

"So we take your car. Problem solved."

"You mean Mom's car? She'd kill me."

"She wouldn't kill you." She waved her hand. "Anyway, it's the family car, you're entitled. Where's your mama?"

"She went to the beach with her friends, she'll probably be there all day."

"So what are we waiting for?" She hopped off her chair and started pulling my arm.

"You sure we're—"

"Guard the house, Birdchik!" she called as she dragged me into the wilderness.

I took the car key out of the box by the side door and we crossed the walkway to the garage. It was a two-car garage, but somehow one half got filled up with things like the lawn mower, wheelbarrow, ladders, rakes, and rolled-up chain link fencing, which was why Dad had to park the pickup out front.

There it sat, Mom's sleek red Buick with its toothy chrome grille. I opened the driver's-side door for the Boarder and helped her in, then went around to the passenger side and climbed in myself, feeling a surge of optimism.

"We'll kidnap Marilyn and be back in no time," I said.

"You should excuse my asking," the Boarder said, "but what's that big dial in the middle?"

"I thought you knew how to drive."

"Driving? It's easy. Just give to me a little assist."

"That's the speedometer. Those numbers tell you how many miles an hour you're driving."

"Hoo-ha!" She flung her arms up. "So I can go a hundred and twenty !"

"That's much too fast! Don't go more than sixty." I stuck the key in the ignition, turned it, and the engine sprang to life.

"Nu." She grabbed hold of the steering wheel. "I'll give it a start."

"Wait." I got out, unlatched the garage doors, swung them open, then got back in the car. I spread the map out on my lap.

"Okay, we're all set. I know a shortcut to the Belt Parkway on the back streets. That way you can get used to the car before we hit the highway. It has automatic gear shifts, so you just have to put it in drive and pull out. Then turn right."

She looked under the dashboard.

"Oy-yoy-yoy."

"What's wrong?"

"Hau boy! They made this car for giants."

I looked and saw her skinny little legs in their thick beige old-lady stockings flailing around. She slid down further and further, her clunky black shoes stretching towards the pedals, until she was practically on the floor.

"Mazel tov!" She hit the accelerator. It's a good thing the car was in park, because the engine revved like crazy.

"STOP! You can't see out the windshield from down there."

"Ay-yay-yay." She hoisted herself back up. "That I didn't think of. Now we're in a pickle."

I bit my thumbnail. Why hadn't I thought of this?

"We can't just give up!" I cried.

"Give up-schmive up." She waved her hand. "You think I got immortality by giving up?"

She jumped out of the car, scurried around to the passenger side, and opened the door. Then she shoved me over until I was behind the huge steering wheel and sat in my place.

I took Mom's back cushion and sat on it the way I usually did so I could see out the windshield. I looked at the Boarder.

"Go already." Another hand-wave. "Before your mama comes home."

"But I'm a *kid*!"

"Go! Go! Go!"

I put it in drive and released the parking brake. The Buick lurched forward. I gave it a smidgen of gas and we rolled down the driveway.

The street was full of kids, hanging out, playing, riding bikes, Joanie galloping on her imaginary horse. Bernie ran toward us, pop beads swinging across his flowered shirt, a look of amazement on his round face. We hit the road with a slight bump and cleared the parked cars. I turned the steering wheel sharply to the right and like magic the car followed.

"Hoo-ha!" The Boarder smacked me on the shoulder. "Hit the gas."

I gave it some gas and vrooom, the car leapt forward. But almost immediately I had to slam on the brake for the stop sign on the corner. The Boarder flew forward, breaking the impact with her hands on the dashboard.

"Oy!" she shouted. "Take it easy, I'm an old lady."

"Sorry." I looked both ways then gave it a little gas. This time it moved more smoothly.

"Get a move on, like an alter cocker you drive."

"You just told me to take it easy." I gave it a little more gas and we sped up. I was hoping nobody would notice me behind the wheel, but all along the block kids were pointing and waving and looking amazed. I saw a group of moms sitting on a stoop. My friend Sammy's short, plump mom jumped up and ran down to the curb.

"Stop!" she shouted as we passed. "You'll kill someone!"

"Oy gevalt!" the Boarder shouted. "Drive faster!" But I had to slow down and stop at Neptune Avenue.

"I'm sorry," I said. "I have to look both ways for cross traffic."

I glanced behind us. There was a whole swarm of mothers now, maybe eight or ten, chasing the car, waving their arms, screaming for me to stop.

The Boarder rolled down her window and shook her fist at them.

"Farschtinkener yentas! Mind your own business!" She rolled her window back up.

Linda's mom reached us first. She ran up and tried to open the passenger-side door, but the Boarder had locked it. Sammy's mom arrived out of breath and started pounding on my window with her fat little fists.

"Go already!" the Boarder shouted. "The coast is clear."

I pressed the gas pedal and we sped across Neptune Avenue. A car appeared out of nowhere and swerved, narrowly missing us. But soon the moms disappeared in the rearview mirror.

On I drove, toward the highway, past bungalows on the right and the police department horse stable on the left.

"You were right." I couldn't help grinning. "Just like bumper cars."

"Make like a racing car." She was bouncing up and down, pounding the dashboard.

I glanced to my left and saw a lot of traffic zipping along Ocean Parkway—I was glad we'd avoided that route. I turned the steering wheel to the right. Driving was a cinch, just turn the wheel and the car follows. I continued along the access road between brick apartment buildings and the highway, just like my parents always did, and in no time we were driving up the entrance ramp.

"Hold on," I said. "We have to merge."

The Belt Parkway was six lanes, divided in the middle by a short metal barrier. I slowed down and stopped at the top of the ramp. Cars were shooting past us faster than bullets—my hands on the steering wheel were shaking.

"I can't do it," I said. My voice was shaking too. "The cars are going too fast."

"Fast-schmast. What did you expect, bicycles?"

"I can't. I'll kill us."

"Just wait for an opening and mash your foot down on the gas."

"But how will I know when?"

"I'll give to you a little assist. Wait... wait... wait... Now, maybe?"

"Now?"

"No, wait!"

There weren't that many cars, but they were all speeding.

"Now!"

"Now?" I said. She punched my shoulder.

"Go already!"

I stepped on the gas, and vrrrooom, we whooshed onto the

highway—but all of a sudden a car was right behind us, brakes squealing. If that wasn't bad enough, the driver started honking his horn like crazy. What did he want me to do? My whole body was shaking, teeth chattering, heart hammering. The Boarder stuck her head out the window and shook a fist at him.

"Stay back, you meshugana!" she yelled. "You're tailgating!"

Just like that the driver switched into the middle lane and drove up alongside us in a blue Cadillac. He stuck his middle finger up, his face contorted into a snarl. My throat clogged and my eyes stung. Wasn't it hard enough just staying in the lane and not hitting anything?

I took another quick glance. He was waving his arm forward.

"What does he want me to do?" I said. "Stop? Get off the highway?"

"Who cares what he wants? From strangers you don't take directions."

Finally the man stopped waving and sped away.

We were tootling along now at a good clip, the engine purring. I could feel every little bump and crack in the road. A shadow fell across the dash. I looked up: we were passing under the Coney Island Avenue bridge. Then it was behind us. Wow!

I felt so grown up, so responsible, a better driver than some of my parents' friends. More important, I was saving Marilyn.

"I'm so glad you talked me into this," I said.

Just then I looked to the right and saw the striped awnings of Lundy's, in Sheepshead Bay.

"Uh-oh," I said. The Boarder grabbed my arm.

"What-oh?"

"We're going in the wrong direction."

"Oy vey iz mir." She cupped her face in her hands and rocked her head back and forth. "I thought you made for us a plan on the map."

"We're on the wrong side of the highway. We're headed toward Canarsie but we should be headed toward Manhattan."

"So turn us around and it wouldn't matter."

"We have to get off at the next exit and get back on going the other direction."

"You couldn't turn around here?"

"Are you crazy? There's a barrier in the middle."

"What a head you have on you." She pinched my cheek. "Kayne horeh."

"Could you help me look for the next exit?" I said. "I have to keep my eyes on the road."

"Whatever you want, Brookileh." She pinched my cheek again. "This much fun I haven't had since I tricked your mama out of that birdcage."

From far away a shrill, high-pitched whine caught my attention.

"Do you hear that?"

"Hear what?" she said.

"I think…" It was getting louder. "I think it's a police siren."

"Ay-yay-yay, the police." She put her hand to her face. "Nu, I hear it too."

"You think they're coming after us?"

She thought for a minute, then shrugged.

"If they stop us," she said, "you tell them I'm senile and I'll tell them I kidnapped you."

"Good plan." I looked in the rear view mirror, then the side view mirror, but I couldn't see any cops.

"Could you look out the back window?" I said. "I'm afraid to take my eyes off the road."

The siren was really loud now.

"For what reason I should look? We know already they're there."

"Please just look. See if they're signaling us or something."

"Okay, okay already." She turned around and screamed, "Oy gevalt!"

"What?"

"This I never expected. Look, in the police car!"

"What? I can't take my eyes off the road!"

"It's HIM!"

"Who?"

"Who do you think?"

"Not—"

"The Molech!" she wailed.

Suddenly the siren was deafening, my heart pounding like crazy. I took my foot off the gas to slow down.

"Gey fast!" she yelled in my ear. "Gey! Gey! Gey! Faster! Faster! Faster!"

But it was all I could do to steer straight. I looked at the dashboard. For some reason the AMPS dial, whatever that was, was going crazy.

She jumped on the seat and stuck her face in mine. I saw furious green eyes, knotted eyebrows.

"Hit the gas!" she yelled.

"Get out of my way, I can't see!"

She latched onto the steering wheel with her knobby fingers and tried to wrestle it away from me, but I swung my arm out and slammed her back against the seat. Sirens shrieking. Oy-yoy-yoying. She grabbed the wheel again, I shoved her back again.

"Faster! Faster! Faster!" she shouted, punching my arm. "The Molech's right on top of us!"

"NO!" I yelled. "We have to stop, we can't outrun the police!"

The police car pulled alongside me, a frowning cop at the window, mouth moving, hand pointing to the side of the road.

"Gey aveck!" She shook a fist at him.

He cut in front of us and slowed down. Was he trying to get us killed?

"Farschtinkener driver!" She started hitting the windshield with her shoe. "Khazers!"

"Hold on!" I shouted.

She grabbed my arm, fingernails digging in.

I lifted my foot to brake, but… but… suddenly I couldn't remember, which pedal? Mom would kill me. I stomped down—but the car didn't stop, started skidding. I yanked the wheel to the left so I wouldn't hit the police car, every nerve in my body sizzling, frying.

"Oy vey iz mir!" the Boarder howled as we swerved, flying across lanes of traffic, cars squealing, screeching, hammering their horns, fishtailing all over the road, smoke billowing, rubber burning, sirens wailing, two more police cars rushing toward us, a fire engine bearing down on our left.

I gripped the wheel tighter, can't catch my breath, can't breathe. *Brooklyn, you can't hide.* This is it. The big goodbye, Lenny's threat, Mississippi's warning. The metal barrier rushed toward me—

Twenty-Six

Okay, okay, I should have pulled the emergency brake, but every-thing was happening so *fast*. The police took me to the emergency room, then went to the house, but Mom wasn't there. She was still at the beach, relaxing on her webbed lounge chair, showing off her new figure, surrounded by Sadie, Etta, Red Ethel, and Rae. I could just picture it. She's telling them how she has to watch me like a hawk ever since Bubbie passed away and her nerves just can't take it any more. Her friends are clucking their tongues and shaking their heads when the police officer's deep voice breaks in: "Excuse me, ladies…" By the time Mom burst into the emergency room, sandy and disheveled, her face was white with rage.

"You could have killed somebody!" she shouted, so loud everyone stared at her.

I acted like I was at death's door and in way too much pain to talk, but she wasn't buying it—she'd spoken to the doctor. So she kept say-ing I could have killed somebody, and I kept saying the Boarder was senile and had kidnapped me. But the Boarder had vanished after the accident, so there was no one to back me up.

Not that it mattered what my stupid excuse was, the police blamed Mom for everything. She should have kept an eye on me, they said.

She told them she'd left me with an elderly relative who seemed to have disappeared, and it was all *her* fault.

The good news was, only one person had been injured, and that was me. I don't remember the aftermath of the accident or the police driving me to the hospital, but a tender red bump the size of a lime had risen up on my forehead. There was a blurry edge around everything and I had the oddest sensation, a dull pounding pain I'd never felt before. I'd always wondered what a headache felt like.

The other good news was that the car was only slightly damaged, where the metal barrier had wiped the grin off its toothy chrome grille.

Oh, and I made the five o'clock local TV news. Not me in person, just a mention of the accident accompanied by my school photograph—the one with messy hair.

No fresh-squeezed orange juice or bacon and eggs for me the next morning. Mom just threw a loaf of Wonder Bread on the table when I sat down, then stomped out of the kitchen. I couldn't eat anyway. I was nauseated and dizzy and my head felt like it was being beaten by a meat mallet. The Boarder hadn't returned, so on top of everything else—Cerbie, Mississippi, and Marilyn, all gone—I now had to worry Lenny might have schlepped her off to death.

The telephone rang in the living room.

"You want to do what?" Mom said. "You have a lot of nerve. Okay already, I can't stand being trapped in this house another minute anyway." She stomped back into the kitchen and told me she was going out.

"You're just going to leave me here alone again?" I said. "Aren't you afraid I'll do something worse?"

She told me I couldn't possibly do anything worse, and anyway, she'd padlocked all the doors from the outside.

"But what if there's a fire?" I cried.

She narrowed those green eyes of hers and glared down at me.

"You should have thought of that before you stole my car." She marched out the kitchen door, down the hall, and through the side door, which she slammed. I heard the padlock click. I looked through the window and saw her opening the side door of the garage.

Locked in like a criminal, totally alone. Mom had finally come up with a punishment that was worse for me than it was for her.

And she'd left me in serious pain—I felt as if someone had stabbed a screwdriver through my eyes. I opened the Frigidaire, squirted some seltzer into a glass, and downed five or six orange-flavored baby aspirin. Then I just sat there on a red vinyl chair, elbows planted on the map-of-Florida tablecloth, propping up my destroyed head.

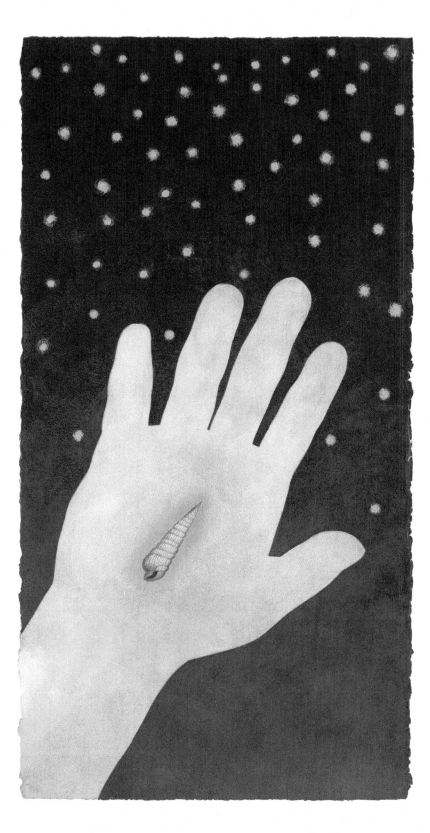

Twenty-Seven

Hours and hours went by, an eternity. It was way past my three-o'clock milk-drinking torture and still no sign of Mom. It was a hot day, so I was sitting in the living room on the plastic-covered couch. The fact that we never opened the drapes kept some of the heat out.

The headache had eased up but left me dizzy—the world swimming, waving and wiggling before my eyes. The green wallpaper looked especially bilious today. So did the tangerine-colored lampshades and the painting of the topless native woman. But the worst thing I felt was alone in a new way. Empty.

I telephoned some of my friends, but none of them could come to the phone. Then Bernie did, and I found out why. He said all the moms on the block had banned their kids from ever talking to me again.

"Anyway I'm sick, real sick, and I can't talk right now," he said and hung up.

I tried the kitchen radio, looking for the blues station, *my* station, but it was just static today. Then I looked through Mom's records again: Frank Sinatra, Dean Martin, Tony Bennett. But I didn't like them anymore—they seemed to be on Lenny's side— and I'd already played my Elvis singles so many times they made me want to puke.

There was a scattering of books on the bookshelf: *Peyton Place, Anna Karenina, The Long Goodbye, Sodom by the Sea.* I'd read them all.

I checked the TV to see if there were any movies on, but no, just Arthur Godfrey, yuck, and other talk shows. Not that I felt like watching television anyway.

If only I could hear Marilyn's voice again, just for a minute, or Mississippi's, or the Boarder's, just to know they were all right. I stared at the big black telephone on the Formica side table for a long time. I picked up the receiver, then slammed it down.

"Ring!" I shouted at it. "Just ring!"

I went back to the kitchen, turned the radio on again. Static, static, static. I tweaked the dial. Come on, all I need is a few bars…

Then I heard it—a twangy guitar and a gravelly voice: *Hey little gal/ Hey little gal…* I could barely make it out, but it sounded like Mississippi. More static, then: *train tracks…* Mumble, mumble, mumble, then: …*come down here/ Whatever you do, whatever you* (unintelligible) *come down here…* Then static consumed it.

I sat there for a long time listening to static, hoping for more. Come down *where?*"

I realized I hadn't eaten all day, so I opened the Frigidaire and took out a triangle of Laughing Cow cheese, peeled the foil back, and took a bite. Yuck. I spit it out. I took a Mallomar cookie out of the cupboard, licked the chocolate off, and threw the rest away. My head pain was coming back and my ears were ringing, so I took a few more baby aspirins.

I looked at the round white kitchen clock. 5:45. The second hand crawled.

One of those Coney Island fires could be starting right now in the basement, down among the dusty rags and paints, the cardboard boxes, the old mattresses, creeping through the walls until suddenly the whole house would burst into flame.

Everything I looked at seemed sharper but at the same time less real. I could almost see Lenny sitting at the kitchen table singing "Thank Heaven for Little Girls," then pointing at me and winking. I wondered if there was any way to trick him like the Boarder had.

I could easily climb out the window if I could just get the screen off. I examined its hinges. There were dozens of them, all painted over until they were thick green bumps on the inner window frame.

I ran to the overstuffed kitchen drawer, pulled out a hammer, ran back, and hit one of the bumps a few times. Who was I kidding, I could never budge it in a million years. Then I had a better idea. I ran back to the drawer and rummaged around through the masking tape, nail clippers, screwdrivers, and rubber washers until I found a utility knife. Back to the window, where I stabbed the screen on the bottom and hacked out a small incision. The blade was dull, so I didn't get very far.

I scrounged around some more in the drawer and grabbed hold of something that should work. Back to the window. I plunged the wire cutters into the hole I'd made with the utility knife and snip, snip, snip, I cut around three sides so I could flap the screen open. Then I flattened the screen back against the frame with my hand. I'd done such a good job you could hardly see the cut marks.

Brrrrring!

I grabbed the receiver off the wall phone.

"Hello?"

"Would that be Miss Brooklyn?" a man's deep voice with a Southern drawl came through the receiver.

"Doc Markowitz! You know, I think I just heard Mississippi on the radio, but there was a lot of static."

"Hold on…" I could picture his eyebrows folding in, practically hear him thinking. "I know what it must have been. There were some poor quality recordings made about ten years ago. What station was it?"

"I don't know. It moves around a lot." It seemed like he did too. "Where are you?"

"I'm on Mermaid Avenue at Woody Guthrie's house. I thought you'd like to know, you were right. Mississippi was here." It took him forever to get all that out, stretching the words like bubble gum.

"That's great!"

"Woody tells me he stayed a couple of days after his shack was torn down. Then that singer Lenny showed up."

Oh God.

"Lenny told Mississippi he'd seen his dog," he said, "so they walked out the door together. Strange thing is, he hasn't come back since. He took his guitar, but his suitcase is still here. Do you have any idea where he might have gone?"

"Oh, no." I couldn't tell him Lenny was the Molech, he'd never believe me. "Lenny's very dangerous. I don't think he's what he seems."

He laughed his jolly laugh.

"I'm sorry," he said, "I shouldn't laugh, but I think your imagination is getting the better of you. Sounds more like they were friends. Maybe Mississippi's staying at his place."

"Then why didn't he go back for his suitcase?"

"I've been wondering about that. Maybe he had a notion someone was watching the building."

While he was talking, the bump on my head started throbbing real bad. I put my hand on it. It felt alive, like a restless little hedgehog curled up under my skin.

"What are you going to do next?" I asked.

"I'll start by talking to that uncle of yours. Maybe he can give me Lenny's address. If not I'll keep trying to catch Lenny on a night he's singing."

I didn't have any better ideas. We said goodbye and hung up.

Brrrrring!

"Yes?"

"What, you going to talk on the phone all day?"

It was the Boarder.

"Where are you?" I said.

"I'm right here."

"Where?"

"Next door at Suzileh's, the schlimazel husband let me in."

"Where did you go after the accident?"

"I want I should come home, but some meshugana locked the house up."

"Come around to the side window."

I lifted the flap of screen, dragged the red kitchen step-stool over to the window, and lugged it over the sill and onto the walkway.

Soon I saw her bouncing along, swinging a brown paper bag, practically skipping through the gate and across the patio, smiling big until she looked up at me.

"Oy gevalt!" she cried. "What happened to your head?"

My hand went up to it. "I hit it on the steering wheel."

"I never saw such a bump, red like a tomato it is. You should be in the hospital."

"It's just a concussion. I was in the emergency room yesterday, the doctor said I was lucky to be alive."

The Boarder climbed up the step-stool.

"Oy," she said. "It's not so easy for an old lady like me to climb in a window." She handed me the paper bag and I helped her in.

"Where did you disappear to after the accident?" I said. "I was *worried*."

She waved her hand. "So much worry, it's not good for you. I got out of the car."

"But then where'd you go? I don't remember anything after that."

"I ran away. I told you I was leaving."

"You just left me there to take the blame all by myself?"

"It's not the blame I was worried about, it was the Molech. He was in the police car."

"Lenny was in the front seat?"

"Nooooo." She waved her hand. "Those were just regular policemen. The Molech was in the back seat, but he couldn't grab me." She smiled big. "I ran away too fast."

"But it's *me* he's after." I don't know why I hadn't figured this out before. "This is my third brush with death and Lenny asked if I had a headache and now I do."

"Look at the bright side."

"Bright side! He could have grabbed us both! And now the car is damaged, my head is killing me, and we didn't even come close to rescuing Marilyn."

"Yes, but it's not every day I outrun the Molech and you he didn't grab."

"Did he see you? How do you know he didn't follow you home?"

"That…" she held up a finger, "is what took me so long. I had to cover my tracks. Just in case. So what else is new?"

"Well, you should know the police are looking for you. Mom may press charges for stealing the car."

"But— "

"They might also charge you with leaving the scene of an accident, corrupting a minor, and other things I don't remember. And Mom says if the police don't put you in jail, she's kicking you out."

She grabbed her head.

"Oy-yoy-yoy-yoy-yoy-yoy-yoy. Better I should go to jail."

"I think you should hide in your room until this whole thing blows over. I won't tell anyone you came home."

"What a smart girlchik." She pinched my cheek. "Kayne horeh."

"What's in the bag?"

"This…" She held it up and pointed. "Is a very special present." She stuck her hand in, rummaged around, and pulled out a half-eaten seed bell. "For Birdchik. I found it on a tree. He bites me when I leave him alone."

"I went up to feed him this morning but I couldn't find him."

"Where would he go? He's a birdchik, he must be…" She sucked in a breath. "Gevalt!"

"Now what's wrong?"

"I think… I may have…" She slapped her head, ran into the hall, then turned back to me. "The window, I left it open."

Up the stairs she ran. I followed, then remembered I'd left a window open myself and dashed back to the kitchen to pull in the step-stool and pat the screen back down before Mom came home.

Twenty-Eight

The search was not going well.

I'd had no idea of the extent of the Boarder's apartment, how endless the corridors were, how dusty and dark. We did locate the window—I'd never seen it before, but of course the Boarder knew right where it was. It was wide open, without a screen, but Birdchik?

"Maybe he's still here somewhere," I said.

"So what are we waiting for?" She handed me a flashlight.

On and on we searched, calling over and over: "Birdchik! Come back, Birdchik!"

We came to a clearing she called the master bedroom. I shined my flashlight in to reveal a massive bed set covered in a thick quilt of dust, with great tents of cobwebs hanging everywhere.

We walked on, the path branching this way and that.

"How do you find your way around?" I said.

"It's all up here." She tapped her head. "Except for some sections. Them, I had to close."

After a while we came to a room that actually had a door on it. I turned the knob and pushed.

"Oh!" I cried when my flashlight hit the walls. They were hung floor to ceiling with bright Mexican paintings—cacti, skulls, sombreros.

"Where'd they come from?"

"Who remembers? I forgot this was here, even. But these I maybe can sell. I know an art dealer."

We walked some more. There was a noise, and I sucked in a breath.

"Did you hear that?" I aimed the flashlight down a narrow passage. "Birdchik, are you in there?"

"That section?" she said. "That's where the giant rats live, they bite your toes. With rabies they are."

"I'll just take a look." I squeezed in and forced my way around a bend, but then I couldn't move, stuck between something big and fuzzy and something big and hard.

"Brookileh? Come out from there already, he's not in there."

I started squirming this way and that. When I finally managed to turn around, something crashed to the floor. I squeezed out.

We stumbled along, every now and then calling, "Birdchik? Where are you, Birdchik?" After a while we came to a narrow staircase. I followed her down to what she called the lower annex: more hallways, more rooms, and more dust.

Then it came to me, why the house looked so much bigger from the outside: this part of the building must have been rented to boarders when my grandparents first built it. Over the years, the Boarder had taken over their rooms.

Eventually we were back in the den, covered in dirt. I picked up a napkin and blew the dust out of my nose.

"He was such a good birdchikel," the Boarder cried. She put her hands over her eyes and rocked her head from side to side. "Out of this world, he was. Never kvetched, never nudzhed. He laughed at my jokes."

My headache was worse. I felt as if a pulsing space alien was squatting on my skull, sucking my brains out.

"Could I have a little schnapps?"

"A drink? This I need too." She hefted herself off the armchair, went over to the sideboard, and got the ornate bottle and glasses. She clunked them down on the table and poured us each a shot.

"Do you have any aspirins?"

"Aspirins? Feh. You Americans, always with the aspirins." She took a little amber bottle off a shelf, dusted it off, and handed it to me. The label was brown around the edges and written in an alphabet I didn't know.

"What is this?"

"This? It's some kind of medicine, I got it from the doctor on the ship to America."

I tapped a few into my hand. Little gray pills.

"How many do I need for a headache?"

"What do I know? Since I died, I haven't had one."

I flung two into my mouth and washed them down with the schnapps. Then I heard it again, the noise. It was very low, muffled, but it sounded like someone calling for help.

"Do you hear that voice?"

"Stop with the voices already."

"Help!" the muffled voice cried.

"You heard *that*, didn't you?"

"Ay-yay-yay." She put her hand to her face. "Deaf, I'm not."

"Help-help! help-help! Squawk! Squawk! Squawk!"

I got up and walked around the room with my ear cupped.

"Squawk! Squawk! Squawk!"

"It's coming from here." I pointed at an opening with a peeling red door propped up in front of it.

"Oy-yoy-yoy. That one's dangerous. I had a pussycat once, she went in there and never came out."

"But we have to go in." I grabbed the door and dragged it to the side. Moths fluttered out, cockroaches scattered. The smell of decay hit me in the face.

The Boarder came over and we peered into the opening. I shined my flashlight in. Giant cobweb tents hung everywhere.

"Help! Help! Squawk! Squawk!"

"It's getting louder," I said. "He must see the light."

"Come to Grandma!" she called into the abyss.

"We're out here, Birdchik!" I shouted.

"Squawk! Squawk! Squawk!"

Something started taking shape in the tunnel but I couldn't make any sense of it. As it got closer, pushing its way through the dark veil of cobwebs, it started to look kind of human but ghostly, gray, and out of focus. I pointed.

"Do you see that?"

"Oy-yoy-yoy."

"What do you think it is?"

She waved her hand. "Don't even ask."

It was getting clearer. Definitely human-shaped, but lopsided and two-headed.

"It's like some kind of monster," I said.

The human shape was starting to look familiar. A short creature with something on its shoulder, something parrot-shaped.

"*That's* Birdchik," I said.

The parrot shape puffed up and shook itself out, releasing a cloud of dust. The human shape stopped, coughed, then resumed trudging our way, until it was right in front of us, covered in cobwebs, glaring at us with big brown eyes.

"Will you get this thing off my shoulder?" Marilyn said.

Turns out Mom had driven Evil Aunt Suzie to Budd Lake to get Marilyn.

"Did you have to scrub floors?" I said.

At this point we were sitting in our usual seats in the Boarder's den—all of us, including Birdchik, powdered in so much dirt we looked like giant animated dust bunnies.

"Of course not." She giggled, then tried to brush the dirt off her face but ended up only rubbing it in more. "They have a maid. We ate real vegetables from the garden and all the ice cream we wanted. And we went swimming every day at the lake. Eric and I measured everything in the bungalow and wrote it all down in a notebook. He let me keep it."

"And you say *I'm* weird."

She grinned. "It was so much fun."

"So Aunt Anna isn't really a slave driver?" I scratched my filth-encrusted, swollen head.

"She's very hurt your mom keeps saying that. Really, she says, she just wanted her to baby sit when they went out. She says your mom is ungrateful and a liar. And my mom? Auntie Anna says she should be locked up before she hurts somebody."

"But why did your mom all of a sudden want to drive up to Budd Lake to get you?"

"Because Auntie Anna drove into town, and... why are you grinning like that?"

"Like what?" I touched my mouth. My lips were stretched all the way across my face. This was so funny I found myself laughing until tears were running down my cheeks.

"Maybe it's the bump on your head," Marilyn said. "How did you get that? Does it hurt?"

"No. I mean yes. I mean who cares?" I jumped up and danced around the room twirling, kicking up a cloud of dust. "I'm so happy!" I called out. Marilyn and the Boarder looked so cute, gawking at me, all covered in dirt, I just couldn't help myself: I ran over and gave them a bunch of hugs and kisses. I even tried to hug Birdchik, but he bit me.

The rest of the story is a little fuzzy, though I thoroughly enjoyed it at the time. It went something like this: Aunt Anna had driven into town to call Evil Aunt Suzie and tell her how well Marilyn was doing and how much fun she was having. Anna was especially proud of all the fresh vegetables she'd cajoled down Marilyn's gullet, and she couldn't help mentioning that she, Anna, was the best mother of all the sisters. That's when Suzie slammed the phone down.

Anna didn't think anything of it, in fact they all laughed about it—until bam! Suzie and Mom burst into the bungalow and tried to snatch Marilyn away. They seemed surprised Aunt Anna wasn't willing to give her up without a fight. Mom-and-Suzie grabbed one of Marilyn's arms and Eric-and-Anna the other and they had a tug-of-war, Marilyn screaming the whole time. But since Eric was only eight and Anna was no spring chicken, or maybe she just didn't want to rip Marilyn's arms out, Mom-and-Suzie won. As they were dragging Marilyn out the door fighting and screaming, Aunt Anna shouted that Evil Aunt Suzie was a child torturer and she was going to sue her for custody.

When they got back to our house Mom couldn't find me, so she sent... oh, who cares.

Twenty-Nine

Day after endless day crept by. By now the bump on my forehead had turned dark purple with a hideous ring of green and yellow around it. It was still pulsing, but the headache was better. The pupil in one of my eyes seemed a little bigger than the other, but maybe I was imagining it.

I was sitting in the big shadowy kitchen in shorts, squirming around, trying to get comfortable. At least I had something new to stare at: Mom had placed a bud vase with a single red rose in the middle of the table. Both of undying plastic. "To brighten things up," she said.

On the other side of the screened front windows, it was an unreasonably sunny morning. Lainy, Linda, and Elaine walked by, giggling, towels around their shoulders. I could almost smell the Coppertone. I heard a joyous squeal, happy shouts, all set to the tinny tune of the Good Humor truck, which was getting louder by fits and starts. Since I'd been imprisoned, it seemed as if every kid I'd ever known had run, skipped, or biked past our windows. Everyone but Marilyn, that is. Mom wouldn't let her in because I was being punished and she wouldn't let me talk to her on the phone, either.

I made good use of all my aching loneliness writing blues song after blues song, belting them out, driving Mom nuts. I'd used up all the pages in my notebook, so I picked up the message pad by the phone. My next song would be about dragging that old ball and chain for shooting a sheriff in Memphis. I figured I was entitled, since I was now under house arrest for the rest of my life. No phone calls, no TV, no music, and especially no Boarder. Not that my parents knew she'd come home, but Mom had put a padlock on the door to keep me from going in, and I'd been looking high and low for the key ever since. Dad had taken the padlocks off the outside doors—unsafe, he said—so Mom had to ruin her life watching me again.

"Oh oh oh oh," I wrote. I gazed out the window. "Oh-oh, oh-oh," I sang out, "I'm sad and blue. I shot the sheriff, I shot him through and through…"

A man on the street walked into my line of vision. The bump on my forehead started pulsing faster. When he got to our house he pushed through the gate and walked toward the door.

I ran into the hall and flung it open. There stood Doc Markowitz, filling the doorway like a white-suited Santa Claus.

"Doc!" I cried. "I'm so happy to see you."

"Well, hello there, Little Miss Brooklyn," he drawled, slow as the last day of school.

"Did you find Mississippi?"

"Not yet." He squinted at me. "What happened to your head?"

"I was in an accident. It looks worse than it is." I gave him Dad's goofy grin and stepped aside. "Come on in."

"Who's there?" Mom called down from upstairs.

"It's Doc!"

"Who?"

"Doc Markowitz!"

"Why didn't you say so?"

"I did!"

"Did you ask him to come in?"

"Just come down, I'm getting hoarse from screaming!"

"So stop screaming!"

I smiled at Doc.

"If this is a bad time," he said, "I could—"

"No!" I grabbed his sleeve and pulled him into the kitchen, where we both sat down at the table.

"By the way," he said, "what was that record y'all were playing?"

"What record?"

"I heard a blues song coming from your house. I just caught a few words, something about shooting a sheriff. It was a female vocalist with a distinct style. I don't believe I've ever heard her before, and I thought I'd heard them all."

"That was me!" I couldn't believe my ears. "Did you like it?"

"Couldn't be, it was too..." He looked into my eyes. "That was *you?*"

"Yeah." I sang out: "Oh-oh, oh-oh, I'm sad and blue. I shot the sheriff, I shot him through and through." I smiled. "That's as far as I got. Mississippi taught me how to write songs and sing." A wave of sadness passed through me.

"You're very lucky," he said. "I wanted to be a singer once, but..." He shrugged. "Not everyone has the talent. And to learn from the master..."

That proves it! I was going to be the greatest girl blues singer in the world, and I'd be able to sing at Uncle Max's as much as I wanted, and Mom would be so proud of me.

I heard clopping, then Mom appeared on the stairs looking like a stick insect in Bermuda shorts and high-heeled mules. She pressed her bright red lips on a tissue, then ran her fingers through her short permed hair.

"Did you find Lenny?" I asked Doc.

"I sure enough did."

"What did he say? Did he tell you—"

"Just a minute." He held up a finger.

Mom was standing there with her hands on her waist. She shot me a dirty look, then smiled at Doc.

"What can I do for you, Dr. Markowitz?" She sat down at the table.

"My friends call me Doc." He smiled back.

"Would you like a cup of coffee, Doc? I could make percolated—"

"No, thank you, ma'am. It's very kind of you, but I can't stay long."

"Stop calling me ma'am, it makes me feel like an old lady." She jumped up. "A cup of coffee won't take a minute." She took the step-stool, put it in front of the cupboards, climbed up, and started rummaging around.

"What did Lenny say?" I asked.

"His story was essentially the same as Woody's. He said he went to Woody's to tell Mississippi he'd seen that dog of his. It ran into the subway, he told him."

"That's strange," I said. "What else did Lenny say?"

"Said Mississippi wanted to look for his dog right then, so they walked over to Surf Avenue together. When they got there Mississippi headed for the subway and Lenny continued on toward the boardwalk. That's the last he saw of him. His guess is Mississippi found his dog and left town."

I narrowed my eyes. "You don't believe him, do you?"

"Why wouldn't I?"

"But... how did he know where to find Mississippi in the first place? Don't you think it's suspicious?"

"Not at all. A lot of performers go to Woody Guthrie's house. They play together, trade songs."

"But if Mississippi's okay, why hasn't he gone back for his suitcase?"

He frowned at this, shook his head.

"Unless he thinks the sheriff is watching the building," I said.

"I suppose that could be, if he actually believes that old story."

"But how are we going to find him?"

"One of the things I've been trying to do is get hold of the names of his neighbors in the shanty town before they tore it down. I have a feeling they'd know about the places he might go. If I could only find one of them, they could lead me to the others." He heaved a sigh. "But no matter how deep I dig, I can't seem to come up with a single name."

"Jones," I said.

"Beg your pardon?"

"Jones and Washington." I told him all about the Jones family and Mr. Washington, and how Mississippi went to church with them, and how Mr. Jones got a job at the Brooklyn Navy Yard, so they moved near there.

"Good Lord." He rubbed his face and took a deep breath. "This could break the whole thing wide open."

"But they moved before Mississippi disappeared, so how would they know where he is?" Then I remembered something else. "They did invite him to dinner the next Sunday."

His face brightened. "See? You're getting the hang of it."

"It's not up here," Mom called to us, then climbed down the stepstool. "I think it's upstairs." She walked over to the staircase and clopped on up.

"If you don't find Mississippi," I said, "what will you do then?"

"There's a singer named Memphis Mae I'd like to track down. She was last seen singing in a juke joint in Greenville, Mississippi. After that, I heard Blind Billygoat Brady turned up in Paris, singing on a street corner. I sure would like to record him."

"Can't you stay in New York?" I leaned forward. "I can help you hunt down blues legends. I'm getting really good at it, right?"

He smiled. "Why, Miss Brooklyn, I'd be honored to have you as an assistant, but in my line of work, you have to stay on the road."

"Found it!" Mom called as she came back down the stairs. She walked over and plopped a framed photograph in front of Doc. I was surprised to see it was her and Dad's wedding picture.

"See how happy he is?" She pointed at Dad's goofy grin.

Doc nodded.

"What you need," Mom tapped the glass, "is a wife to settle down with."

Thirty

Mom said I was about to give her a nervous breakdown with my depressing songs, but at least she was rid of the Boarder.

If only I wasn't under house arrest and I could break the Boarder out of her room, everything could go back to what passed for normal around here. Everything, that is, except the bruise on my forehead, which still throbbed like a broken heart and seemed to be getting more hideous—all yellow-gray and green now—by the day. If it wouldn't go away, I wished it would at least turn a nicer color.

I was hugging my knees, bare feet sticking to the crunchy plastic covering the living room couch, just sitting there in the pink light of the tangerine-colored lampshades, feeling dizzy and unfocused.

What to do? I got up, slid the big wood-covered family album off the shelf, and flopped back down on the couch with it, wondering who I looked the most like. I flipped open the book and decided to search for myself in the pictures.

Right there filling the whole first page was Mom, standing on the boardwalk with the beach behind her, wearing a rhinestone tiara and a black bathing suit crossed with a banner: Miss Coney Island. Her face and figure looked great, but the most appealing thing about her was

her childlike smile, happiness radiating from her eyes. I'd never seen her that happy.

Did I look like her? Now that I looked carefully, I realized I did. I never noticed before, but we had the same shaped mouth, the same arching eyebrows. The biggest difference was our teeth. She had big white straight ones and I had pointy vampire teeth, which I loved, but she hated.

I'd seen this picture hundreds of times, but a new thought struck me. She had shoulder-length hair back then, cut into a 1940's style, a smooth pageboy with a loop of hair over her forehead. So why was she dying to chop mine off?

The next photograph was a studio portrait of Grandma Lena when she was young. It was like a fountain of youth, this photo album. She was beautiful too. It was black and white, but I know she had green eyes like Mom's, and mine.

The next page had a photograph of Dad in his U.S. Air Force uniform, hat cocked to one side on straight red hair, smiling his goofy grin, which I was glad I inherited.

I flipped through more pages. Many of these people were dead, out of reach forever. My eyes settled on a studio photograph of Bubbie when she was young. I ran my finger over it. She looked like a gypsy—beautiful, dark, intense. She's who I wanted to look like more than anyone. I stared at it for a long time, and the more I looked at her face, the more I could see my own in hers.

The opposite page showed a picture of her husband, my grandpa Chuna, standing in front of their tailor shop on Mermaid Avenue. I wished I'd known him. He looked a lot like Dad, but no freckles. Why did they come to this country? Did we still have roots back there in Poland? You'd never know it from Dad, who had no interest in the place. He spoke only English now, didn't even have an accent any more.

An odd rhythmic noise, something like rough sandpaper on stone or somebody snoring, poked into my thoughts. I realized it had been going on for some time. It seemed to be coming from upstairs, probably just Mom cleaning or—

"Brooklyn!" Mom yelled so loud her voice cracked.

I ran up the stairs two at a time. She stood in the shadowy hallway, hand on neck, gaping at the Boarder's padlocked door and pointing.

There on the lower part of the door was an almost complete rough circle, a rusty power saw going in and out of it.

"It's only the Boarder," I said. "She's—"

Plop! The piece of door flew out of the hole in a burst of sawdust and landed at our feet.

"What's she—"

"Oy!" The Boarder stuck her head out and blinked at us. "The door was stuck like glue."

Bizz! Bizz! Bizz! Bizzzzzzzzzzzzz!!!!!! rang the downstairs doorbell.

Mom slapped her hands over her ears.

"I can't take it! Not another crisis!"

I heard yelling from outside.

"HELP! Is anybody home? Let me in!"

I raced down the stairs, Mom following and the Boarder right behind us, scattering sawdust and screaming "oy-yoy-yoy!"

I got to the door first and flung it open.

Marilyn stood there gripping the door jamb, looking pale and shaken. Her shirt was on inside out and her sneakers were untied.

"It's my mom," she said. "She's... she's... just *come!*" She turned and started running down the path.

I dashed out barefoot right behind her as she stumbled along with her untied shoelaces.

"Wait!" Mom called after me, "you have to put on your..." but by this time we were running up the stoop and through Marilyn's peeling front door.

I could feel sand on the linoleum under my bare feet. For a minute it was very quiet. The smell of Brussels sprouts, wet dog, seaweed, and tar filled the air. There were sandy beach towels all over the place along with flip-flops, plastic pails, and twisted-up pizza boxes.

Mom walked in behind us, then the Boarder came huffing and puffing up the steps and into the hall.

"What's going on?" Mom asked.

"I think she's in the basement," Marilyn said.

Two teenagers—a boy and girl in shorts and flip-flops—came galloping down the stairs, grabbing towels off the banister. They ran past us and out into the world.

Then Uncle Nat came wheeling in from the living room, barefoot, hair messy, his hearing aid batteries on his lap.

"Take it easy," he said, "I've called an ambulance. They should be here any minute."

"Is Suzie sick?" Mom asked.

The renter from the basement came running up the stairs, clutching her little boy to her huge bosom. Her hair was in rollers and she was wearing a billowing chartreuse nightgown. One of her slippers fell off as she kicked something out of the way.

"Save yourselves!" she cried, then flew through the front door, out the gate, and just kept going.

We all looked at each other.

"Hoo-ha!" The Boarder started jumping up and down, clapping her hands. "Always with the drama. Next time we should sell tickets."

"What's going on?" Mom asked Uncle Nat.

"I don't know," he said. "It's Suzie, she seems to be—"

We heard an unearthly howl, then Evil Aunt Suzie came bursting out of the basement, growling and barking.

We jumped back.

I'd never seen Aunt Suzie this bad—lipstick smeared across her jaw, dark hair in a wild tangle, nylons bunched up around her ankles, house-dress ripped to shreds. She was hiding something behind her back.

"For crying out loud," Mom said, "will you cut it out? You're scaring the kids."

Suzie didn't seem to have heard her. She was curling her lip, baring her teeth, glaring at us with a look of hatred pure as snake venom—then suddenly she grabbed her head and shouted to herself, "Shut up already!"

"Suzie, hon," Uncle Nat said, "just calm down—"

"What got her started?" I asked Marilyn.

She whispered in my ear: "Auntie Anna came by. Wanted to take me back, but Mom went berserk and Auntie Anna ran away."

"You!" Aunt Suzie pointed at the Boarder. "I'm gonna kill you! You stole my family!"

The Boarder started inching backward toward the door.

"Nice Suzileh." She raised her hands and plastered a grin on her wrinkled old kisser. "What is it you have behind your back? You should maybe…" She reached the door and fled.

Just then poor little Duchess came pitter-pattering down from upstairs, tail curling, smiling a doggy smile.

Suzie made a horrible noise, part hiss, part growl —.

"Oh, my God!" Mom wailed. "It's rabies. Suzie has rabies!"

"Drop dead!" Suzie yelled at her. "And you!" she pointed at Marilyn. "You'd go with Anna if I let you." At last she whipped out what she'd been carrying behind her back: a tarnished carving knife.

Duchess ran down the rest of the stairs, barking, and when she reached the hall flew into a frenzy, running back and forth in front of the evil aunt, growling and spitting, snapping at her.

Suzie tried to stab the dog but kept missing.

Then Duchess lunged and sank her teeth into Suzie's arm. The knife fell to the linoleum with a metallic clank.

"Aaaaaarghhhh!!!!!" Suzie screamed, blood spurting. She grabbed a frying pan off the floor and hit Duchess with it, slammed her against the wall. The dog dropped to the floor in a heap.

"You *killed* her!" Marilyn cried.

Suzie froze, blood splattered all over the place, then bent down for the knife.

Inside my head came a whisper of Lenny's voice: *Thank heaven for...* followed by faraway growling.

"Run for your lives!" Mom yelled.

The three of us bolted. Marilyn hesitated on the path, but I yanked her along. We came to a halt on the other side of the street.

"I feel sick," Mom said. She was holding her stomach, shivering. Marilyn was crying, and I was trying to catch my breath. I looked across the street at the open front door, but the hall seemed empty now.

A tortured scream, unlike anything I'd ever heard, came from the house.

"My dad!" Marilyn cried. She ran back, still tripping over her shoelaces, up the stoop and through the door. I tried to follow, but Mom grabbed my arm.

Then I heard the siren. The ambulance flew around the corner and pulled up in front of the building.

I broke free and ran, but just before I got to the gate, two burly men in white jackets jumped out the back of the ambulance, pushed me aside, and ran into the house.

I'd like to say the men in white jackets got there in time, wrestled Aunt Suzie into a straitjacket, and hauled her off to a padded cell where she belonged. But no. All they found was poor Duchess dead on the floor, blood all over the place, and Marilyn hugging her dad and crying while he patted her on the back, saying, "There, there."

Following the trail of blood, we saw that Suzie had run down the hall, through the kitchen, out the back door, across the cement backyard, and into the wild forest of the vacant lot. From there she was free to prowl the alleys, howling and brandishing her carving knife.

Thirty-One

After Evil Aunt Suzie murdered Duchess and ran off, all the board-ers packed their things and fled, leaving behind a sad wake of mismatched flip-flops and torn towels. Even Marilyn couldn't take it any more and asked Aunt Anna to come and get her, abandoning me just like that. She would stay in Budd Lake until her mom was found and brought to justice.

I walked into the kitchen to make myself lunch and was met by a cloud of cigarette smoke so thick it made me cough. Mom was sitting at the table sighing into a cup of black instant coffee. She'd given up whiskey sours—too many calories—and started smoking a lot of cigarettes instead because they killed her appetite. There was a bottle of Happiness Pills sit-ting on the map-of-Florida tablecloth next to an ashtray full of butts.

"I'm going to make a Swiss cheese sandwich," I said. "You want one?"

She snorted. "Don't even mention food or I'll puke."

"Mom, I really think you should eat something. How about a cookie?"

"Yuck."

I put a few Mallomar cookies on a plate and set it in front of her.

"Look," I said, "they're really good. Just try one."

She swiped it away. "I told you I can't eat."

"And cookies go really well with milk." I poured a glass and put it on the table in front of her. "Yum, yum, yum, it's so tasty." Okay, I was being sarcastic, but she didn't seem to notice.

She frowned at it. "Are you trying to make me sick?"

"How come it's so good for me but not for you?"

"Because you're a kid. Now could we talk about something else?" She picked up the milk and emptied it in the sink, sat back down. "I don't know why, but I'm so tired."

"Because you haven't eaten anything."

She poured a few Happiness Pills into her hand and gulped them down.

"I think you're taking too many of those, Mom."

"Don't worry. I know how many to take."

I shrugged, made my sandwich, squirted some seltzer into a glass, and sat down at the table.

"Where do you think Aunt Suzie is?" I asked. This was not a new subject.

"Who knows?" She put her hand to her forehead, looked like she was about to cry. "I'm so worried about her."

"What! You're worried about *her*. What about everyone else? She might kill someone."

"Don't be silly." She waved her hand. "She'd never hurt anyone."

"She murdered Duchess, she imprisoned Marilyn, and now she's running around the neighborhood with a carving knife!"

"She might starve to death out there." She sighed.

A strange thought came to me—maybe she didn't hate Evil Aunt Suzie after all. Maybe she cared about her in her own way—maybe they needed each other. Grownups were hard to understand.

"I'm more worried about you starving to death," I said.

"Me? I eat too much. Look at that." She tried to pinch her skeletal ribcage.

"Just eat a cookie." I pushed the plate towards her again. "Please?"

"Not right now." She gave a deep sigh. "I don't know why, but I'm dead tired. I feel as if I could sleep forever." She curled her arms on the table, put her head down, and closed her eyes.

A moment went by before it hit me. I could almost see Lenny, walking over, touching his finger to her forehead while I was supposed to be keeping an eye on her. I felt all jittery inside, and with that came a flood of warmth, of love for Mom, and this surprised me more than anything. Maybe *my* feelings were hard to understand too.

"Mom!" I started shaking her arm. It felt limp and cold. "Wake up!" I cried. "Please wake up!"

"Ahhhhh!" She jerked up with a start.

I jumped back, heart racing.

"What the hell's wrong with you?" She glared at me. "You scared the bejeezus out of me."

I let out a breath that was almost a sob.

"Nothing. I was worried." I was still trying to catch my breath. "You looked…"

"I'm so tired," she said.

I put my arm around her shoulders. They felt like hollow bones.

"Come on, Mom, I'll help you upstairs so you can lie down and I'll bring you a nice cup of tea."

She picked up the bottle of Happiness Pills. I gently took it out of her hand and set it on the table.

"Why don't we leave these here?"

She frowned at me but let me lead her up to her room.

That worried me more than anything.

Thirty-Two

I suck in a breath and sit up in bed.

Train tracks. Come down here. Of course—the subway! But why would Mississippi want me to go there?

I look at my bedside clock but the numbers are out of focus, all jumbled up. It doesn't matter—I know it's late, I can feel it.

I swing my legs out of bed and tiptoe downstairs and out the front door.

I seem to have gotten to the wide open subway entrance on Surf Avenue. It feels like the whole night's gone by, even though it couldn't have, because it's still dark. I stare at the cream-colored ceramic tiles and green BMT LINES built into them. It's the last stop in Brooklyn—the end of the line.

I feel compelled, sucked into the hollow cavernous terminal, pushing through the turnstile, running, flying down flight after flight of stairs, ending up in a round-ceilinged corridor of cracked white tiles, everything blurred like I'm watching it through a moving camera.

I feel a stab of pain on my forehead, hear a voice that sounds far away.

"Brooklyn," it calls out, urgent, yet muffled. It's confusing, seems to come from above yet inside my head.

"Who's there?" I say.

"Brooklyn," it calls again, but faintly. "Brooklyn…" fading away.

I realize who it is. "Mom!"

"She's not here," a voice whispers. It sounds like my own voice.

I hear something else. It sounds like an ambulance.

"That's not here either," the voice says.

The siren gets louder and louder, reaches a crescendo, then fades away.

I start walking, following signs. Upstairs, downstairs, through tunnels, on and on for the longest time. I don't know what I'm looking for, but if Mississippi told me to come here, it must be important.

At last I find a platform. I sit down on a bench and wait and wait, but trains just keep speeding by. Maybe I'm supposed to go back upstairs. I try, but the stairway's bricked up, so I climb down the steps at the end of the platform and walk into the dark train tunnel. I walk and walk and as I walk I run my fingers along a snaking yellow pipe, like a handrail on the sooty wall. The tunnel gets narrower and narrower and then it's painted with red and white stripes and the words: Danger. No Clearance.

The ground starts shaking. Two lights like yellow eyes rush at me, getting huge, filling the tunnel. I slam back into a niche just as the train rushes by, rattling and clanking. In the cars whizzing past I glimpse blank-faced people, mostly old, not one of them looking out of the dirty glass windows.

I ramble from one track to another as they crisscross, getting deeper and deeper into the system, resting in holes in the walls until I'm so tired I could die.

My eyes focus on a point of light at the end of a tunnel. I get a whiff of disinfectant and dying flowers, hear the murmur of concerned voices. "Stay with me," one of them says before the voices fade away, replaced by drunken laughter that shakes the sooty walls. I smell whiskey, beer, cheap perfume. Smoke seeps through cracks. Lenny sings:

Come to me, little Brooklyn
I'm so close, oh can't you see—

I hear running, nails clicking on the tracks, but I can't turn around, can't move. Thrashing and growling, barking, singing: *...come down here! Whatever you do, whatever you do, don't—*"

Static.

"Mississippi?"

Oh, no. He wasn't telling me to come to the subway, he was warning me not to.

"Go," he says, "before—"

I open my eyes.

I'm on my back, everything hazy, squinting into a bright white light. A shape formed out of the whiteness—

I blinked it into focus.

It was Dad's freckled face, which surprised me. After all, it was the busy season.

"You okay, Princess?"

"Where am I?"

"The hospital."

Mom was there too, sitting next to my bed, her face blotchy, her eyes red as if she'd been crying, I assumed over me, and this surprised me too.

Dad explained Mom couldn't wake me up this morning, so she called an ambulance. The doctors in the Coney Island Hospital emergency room told them that as a result of my concussion, blood had built up under my skull, putting pressure on my brain. That's why I was unconscious, why they couldn't wake me. Intracranial hematoma, they called it. They were waiting for a big brain surgeon to come down from Mount Sinai Hospital to help them decide if I needed surgery.

Thirty-Three

They decided not to operate, so they sent me home. The doctors figured my body must have reabsorbed the blood around my brain. Why else would I suddenly wake up like that? Wait and see, that's what they told my parents. And report any strange behavior on my part, especially if I seemed to be seeing things. And don't give me any aspirin, worst thing for an intracranial hematoma.

I felt fine, a little lightheaded maybe, and the way I saw things seemed different. I know it sounds crazy, but I felt almost as if I could see under the surface of things. The bump on my forehead was just about flat and the bruise had faded to light brown, so I finally looked more or less like a normal person.

Mom was having nervous day after nervous day. She couldn't even hold down the little food she ate. I'd given her the scare of her life, she said. She thought I'd died in my sleep.

I could almost see her touching my shoulder, saying "wake up," feeling a stab of fear, realization, panic.

And she was worried about Aunt Suzie, too.

So she just stayed in her room, smoking, talking to the mirror, popping Happiness Pills. She seemed to have forgotten all about house arrest and milk-drinking-torture. Absolutely no singing, she said, and don't pester me.

The Boarder wasn't in her room. I hadn't been able to find her for three days, which worried me. "Guard the house! Guard the house!" Birdchik kept squawking every time I went in.

I tried to call some of my friends from the plastic-covered couch, but they still weren't coming to the phone. Lainy's mom told me never to call again. I was a bad influence, she said, and my whole family was criminally insane.

I smelled gas, checked the stove for the hundredth time. Then I checked all the doors, not to see if they were locked, but to make sure they weren't. Suddenly I couldn't catch my breath, had to get out. I put on my red Keds and headed for Uncle Max's.

On the boardwalk there was the usual clank, clank, clank, eeeeeeeekkk! of the Cyclone, hurdy-gurdy music blaring, the Wonder Wheel turning, people talking and laughing, but none of it seemed real, more like a world I no longer belonged in.

I was dragging my feet, looking from lamppost to lamppost at the posters of Evil Aunt Suzie. These featured a snapshot of her posed with a carving knife, ready to strike, but in this case at a birthday cake. Armed and Dangerous, the posters read, and gave the public a police number to telephone if they spotted her.

"Yoo-hoo!" someone called to me, waving, from one of the benches.

I dragged myself over. She was a pretty lady with dirty blond hair in a short pixie cut, wearing Bermuda shorts and a crisp white blouse.

"Don't you recognize me?" She smiled.

"Sorry, but…" I blinked a few times, trying to place her. Then it came to me. Not her face but her accent. "Madame Clarissa?"

Her smile widened and she nodded.

"I'm on my lunch break," she said. "Want a hot dog? I shouldn't eat two anyway."

"Sure." I plopped down next to her on the bench.

She handed me one wrapped in a napkin. Just one bite and I felt better.

"You lost weight," I said. "And dyed your hair and cut it short."

"Nope." She ran her fingers through it. "This is my natural color, the black mop was a wig. It's part of my spiritualist costume, like the dress and that awful makeup."

"You look great."

"Thanks. I feel so much better. I've been swimming and playing handball."

"I thought only men played handball."

"Let you in on a little secret." She cupped her hand to her mouth and whispered, "The best-looking fellas hang around the handball courts."

"So how's business?"

"Not great." She rubbed her eyes. "Houdini left me."

"Oh, no! Did your husband drive him out?"

"No, he just got tired of trying to come back from the dead. Some escape artist, he couldn't even make it out of the building. Besides, all his friends are dead by now, so there's no one left to impress."

"What about Harry-the-husband?"

"He deserted me too. A new guide showed up, helped him get over his jealousy and move on from the Place between Life and Death."

A new guide… something tugged at my memory, but I couldn't pin it down.

"So what are you doing for your act?"

"It's awful—I call and call but no one answers, so I have to fake it. I feel so guilty. My best bet now is to snag another husband, one with a real job." She glanced at her wristwatch. "Holy moly!" She jumped up. "I have a busload of tourists coming in from Westchester for a séance."

She started walking away, then slapped her forehead and turned back.

"I almost forgot, I have a message for you, over a month now. You were supposed to come by for it, at least that's what I thought."

"Who's it from?"

"That fella Mississippi from the boardwalk."

"Oh my God. Where is it?"

"Up here." She tapped her head. "It came to me in a sitting, kind of a trance-o-gram."

"Does that mean he's dead?"

"Who knows? Maybe he's just telepathic."

"What did he say?"

"He sang it." She held up a finger. "It's been a while, give me a minute."

"You have to remember, it's really important."

"It's coming back to me." She closed her eyes and put her fingers to her forehead. "Okay, here it is."

Don't you worry yourself none, least not about me
No, don't worry yourself none, least not about me
I finally come home, to the place I need to be.

Now I remembered—in one of his secret messages, Mississippi sang that he was going to "be the guide down there." So that's where he was: the Place between Life and Death. But—did that mean I'd never see him again?

"Well, that's it," she said. "I really have to run." Which she did, literally.

I continued down the boardwalk until I got to Uncle Max's. The accordion doors were mostly open, Uncle Max sitting on one of the red crushed-velvet chairs at a table near the front. He was wearing his black shirt with the sleeves rolled up, his cigar clamped between his teeth, pounding away at an adding machine, a big pile of papers next to him.

"Hi." I waved. "Can I come in? Pleeeease?"

He let out a quick snort of laughter. He *was* warming up to me.

"Just this once," he said. "But I don't want you hanging around all day."

I ran over.

"What are you doing here?" he said. "I thought you were in the hospital."

"They let me out." I gave him my most winning smile. "Uncle Max?"

"What?"

"Can I sing here again?"

He laughed. "You never give up, do you? Come back in ten years and we'll talk."

Just then, Lenny, wearing his sports shirt and black slacks, stepped in through the door to the back carrying a large corrugated box — which he dropped the second he laid eyes on me. There was a loud crash and the sound of glass breaking. Liquid crept up the cardboard and seeped onto the red carpet.

"Goddammit!" Uncle Max shouted. "What's wrong with you?"

But Lenny didn't seem to hear him. He locked his dark eyes on mine with white-hot intensity—hatred, anger, frustration, I couldn't tell.

"I don't care who you know," he said. "I've had enough of you!"

"What are you talking about?" Uncle Max said.

But Lenny ignored him and started walking toward me. I wanted to run, but I was paralyzed with fear.

Uncle Max jumped up and shouted at Lenny.

"Have you lost your mind?"

Something shot in through the door— a flash of silver fur, glinting teeth, amber eyes. Lenny practically leapt out of the saloon, the creature chasing after him.

I ran outside.

"Cerbie!" I shouted. "*Wait!*"

They shot down the ramp at Stillwell Avenue, around it, and under the boardwalk.

I flung myself after them, down around the ramp and into the world of damp shadowy dunes. Lenny and Cerbie were nowhere to be seen. I started running over the sand through the corridor of cement columns, then stopped, turned, and ran back the other way before coming to a halt right where I'd started. Then I just stood there, catching my breath, not knowing what to do. There was nothing there, not a clue, just the dark brick wall of Uncle Max's building.

Thirty-four

I was working my way through the Junkland Jungle when I saw the yellow glow from the Boarder's den and heard her Yiddish accent. Good, she was finally home. I picked up my pace, turned the bend, and headed into the den.

I yelped when I saw who was there.

Evil Aunt Suzie sat on a chair, staring straight ahead, the whites of her eyes in sharp contrast to her filthy face. I was shocked to see how much weight she'd lost—she looked skeletal. The wound on her arm was red and filled with pus, and she was covered in leaves, seeds, mud, and dried blood. Her housedress was in shreds and a Bazooka bubble gum wrapper was stuck to what was left of her sleeve. Her hair looked like some crazy bird's nest. One sensible brown shoe was on the floor.

"Brookileh." The Boarder waved at me from her ratty armchair, grinning. "Look who I found."

"Oh, my God," I said. "Aunt Suzie? Are you okay?"

She looked around. "You talking to me, little girl?"

"Don't you recognize me?"

"What'd you call me?"

The Boarder pointed at Suzie, cupped her knotted old hand, and

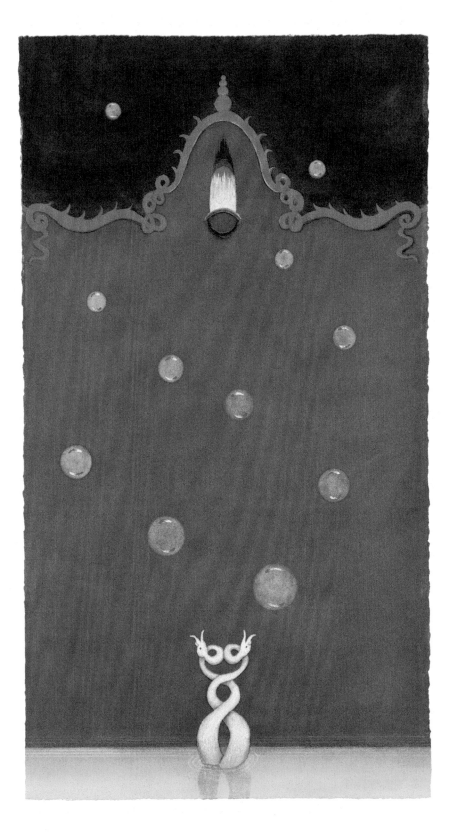

whispered, "She doesn't remember a thing." Then she started thumbing furiously through a book on the arm of her chair. "Psalms? Ram's horn? Oy. What did I do wrong?"

I ran over and sat down on the ottoman.

"How did she get here?"

"You think it was easy? For days I've been looking, then it came to me an idea. I followed the trail of blood, and—"

"I should be going now," Suzie said. She put her shoe on and got up.

"Wait," I said. "Where are you going?"

She scratched her head. "Do I live somewhere?"

"You live right next door. Brick house with a rose garden in front."

"Oh, goody." She clapped her hands. "I love roses."

"Stay on the main trail until you come to the door," I said. "If you don't, you may never find your way out."

"It was nice meeting you, little girl. And you too, teeny-weeny old lady." And with that she stumbled into the trash maze.

"Where did you find her?" I asked.

"Ay-yay-yay." She hit her forehead. "I followed the trail of blood though Suzileh's backyard and into the vacant lot. A regular jungle it is back there. I walked and walked until finally I found a big Frigidaire box. I looked inside, and pssh! There she is."

"She was living in a box all this time?"

She shrugged. "This I wouldn't know."

"Poor Aunt Suzie. She looks horrible."

She nodded. "They bury better-looking ones."

"Why can't she remember anything?"

"It's all this cockamamie book's fault." She tossed it on the table, now covered with Dad's plaid sports shirt. The book landed next to what I recognized to be a shofar, a long, graceful ceremonial ram's horn used in synagogue.

The book was thin, worn out, leather-bound. I picked it up and flipped through the pages. They were brittle, brown-edged, all written in Yiddish.

"What's this?"

She tapped my hand. "I found a book on how to exorcise a dybbuk."

"So you can exorcise Evil Aunt Suzie's?"

"This I did already."

"But how?"

"It's not so hard, any schmo can do it. It says here…" She opened the book. "You say Psalm Ninety-one three times. Then you tell the dybbuk it's safe to come out. Then you give a toot on the shofar." She picked up the ram's horn and blew out a loud wailing noise. "This shakes loose the dybbuk from the body, so if it wants to, it can escape. Then, if you're lucky, it flies out from the host's little toe. The only problem is for some reason it took Suzileh's memory with it."

"Do you know who the dybbuk was?"

Her green eyes crinkled. "Give a guess."

Suddenly it all made sense. "Oh, no. Not my real—"

"She jumped in right here." She knocked on her temple. "She's in my head now, aren't you, Rivaleh?"

"So she's trapped in *your* body now?"

"I wouldn't say trapped. She wanted to come in." She shrugged. "She's entitled."

"So now you really are my great-great—"

"Grandma!" She threw herself at me in a big bear hug, almost knocking me off the ottoman.

Thirty-five

Labor Day. Just a few more hours to the end of summer and nobody had died yet.

Mom hadn't gotten dressed this morning, just sat on the bed in her pink satin pajamas all day, her hair uncombed, purple rings under her eyes like bruises. Just looking at her made me tired. She didn't even have the energy to talk to the mirror. And when I went to her room to ask if she'd take me to the Mardi Gras parade she just shook her head.

"Please." It was getting dark out, and I was dying to go. "We always go together, Mom. You'll enjoy it."

"Call some of your friends." She shuddered. "Go with them."

The kids on the block still weren't allowed to talk to me, and Marilyn was still at Aunt Anna's. In happier years we all went together: Mom, Bubbie, Marilyn, Aunt Suzie, Uncle Nat, and even Dad always found time. We threw confetti and laughed.

"Please," I said.

If I could just get her there she'd be all right—that's how I felt—and everybody would just show up and it would be just like it used to be.

"I can't," she whispered. "I feel like I'm going to die."

I sat down on the bed.

"Do you want me to stay here? Keep you company?"

"Just leave me alone." This she whispered so low I could hardly hear it.

I went back to my room, put on my Keds and dungarees, and tied my hair in a ponytail with a rubber band. Then I changed my mind and let it loose, wild and messy.

I dragged myself through the Junkland Jungle to see if the Boarder would go with me, but when I got there the clearing was wrecked—the table overturned, random stuff strewn on the floor, the ottoman covered in yellowing newspapers and dishes, and Birdchik perched on the back of the armchair, feathers dirty, a few falling off.

The Boarder jumped up from her chair.

"Brookileh!" she called out, but not in a friendly way. "What is it you want now?" Then she smacked her hands over her ears and shouted at the ceiling: "Shah! Shah! Shah!"

"What's—"

"Now I know how Suzileh felt. Riva never shuts up. She wants this, she wants that. She keeps screaming I murdered her and stole her family. I give her immortality and still she's kvetching. "

"But she's right," I said.

"Gey aveck!" she shouted.

"You mean me? Or…" I pointed at her head.

"Gey aveck! Gey aveck! Gey aveck!" Birdchik squawked, followed by a deafening shriek.

"But—"

"Gey! I'm telling you!"

I left.

I didn't have a friend in the world, so I did something I'd never done before: I headed for the Mardi Gras parade all by myself.

The curlicued wrought-iron lampposts were strung from one side of Surf Avenue to the other with strings of purple and red lights, a glowing yellow star at the center of each strand, suspended in the night sky.

I'd pushed my way to a good spot in front of the B&B carousel. I was especially proud of this ride because Dad had built the frame as well as the engine. It was the most beautiful ride in Coney Island, with its mountain scenes, beveled mirrors, and medieval lion chariots. Its brightly painted hand-carved horses threw their heads back, manes flying, galloping up and down to the Gebruder Band organ with its hundred and ninety-seven wooden pipes, bass and snare drums, tubas, trumpets, piccolos, flutes, and clanging cymbals, mechanically rolling out "The Carousel Waltz" on this clear, warm, last night of summer.

I was standing on the curb, squashed between a frail middle-aged lady and a heavy-set man. All around me was a crush of families, teenagers, and thousands of kids, some holding on to their mom's skirts, some perched on their dad's shoulders, older ones hanging out with their friends.

And through it flowed the parade of floats—trident-waving Neptunes, jitterbugging lobsters, belly dancers, skeletons, ghouls, sea horses, mermaids. Jazz bands were swinging, acrobats somersaulting, majorettes twirling, everybody throwing confetti.

It always thrilled me, but not now. In fact I felt more lonely than ever.

I tapped the arm of the lady next to me.

"Hi," I said. "My name's Brooklyn."

She blinked at me with sad gray eyes.

"What's wrong?" she said.

"Want some confetti?" I thrust the bag at her, which caused her to jump back.

"No thanks." She blinked some more. "You're not here all by yourself, are you?"

"Yeah, but…" I looked around at all the kids with their parents, felt a stab of jealousy. "I live around here."

"Your parents know where you are?"

"Yeah."

She shook her head and tsked.

"I don't think it's safe. One time…" Her voice trailed off.

I turned back to the parade. A float carrying a giant swan made of white paper flowers was passing. On its throne were three beauty queens in bathing suits. One of them wore the sash of Miss Coney Island.

Then there were majorettes in short white dresses and white boots, twirling batons like wind-up toys.

A two-headed winged dragon was passing. One of the heads followed me with its eyes.

I turned to the lady next to me, pulled on her sleeve.

"Does everything look normal to you?" I asked.

"What do you mean?"

A troupe of skeletons came tumbling toward us. I watched them for a minute, then looked back at the lady. Now her face was painted white and she had big fake red lips.

I felt a pain in my forehead, put my hand on it. I was getting scared.

"Don't worry," she said, "Just stick by me until the parade's over, and I'll walk you home. Oh, look!"

She pointed at a float gliding past the Cyclone. It had a canopy over it with gilded baroque scrolls, and the whole thing was entwined with garlands of red roses. On it rode the king and queen of Mardi Gras, tossing handfuls of rosebuds to the crowd. The queen had on a frilly white gown and diamond tiara and the king a purple velvet cloak and white ruffled collar.

"Look at the king," the lady said. "Isn't he handsome?"

He turned his head. His eyes met mine, and I broke out in a cold sweat.

It was Lenny.

My knees buckled. The lady flung her arm around my shoulders, holding me up.

"You all right?"

Lenny walked to the back of the float, hopped off, and sauntered over to us.

"I'd better take her to the hospital," he said, white teeth flashing. "She's my boss's niece."

"No!" I tried to scream, but barely a squeak came out. Everything looked blood red. My stomach felt as if it were full of steel filings.

He scooped me up in his big arms. I tried to fight—kick, punch— but I couldn't move. "Help!" I tried to shout, but no sound came out, just a hiss of air.

"Just a minute." The lady held up her hand. "I don't think—"

"Coming through!" Lenny shouted. "Emergency! Sick child!"

I could see faces all around, looking down at me, but they'd all turned into white plastic masks. Couldn't they see he was kidnapping me? Hot tears rolled down my face.

I heard a man shout, "Wait! I'm a doctor!" but Lenny just kept going.

He carried me to the back of the crowd, then made his way along the store fronts on Surf Avenue, calling out, "Emergency! Sick child!" over and over as he pushed his way through. An ambulance siren wailed somewhere in the distance. Red, pink, and green neon signs lit our way past the Wonderland Side Show, the Scooter, the Whip, Crazy Ghosts. And all I could do was stare up at the black sky, not a star in sight.

At Phillip's Candy Store Lenny swung his purple cape out in a dramatic swoosh, then carried me into the deserted subway terminal.

Outside I could hear a brass band playing, "When the Saints Come Marching In," could almost see the confetti flying. But in here the world seemed to stop.

Lenny pushed through the turnstile and carried me down several flights of stairs to the round-ceilinged corridor I'd seen in my coma.

He stopped and looked around.

"Not at his post," he said. "Just as well. Now let's get this over with before some buttinsky interferes again."

He set me down against the cold tiles. I could feel the machinery of the place—rumblings from deep below.

He started singing: "Strangers in the Night" moving his right index finger toward my forehead. It looked magnified—short black hairs, manicured nails, whorls on his fingertip like a maze.

But just before he touched my forehead I heard a half bark, half growl, and something wild and furious charged down the corridor—

"Ha!" Lenny shouted. "The loyal mutt to the rescue, but I'm ready this time." He reached into his cape and pulled out a gun.

Cerbie leapt into the air.

Bang!

He let out a yelp and fell to the ground.

My insides turned to dry ice. I wanted to run to him, but trembling was the only movement I could make.

Cerbie struggled to get up. He lifted the top of his body, let out a sharp bark, then collapsed.

I glared at Lenny through the tears pouring down my cheeks.

"Hate me all you want," he said. "It only makes me stronger." He picked me up and flung me over his shoulder like a sack of potatoes. I tried to kick, punch, bite, but it was still no use.

"You've been a real pain in the neck." He laughed. "But I like a challenge every now and then, breaks up the monotony."

He strolled to the end of the corridor and stepped on an escalator going down. The way he was holding me, everything was upside down and my head was spinning, pounding.

And thinking. This is it. I'll never see Mom or Dad or Marilyn or the Boarder again. It's not fair. Lenny should be the one to die, not Cerbie, not me.

My tangled hair was hanging over my face like something out of a swamp-creature movie. I stared at the steel lines on the escalator steps but soon got so dizzy I closed my eyes and felt the soft velvet of the back of Lenny's cape on my cheek. It smelled like smoke and Old Spice.

He started singing, "I Could Have Danced all Night."

No secret messages this time—he was singing just for the joy of it.

When he was done with that song, he launched into, "A Little Bit of Luck."

His voice echoed off the tile walls. For all I know he sang all the songs from *My Fair Lady*—but things got dark and his voice faded in the middle of "I've Grown Accustomed to Her Face."

When my eyes opened, rocks were poking through the tiles and Lenny was humming to himself. We hit bottom. He stepped off the escalator, readjusted me on his shoulder, and started walking down a white-tiled train platform lined with steel

I-beams for columns. It was dimly lit with a few bright spots here and there.

After some more bouncing and humming, he hefted me off his shoulder and set me against the wall again. Down here the tiles were in worse shape, a lot of them missing, revealing black tar underneath. There were stalactites dripping overhead, and rolls of peeling paint showed something dark red beneath the surface. Between the tracks were scattered bottles, toys, candy wrappers.

A light flashed on deep in the tunnel and glinted on the tracks. The platform started vibrating, then rumbling, steel on steel, grinding, squealing, coming at us, louder and louder. Two yellow headlights appeared, then whoosh! the train was speeding by, clanking and banging at its couplings. People sat behind the dirty glass windows, all motionless, beyond reach.

"I love the express," Lenny said, and watched the train until the taillights, one blue, one red, disappeared. "Now I'm really in the mood. Let's give it another try." He pointed his index finger again. "You're the hardest kid to kill I ever met."

"Wait!" A gravelly voice shouted.

Mississippi ran toward us, his footfalls echoing off the tile walls.

Lenny snorted.

"You're too late, old man," he called out. To me he said, "Hate to short-change you, but you've already heard me sing anyway."

He jabbed his finger into my forehead.

I felt a jolt of pain, then nothing at all.

Thirty-Six

When I opened my eyes, I was numb.

Mississippi stood there, white shirt, suspenders, guitar strapped around his chest, just like when I saw him last on the Fourth of July. But now he was scowling at Lenny, fists clenched and planted on his hips.

"What?" Lenny said. "I'm just doing my job."

"We had an agreement."

"No, we didn't." Lenny shrugged. "I said I'd think about it. Bottom line, if I don't jam her in now, I might never get another chance. She might end up being like the crazy old lady who tricked me." He let out a huff. "Two under the same roof. Can you believe it? Must be contagious."

"So what?" Mississippi said.

"So what? So *what*! If I screw up one more time, the Soprano," he pointed up, "might send *me* to the other side."

"But Brooklyn's a singer, like us," Mississippi said, which gave me a thrill.

"No she's not. She's mortal. Her name came up in the book. Doesn't that mean anything to you?"

"But she's just a kid."

"So? I take lots of kids. You know what the most common cause of death among children is? Car crashes, just like your little friend here caused. And the second most common? Drowning. She was asking for it."

"You leave me no choice." Mississippi stepped right up to Lenny. I'd never seen him this way before—angry, fearless.

"I challenge you…" he bit off each word, "to a showdown."

"A *showdown*?" Lenny laughed and laughed. "You've been down here, what? Seven weeks? All you ever do is whine about that hick sheriff, and now you're challenging *me*?"

Mississippi looked Lenny up and down, blew on his fingers.

"You scared?"

"Scared!" Lenny sighed. "Fine, a showdown. Joe can judge."

"When I win?" Mississippi said. "You let Miss Brooklyn go home. For good."

"Sure, but you're not going to win. And *when* you lose, the brat goes straight to the other side. No hanging around. I'm sick and tired of all these entities you let move in here like it's a hotel or something. *And* you have to resign, move on to the other side yourself."

My hands curled into a fist, nails digging in. I wanted to tell Mississippi not to risk it, but I couldn't speak.

"Don't you worry yourself none." Mississippi winked at me. "I ain't never lost a showdown in my whole entire life."

"Joe can be there in about fifteen of your dreary minutes." Lenny swung his cape around. His shiny black shoes made a clicking noise on the cement floor as he walked away.

"Having trouble talking?" Mississippi asked.

I nodded.

"That there's a good sign. It means you still got a foot in the real world."

So I wasn't totally dead, but if he lost the showdown I would be. And so would he.

"You probably wondering how I got here?"

I nodded.

"They sent Lenny to Woody's house to offer me the job." He gave me a proud smile. "I sure do like it—helping people let go of the world they done left behind, easing their fears. The big shots in the afterlife had their eyes on me for years, ever since I was born. That's why they sent me Cerbie, why he guided me here. So when the last guide left and took his dog with him... but I'm getting ahead of myself. Cerbie knew it was time when he saw Lenny on the boardwalk, so he come down here. He has a real important job, keeping live people from wandering in. Took a long time for Lenny to fetch me—kept dragging his feet, wanted to run the whole place hisself, but everything fell apart, lost souls wandering out, some getting stuck here past their time, till he didn't have no choice. He had to come for me." He puffed up his chest. "I'm just as powerful as he is now."

But why didn't Lenny just kill me in the first place? I didn't say it out loud, but Mississippi heard it.

"Because Cerbie was protecting you."

I knew it!

"Every time Lenny tried to mark you, Cerbie took the gravest of risks leaving his post, going up there, fighting off Lenny. After I got here I started protecting you too. I thought I'd talked Lenny out of it, but he went behind our backs, grabbed you when we wasn't looking."

I tried to nod, so he'd know I understood.

It occurred to me that maybe Bubbie was here. Maybe I could see her again.

"After you didn't drown," he said, "your grandma was free to go to the other side."

What's on the other side? I tried to ask.

He shrugged. "Don't rightly know. Nobody does."

Darn. I thought for sure—

"But do you want to know what happened to the Meat-faced Sheriff?"

I nodded again.

"Turns out he's here."

I tried to cock my head. I think it moved a little bit.

"Sneaking around, hiding out in them tunnels." He looked in both directions. "When Cerbie bit him in the arm all those years ago— remember I told you about it, the fork in the road? The sheriff just kept running and running and bleeding and bleeding until he couldn't run no more, then he fell down in the dirt. In the end he wasn't nothing but a fat, red-faced man bleeding to death on a lonesome back road."

My eyes widened.

"Been here all those years, lost and angry. And now they tell me..." He heaved a sigh. "I'm supposed to track him down and guide him to the other side."

I sucked in a breath.

"That's right, Little Sugar." He nodded, a sad smile on his papery old face. "In a way, I'm the one hunting *him* now."

I wanted to smile but couldn't because of what had happened to Cerbie.

"What's the matter, Little Sugar?" It took him about half a second to figure it out. "I know, you worried about Cerbie, ain't you?"

I nodded.

"Well, don't you trouble yourself none. Things ain't always what they seem down here."

They sure weren't.

"Remember how I told you bullets didn't kill Cerbie?"

The last word was barely out of his mouth when a silver streak flew around the bend. It took me a second, then my heart did a somersault. Cerbie was running at us.

When he got a few feet away he started dashing around in circles, bouncing, dancing with his forepaws, poking me with his nose, ears erect, amber eyes glowing, just grinning and grinning.

And I could move!

I grabbed him around the neck and snuggled him close to me. I'd forgotten how big he was, how soft and thick his fur felt. We danced around in sheer joy.

"See?" Mississippi laughed. "Ain't nobody can kill an immortal being. Lenny just slowed him down." He took out a pocket watch and looked at it.

"Come on, Little Sugar." He waved his hand. Cerbie made invitational runs back and forth in front of us. "Don't want to be late for the showdown." He took my sleeve, tugged, and I glided alongside him.

Thirty-Seven

L enny was standing in front of a black-tiled storefront. "Piano Bar," a crimson neon sign glowed in the window. Cerbie eyed him coldly and I shot him an angry look, which just made him smile. He whooshed his cape around and pushed through the padded black leather door. We followed him in.

It was a large joint, kind of hollow feeling, with a black marble floor, flocked red wallpaper, and in the back a pulsing crimson EXIT sign. There was a baby grand piano on a raised stage, now in shadow, and a shiny black counter along its right wall where Joe, Uncle Max's bartender, was wiping glasses with a rag and shelving them.

The place was dotted with customers, mostly gray-haired men and women with a few younger ones mixed in. They were seated here and there at the tables, drinking, smoking, talking in low voices. I was surprised to see two teenagers, a boy in a biker jacket leaning against the wall and a skinny girl biting her nails at a table near the back. All the customers kept glancing at the crimson EXIT sign with mixed expressions: fear, bewilderment, longing.

My whole body was trembling with anticipation.

Lenny slouched against the bar and ordered a martini. He lit a cigarette, took a long drag, blew out a ring of smoke. Joe clunked his drink in front of him and he slugged it back.

"Keep them coming," he said.

Mississippi and I went over to a small round table near the stage. He slipped his guitar over his head and put it down. Then we seated ourselves, Cerbie lying on the floor next to me. Mississippi called over to Joe.

"Shot of Scotch for me and a Shirley Temple for my sassy little goddaughter here." He gave me a reassuring smile. Joe brought us our drinks, but I was too nervous to take more than a sip. Then Mississippi called over to Lenny.

"Losers first." He waved at the stage.

One of Lenny's eyebrows shot up. He sauntered to the front of the room, stepped on stage.

"I hate him," I said.

"Now Little Sugar, don't you go doing that. He don't decide who lives and who dies. Man's just doing his job."

"Yeah, but he likes it."

A spotlight flashed drenching Lenny in brightness. He looked gorgeous, glowing. I'd never seen anyone so full of himself. The hum of voices died away.

Lenny looked to one of the wings. He put his thumb and index finger in his mouth and let out a loud whistle. Three old men came shuffling onto the stage. They were emaciated, covered with dirt, and two of them were carrying chairs and instruments. The third sat down at the piano.

When I realized what he was doing I jumped up. The creep! It wasn't fair, bringing in a band, saving his energy just for singing.

"Don't you worry yourself none," Mississippi said. "Sometimes too many instruments takes the edge off the song."

I sat down, but I didn't like it.

Meanwhile, one of the men had seated himself and positioned his guitar. But the other one was slowly shuffling—dragging the chair, clutching his violin to his chest—toward the glowing red EXIT sign.

"Hey!" Lenny yelled at him. "Where do you think you're going?"

The man froze, stood there trembling, then slowly turned around, a confused, a miserable look on his worn out face. He banged the chair down where he stood, sat, and positioned the violin.

"Where's the drummer?" Lenny said.

The pianist pointed at the EXIT door.

"Who said he could go? I wasn't done with him."

"I did," Mississippi called out. "That's *my* job now."

Lenny gave out an exasperated sigh.

"Okay," he said, "you three'll have to do. He gracefully placed his long fingers around the microphone, lifted it off its stand, and smiled his best smile –- which was really something. "Let's hit it!" he shouted at them.

The pianist tinkled the keys in a short, intriguing introduction, then Lenny joined in:

> There is no death for me:
> I'll never see—behind the curtain
> I am—the boss down here

He threw out his hand.

> Believe no other version

It felt as if he were singing directly to me, slow and sizzling, world-weary and full of regret, taking all the sleaziness in the world but changing it, making it ring with heartache.

I live—a million lives
I sing a million songs and play

He swayed back and forth.

I do—my job down here

He looked straight at me.

Right in this subway

The words no longer mattered, just the layers of his voice, its surface lightness, its dark undercurrents, its buttery smoothness, all the sadness it held.

Mistakes

The piano trilled here.

I've made a few

The violin came in louder and predominated, sadder and sweeter than the piano.

And I've been tricked, but just one time.
There is—no hope for you.

I wondered if Lenny had been human once. He must have been, to sing like this.

I'm not committing any crime.

His voice seemed to be getting stronger, gaining power as he went along. I knew how good he was, but he'd never been *this* good.

I'll win this stupid showdown
You'll never see another birthday.

It was hard to pull myself out of his spell, but I glanced around—the audience was perfectly still, enraptured. I looked over at Joe, standing behind the counter. He was nodding to himself, swaying to the song's rhythm. I looked at Mississippi. A faint crease formed between his eyebrows.

I'll send you farther down
Below this subway.

There was a moment of silence, then the audience started applauding, just clapped and clapped. Lenny replaced the microphone, flashed a grin at them, and took a bow, which made them clap even more. Someone let out a piercing whistle. Lenny stood there, drinking it all in, smiling his conceited smile.

When the applause finally died away the musicians shuffled out and Lenny ambled back to the bar and slouched against it. He untied the top of his cape and loosened his ruffled collar with his finger, then picked up his martini.

"Little warm in here, isn't it?" he said to Joe.

Mississippi stood up, slipped his guitar over his head, and stepped up onto the stage. The spotlight saturated him, made him shine. He waited for total silence before he started strumming.

I'd been a little bit worried, I admit it—Lenny was *so* good—but the first few notes of Mississippi's guitar sent a wave of sound into the room so sweet and sad I could taste it.

I watched the long fingers of his right hand picking, his left pressing down on the strings.

And then he started singing:

> I'm just a poor boy, a long, long way from home
> Such a poor boy, a long way from home
> I ain't never said goodbye, now my poor mama's gone

He went into an instrumental, strumming the strings, banging them black and blue, humming, oh-oh-oh-ing, then singing about hurt so deep it made you cry.

> I seen hard traveling, no place to lay my weary head
> Yes, I seen hard traveling, no place to lay my weary head
> I ain't never set down roots, never slept in no soft bed

His voice held all the rawness in the world, all the loneliness. Mississippi was singing for everyone, pouring out their pain, helping them move on. Lenny, I suddenly realized, only sang for himself.

I looked toward the bar. Lenny's face was impassive. Joe had closed his eyes and thrown his head back.

> My life is over, Lord I've breathed my final breath
> Yes, my life is over, oh Lord I've breathed my final breath

Mississippi must have sung this song a thousand times, a thousand different ways, and every time it moved me deep inside. But the last line was new:

> Now I'm home here at last,
> between the place of life and death.

The final notes washed over us, held us suspended in silence, each of us taking from it what we could. After a time I looked around. A white-haired lady at the next table rubbed her bloodshot eyes. The man next to her let out a sigh of relief. The teenage girl looked at the teenage boy like she was forgiving him for something.

I didn't know if Mississippi had won, but I felt lighter, almost buoyant.

We all turned to Joe. He had his eyes closed as the barest trace of a smile spread across his face.

He gave Mississippi the thumbs up.

Everybody started applauding, standing up, scraping their chairs back, clapping like they'd never clapped in their lives, not just with admiration but with warmth, with release—until SMACK! Lenny slammed his hand on the counter and glared at Mississippi.

"Why do you have to be so damn good?" he said and stomped out.

I felt a rush of pure joy. Mississippi had won, he'd still be a big shot in the afterlife, and I'd be able to go home.

But suddenly I didn't want to leave. I wanted to stay here, get up on stage and sing and sing and sing, listen to Mississippi play, dance with Cerbie, and never have to drink milk again.

I ran up onto the stage and tried to throw my arms around Mississippi, but he put his hands up in front of him.

"Whoa," he said. "I still got my guitar on."

"What did you mean," I said, "when you told Lenny I was a singer like you and him? Am I a big shot in the afterlife too?"

"I don't rightly know what's going to happen after you die, but right now—"

"Please don't make me go back." I started crying.

"Now, Little Sugar—"

"Please?"

"You need to listen to me now, all right? It's important."

"Okay," I said, but I didn't want to listen. He was going to tell me why I had to go back. Of course, if I didn't go back I'd never see Dad again, or—

"You got songs to hear, Little Sugar. And you got songs to sing."

I looked at his face and I knew I had a life to live, too.

I nodded.

He slipped his guitar over his head and laid it on the piano stool. Then he smiled a great big smile and opened his arms to hug me goodbye.

Thirty-Eight

I was floating on my back in a white, bright, blank space. I smelled Pine-Sol and rubbing alcohol, heard the murmur of faraway voices.

I tried to focus. I saw a cloudy sky above me, felt a stabbing pain on my forehead. Something broke out of the clouds. It was Dad's freckled face, shining down on me, lighting up my world. He was grinning like some goofy god in some goofy universe where everything always turns out happy.

"You gave us quite a scare, Princess," he said. "What got into you, going to the parade by yourself?"

He said I'd blacked out just as the float carrying the king and queen was passing, and a lady called an ambulance. I was unconscious the whole time, so it was a lucky thing a doctor at Coney Island Hospital remembered me and my intracranial hematoma, because he called the brain surgeon from Mount Sinai Hospital who'd seen me before, and he rushed right down from Manhattan and operated.

Mom was here too. She was wearing a bathrobe, sitting in a chair next to the bed. Her eyes were bloodshot and her face was red and blotchy. I knew that no amount of staring in the mirror would ever

make her the fairest in the land again, but now I saw in her a different kind of beauty, the sad beauty of the blues.

My forehead started throbbing. I reached up, touched my scalp. It was bandaged.

"Mom?"

She got up, a little shaky on her matchstick legs, and braced herself on the chair. Dad went over, put his arm around her frail shoulders, and led her over to my bed, where she grasped the railing like a sparrow coming to rest.

"What, Alley Cat?" Her voice sounded weak.

"Were you worried about me?"

She looked confused, sniffled back tears.

"Of course. You're my little girl."

Tears ran down the side of my face and soon we were both crying.

"And you don't want to get rid of me?" I asked.

"Noooo. Of course not." She blew her nose.

"I was worried about you, too," I said.

"I'm sorry. They say there's something wrong with me, that I have to eat more." She frowned. "They took away my Happiness Pills." She said this as if I would understand how unfair it was. "They've admitted me to the hospital too. They put me in here with you."

They sent me home a week before Mom, her problems being harder to treat or even understand than mine, so I had Dad all to myself.

"I'm sorry I didn't take better care of Mom," I said in the car on the way home. "I tried to make her eat, but I might as well have been talking to the television. I don't think I can take care of her." I was fighting back tears, sniffling.

"Oh, Princess," he said, "that's not your job. Your job is to be a kid. I'll take care of Mom."

"Will you take care of me, too?"

"Of course. That's what dads are for."

I couldn't hold back the tears any longer, so he had to pull over, even though we were only two blocks from home, and give me a hug.

I bought a guitar with the fifty dollars Uncle Max gave me and was taking lessons. Mississippi was right—I had songs to sing. Marilyn was still trying to decide how to spend hers, maybe do something to rescue abused dogs.

When I told the Boarder that the Molech knew she was living at our house but it didn't matter because he didn't know if he'd ever find a slot to stuff her in, or me for that matter, she decided she could go to Miami Beach for the winter. Turns out my real great-great-grandmother always wanted to go. It was the only way to make her happy, the Boarder told me.

"Like being married, it is," she said. "Only worse."

Turns out some of the paintings she had were by famous Mexican artists. She sold one, and now she was loaded—I mean *really* loaded. She called me when she got to Miami, long distance.

"Ay-yay-yay," she said, "they have here such a swimming pool. And Wolfy's? They make for you a stuffed kishke, it's out of this world." Then she said I could call collect any time I wanted and she'd tell me about her and Riva's adventures.

The best part is they left Birdchik with me, which drove Mom nuts, but at least it wasn't an evil dog.

On Yom Kippur we all put our sins in our pockets and walked to the end of Steeplechase Pier. It was a cloudy October afternoon, so misty the gray-green sea blended into the gray-blue sky with no horizon line.

I was finally wearing the red silk dress Bubbie had sewn for me, with lots of crinolines and patent leather Mary Janes. It was too dressy for the daytime, but Mom wanted to see me in it, and I think Bubbie would have been pleased. The sad thing was, this was probably the last time I'd ever be able to wear it, I was growing so fast.

They'd shaved my head for the surgery, but by now the bandage was off and my hair had grown almost three inches already. The surgeon said he'd never seen hair grow that fast. So in the end, Mom got her way—I let her trim it into a pixie. Actually, she was right, it did look kind of cute.

Mom and Dad were both in navy blue suits, which made them look like happy bookends. Dad was fasting, as he always did for Yom Kippur, but Mom couldn't stop eating. It seemed the Day of Atonement was the one day of the year she was ravenous.

She was seeing a psychiatrist who specialized in eating problems. She'd gotten Mom off Happiness Pills and onto fresh fruits and vegetables and was rooting around in her unconscious to get to the bottom of it all.

Aunt Suzie was wearing a neat beige dress with matching jacket and looked surprisingly trim and healthy. She was pushing Uncle Nat in his wheelchair, bumpity-bump, over the wooden slats of the pier.

The doctors figured Aunt Suzie had had a nervous breakdown. She still hadn't recovered her memory—or personality. In fact, she seemed to be looking to us to tell her who she was, which Marilyn and I were more than happy to do. Uncle Nat decided that as part of their fresh start he'd have the entire house renovated and put in an elevator so he could get upstairs. There would be no more boarders.

Marilyn looked adorable in a flared gray felt skirt with a poodle appliqué and a pink jacket, an expensive outfit Aunt Anna had bought for her as a going-home present.

At the deep end of the pier we reached into our pockets and pulled out our sins, each sin clinging to a bread crumb, and tossed them into the choppy sea. To everyone's surprise, Aunt Suzie whipped out a whole loaf of Italian bread, swung it over her head, and sailed it into the ocean like a zeppelin.

Some days after school, instead of walking all the way home I leave Marilyn and the other kids on the block at the corner of Ocean View Avenue and walk on, down Ocean Parkway, through Seaside Park, past the handball courts, and up onto the wide expanse of lonely boardwalk, whistling in the sea breeze. If I close my eyes and let go of the present I can hear the faraway twangy notes of a guitar, accompanied by a strong gravelly voice, floating on the wind.

I'm just a poor boy, a long long way from home
Such a poor boy, a long way from home

In my mind I take off running.

I ain't never said goodbye...

Then I see Cerbie bounding toward me, faster than seems possible, until he's jumping up on my shoulders, licking my face, his amber eyes glowing with joy. I hug his thick silver fur and he runs back and forth, yipping, inviting me to run with him, and we both fly toward Mississippi who's at his spot on the boardwalk, singing just for me.

Acknowledgements

Most of all I want to thank Renni Brown, my editor, who guided this novel into existence, taught me most of what I know about fiction writing, and had faith in my novels for so many years, and thank you to the many others at the Editorial Department who helped me.

Also, my husband: Jim Blythe—for his advice, literary instincts, proofreading, and support—and thank you to the readers of a very early version of this book: Michael Feldheim—when he was only eleven years old—Annabelle Meacham, Jaynie Cohen, and Ray Berthiaume.

As far as the illustrations go I'd like to acknowledge the feedback of my many artist friends and my art group: Artists' Link, Memphis Area Visual Artists.

For original Coney Island stories, blog, and glowing artwork, please visit my web site: sheilapmartin.com. Also, please like my author's page on Facebook, Sheila Martin, Author.

About the Author

Sheila Martin was born in 1946 and grew up in the Coney Island/Brighton Beach section of Brooklyn. Even before her first finger painting she knew she wanted to be a painter.

In 1971 she graduated from New York University, where she earned a B.A. in fine art.

From 1971 to 1979 she worked in graphic design in New York City.

In 1979 she moved to Ithaca, New York with her husband Jim Blythe. Here she started a successful graphic design business which specialized in not-for-profit organizations.

In 1992, Sheila and Jim moved to Memphis, TN, where Jim landed a job as a medieval history professor. Here she phased out her graphic design business and started painting full time. Shortly thereafter she developed an intense interest in writing.

She has since written and illustrated this novel, written a second novel, and is working on a volume of short stories.

CPSIA information can be obtained
at www.ICGtesting.com
Printed in the USA
LVOW06s1019270916

506286LV00004B/4/P